JENNIFER O'NEILL

CIRCLE *of* FRIENDS

Just off Main

A FALL TOGETHER

A NOVEL

BROADMAN
& HOLMAN
PUBLISHERS
Nashville, Tennessee

Ten-digit ISBN: 0-8054-4195-6
Thirteen-digit ISBN: 978-0-8054-4195-6

Published by Broadman & Holman Publishers,
Nashville, Tennessee

Dewey Decimal Classification: F
Subject Heading: WOMEN—FICTION /
FRIENDSHIP—FICTION / SPIRITUAL LIFE—FICTION

1 2 3 4 5 6 7 8 9 10   10 09 08 07 06

To all the sisters I never had growing up,
but now know in Christ! Tons of love,
Jen   XOXO

Chapter 1

-Lauren-

*W*hat to keep, what to throw away? Pieces of Lauren's life lay strewn across her bedroom like piles of leaves gathered in an autumn clean-up—pictures, letters, even gifts she'd never used but couldn't give away without hurting someone's feelings. Lauren knew letting go wouldn't be easy.

Standing back from her task at hand, she was momentarily mesmerized by the vast display of flickering candles sprinkled across her antique dressers and night tables. Lauren stretched her lithe body like a cat, her auburn hair framing a still stunning face. She definitely did not look her age, which, by the way, she was sure to disclose to all, particularly new acquaintances; she liked being up-front. Frankly, this woman was proud that she had made it to the big "five-0" in one piece, especially given her colorful past. Sinking onto her bed, she was enveloped by comforters and handmade quilts, her body making an imprint like a finger poking the belly of the Pillsbury Doughboy.

Everything was going to be alright, she thought, calling forth her waning enthusiasm. A new life adventure was being birthed, so it was natural to feel some labor pains, right? Besides, Lauren had learned not to panic when God closed one door before revealing which new door of opportunity she was to step through. Yes, she had learned to rely on him when the details of this world seemed overwhelming. Hadn't she?

"Take it easy, one step at a time," she whispered. The mountains of clothes on the floor were scheduled for the local charity pickup tomorrow afternoon, but first she wanted to try all of them on again, just to make sure they were really too tight, too long, too cute, or too old. No! She had to stop being wishy-washy. She wasn't merely cleaning out closets; she was changing her life, and she had promised herself that whatever she took from her past must not inhibit her future. 1996 was going to be her turning point!

Calling forth resolve, Lauren gathered herself up into a seated position as she pulled at the T-shirt that hugged her body like an ad for static cling. "OK, let's go," she muttered, grabbing for her cold cup of coffee; the heavy cream floating on top made a mosaic pattern out of the fat globules. "Oh goodie, that looks healthy." She gulped it down, took a breath, stood, then gingerly stepped over her memories as if walking through a minefield. She conjured up a sudden warning notice: "One wrong move, and you'll simply disappear into your past, never to be seen again."

She couldn't help but be amused by the image she had thought up as she read an imaginary newspaper headline:

Local Woman Suffocated in a Pile of Donated Clothes

As she proceeded across the room, she caught her image in the dresser mirror; she wondered how long she would hold her stomach in when no one was looking. Suddenly, she kicked out in an impressive Bob Fosse spin and pose that surprised even her as one of her oversized fuzzy slippers flew across the room. "Not too shabby, you old dog," she boasted to the pictures on the wall. More family photos of Lauren, her son Tucker, and a variety of animals romping through freeze-framed occasions covered her bedroom shelves. What was conspicuously absent was any record of a man in her life.

She leaned against the door for support as she spun another internal pep talk that had become so commonplace of late. *Hey, you're just a little tired, that's all.* Lauren's head slowly fell back while she fought to control the onslaught of emotions that were increasingly overtaking her. Her breathing quickened, something that hadn't happened in the longest time, at least not that she'd admit. Alright, yes, two summers ago there was that incident when she couldn't find the belt to her dress. Everyone was waiting downstairs in the car ready to go to the fair, and there she was on her bedroom floor, a heap of crumpled humanity, drowning in tears. She couldn't breathe then either. Of course, it wasn't really about the belt. It was just easier to admit that she had lost a piece of clothing than admit that she was divorced for the second time.

She thought, *Oh well, you made your bed. Now you have to make it again.*

She forced her heaving chest to adopt a more reasonable meter as she moved toward the bathroom to wash her face. Despite her best intentions her thoughts made another U-turn; she looked about her bedroom, devouring every detail. A lot had happened there, both good and bad. *Watch out,* she cautioned herself, *the blame game was about to begin.* "No!" She was not going there anymore. "It's all your fault" had not passed her lips in some time. In the last three years of being single, she'd learned that the saying, "If you throw dirt, you lose ground," was a true analogy. Pointing the finger simply wasn't allowed. She had also made strides in conquering some of her feelings, seeing them for what they really were, unreliable at best. In fact, Lauren had begun to identify some of her feelings as an enemy of sorts; a negative mental tape that was capable of taunting her into bouts of depression or luring her into lustful fantasies while focusing on pressures that had the ability to steal her joy and peace. Thank God her friend Susan was mature in her faith, what an anchor she'd been for Lauren. Just the thought of this wonderful woman made her smile. Lauren had come to consider her neighbor a surrogate older sister, especially since she and her real sister, Irene, had grown apart in so many ways.

Whenever Lauren felt a pity party coming on, Susan would calmly remind her that patience was not one of Lauren's virtues and that she could choose to be in Christ, or she could choose to be in pain. Susan also lovingly pointed out that the two ex-husbands in Lauren's past were also her choice as well. Lauren finally had to admit that she was the common denominator in her marriages, and the author of most of her pain. If she chose to invent men, why was she always so surprised that they ended up not being what she wanted or needed?

She considered her expression of dismay framed in the bathroom mirror; she suddenly looked old and worn out—scary, in fact. "Come on, Lauren, where's your sense of humor?" She threw some water on her face. "Remember how you promised that you didn't mind lines around your eyes as long as they turned up from laughing? Liar, liar."

Disgusted, she made her way back to the bedroom. Aha, music. Yes! A little Cole Porter. What a composer. What a master lyricist. His music always worked magic for her mom and dad. She could remember when she and her sister would glue their ears to the wall, listening to their parents party the evening away. Irene was ten and Lauren was eight when they were old enough to pick up on Margaret and Sam's courting rituals that sometimes ended in cooing, other times in verbal blowouts. But no matter, the next morning was a new day, and never a mention was made of the prior evening's escapades. One thing Irene and Lauren did know; their parents were in their marriage for the long haul. They had found something both girls wanted when they grew up, a soul mate. Unfortunately, that was not in the cards for either of these sisters—at least not so far.

Porter's song "Night and Day" oozed from Lauren's stereo like a velvet fog. She spun across the room holding fast to an imaginary partner as the last vestige of a tear escaped her glassy eyes. They were always a little glassy, she remembered some voice telling her in the middle of the night; that was part of her mystery. And that memory was enough to take the wind out of her sails; she simply did not want to think about lost loves.

Lauren turned on the TV so she could watch its light flicker across the room for a minute before getting back to work. It would be dawn soon—enough procrastinating. She forced herself to sit down in the middle of the floor and address a flowered box held fast with a large pink ribbon. Before pulling the top free, she cautiously peeked inside as if its contents might leap out and bite her. She knew she probably should have just thrown the love letters out then and there, but she couldn't bring herself simply to erase her past in one fell swoop.

"Once bitten, twice dumped," or whatever that saying was; she was notorious for decimating a turn of phrase. Lauren scolded herself, thinking back on her failed marriages. It just didn't seem right for her to be in possession of both his-and-her versions of early dating "admissions of amour"; what did he have to pine over? To make matters worse, she had two sets of these letters, Steven's and Brian's, husband number one and husband number two. How could they both have left their letters? Oh yes, Steven moved out in such a huff he didn't even take his golf clubs, let alone his telltale romantic ramblings. And Brian threw all of his letters back in her face during one of their more physical spats.

After a fair amount of hemming and hawing, she decided to open one of the notes to read aloud. Despite herself, she was moved by the promises it held. Steven penned this particular collection of poetic metaphors after their second date:

> *Now that I have met you, I realize what was missing in my life. A deep yearning has suddenly been satisfied. I never want to lose this feeling of love and completeness. Always, Steven.*

She was sixteen; he was twenty-two when they met, and they were made for each other. At least that's what they both felt at the time. It had to be love because it hurt so much when they fought; and boy, did they ever fight. In those days Lauren's teenage logic argued, "If I didn't care, it wouldn't hurt, so hurting must be a good thing." Even when she and Steven were engaged to be married and they made love for the first time, now that was a different kind of hurt. But Lauren told herself that it didn't matter; she wasn't about to lose him. After all, how long would he hang around a high school cheerleader when there were all those wild, older girls at college that he always talked about? Besides, everyone was "doing it," so it must be OK. That "good girl, bad girl" bit was just something her mother put in her head so she wouldn't . . . what? Lauren never really figured that one out. That is, not until she knew God's Word on the subject. Oh, how she wished she'd had her faith back then. So much drama and trauma could have been avoided, so much pain prompted by her lack of discernment and emotionally needy personality.

Lauren stuffed Steven's letter back in the box and cautiously reached for another. This time it was a card with a knight in armor on the cover. "Brian, you always hit below the hip," she snipped. Shaking her head, her eyes scanned the page as she read his words:

And I have never felt such happiness before. You have given my heart direction, my life meaning. With you I can truly believe that love can conquer all. Forever yours, Brian.

"Good one, Bri." She crushed the card like a stale potato chip. Yes, her hands were strong; no long polished nails for Lauren. She was a working girl. She had substance, vision; she was a survivor. *After all,* she thought, *absence makes the heart wander.*

So when she gathered all the letters from the flowered box with the pink ribbon and tore them in half on the first try, she shouldn't have been surprised. But she was. Was she really that powerful? Was she actually doing what it looked like she was doing? Was she really getting up and walking over to the fireplace, pulling back the screen and throwing her past reasons for living into the fire without a second thought?

"Wait!" Her hands fumbled between the flames, grabbing what she could save of the written words. She held two and a half singed letters up for review. Relieved there was one from each ex-suitor, she watched the fire devour the rest in a curl of smoke. *That was close,* she thought. She had to keep at least one letter from each husband so she'd have concrete proof of what does not work.

Despite her bravado, Lauren had to admit that for her self-esteem had always been elusive. Worse than that, Lauren sometimes wasn't sure she would be able to emerge from the disillusionment of her marriages with the ability ever to trust or dream again. And what is life without dreams? Bad ratings . . . or was it bad blood? After all, her sister was going through her second divorce. She wondered, *Does divorce mean you're a bad person, or just stupid, or gullible—or worse, maybe all of the above?*

Lauren looked back into the fire, reminding herself, "You can't be a little bit pregnant." She really didn't need these letters anymore. All she had to do was open her fingers and let them fall into the flames, and that would be that. After all, wasn't that what the move to Tennessee was all about? Finally and truly letting go and letting God take over? What was all this drama about? She was way past this kind of hurt. She was not going to backslide!

When Lauren looked back down at her hands, the letters were gone. Somehow, miraculously and without warning, she'd made the plunge. The last written testimony of her marriages vanished in a ribbon of smoke that lingered in the chimney and then simply disappeared.

After a fleeting moment of final grieving, Lauren felt a wave of liberation flow throughout her body and ignite her spirit. Yes, she felt invincible—free! What a high! Unfortunately, the glorious moment was invaded by a beam of sunlight that sliced through the window shade, making a direct hit on Lauren's face. Her eyes slammed shut in denial. "Oh no, please, not yet!"

She trudged over to the window to see if she was hallucinating. Nope, it was definitely the beginning of a new day, despite Lauren's protests. Resigned, she grabbed a pair of old jeans and a large turtleneck sweater to ward off the nip in the air heralding a change of season. Then she began to give thanks, "This is the day the Lord has made and, in it, I will be glad. I ask for the refilling of the Holy Spirit and the forgiveness of my sins. I repent, Lord. I love and worship you, Father God. Thank you for your grace and favor. I love being your child."

The sound from down the hall caught Lauren's attention, interrupting her morning prayer. Through the entrance of her bedroom emerged William the dog, his black fur melding into the still darkened hallway. His entire body wagged as he traversed the mounds of clothing to greet his mistress with a succession of licks and moans. Lauren bent over to pat him, then staggered back. Catching a whiff of his breath, she pointed an accusing finger in the dog's direction; his ears flattened in embarrassment. "You stole Bingo's food again."

She slapped the side of her leg, in a command for William to follow, and headed for the hall. He stared at her blankly with his one blue/one brown eye, then hurried to catch up. Lauren always said William wasn't the "brightest bulb in the drawer."

Just as the twosome headed down the stairs, the soulful wail from a cat filled the house. Lauren ran her hand along William's wide back. "Don't breathe on her; it's a dead giveaway."

Chapter 2

-Tucker-

As if by heavenly choreography, the rising sun illuminated Lauren's path as she made her way across the living room toward the kitchen. She thought of how much she loved this time of day. Everything was so peaceful and fresh, like God had been up all night spring-cleaning.

Her dog slammed into her like a bus in an ice skid when Lauren suddenly stopped to take in the sun beaming through the windows. He slunk toward the kitchen door to wait while Lauren watched a montage of past Christmas mornings play out in her imagination. They were bittersweet visions; of course, faces were changed to protect the innocent—not that there were many innocent in those days.

After she had her fill of holidays past, Lauren moved purposefully through the swinging kitchen door, which William sidestepped a nanosecond before it slammed shut on his tail.

They were greeted by Bingo, a formidable calico cat crouched on the kitchen counter ready to pounce. The feline's yellow eyes formed slivers above her chiseled features. She was scowling at her empty food dish below her, the very one which William had raided earlier. In the dog's haste to devour the cat's food, he'd left telltale teeth marks on the tiny bowl.

Bingo expressed her next level of annoyance by swishing her tail high above her rump as if a weather balloon in a storm was attached to its end. William stood behind Lauren for protection while Lauren picked up the bowl and refilled it with food. "Alright, both of you, kiss and make up." Bingo simply turned and faced the wall while William slowly retreated to his bed in the corner. "Fine," Lauren said as she went on about her business. "You have no idea how stupid both of you look when you pout."

❦

Pulling some cereal out of the cabinet for Tucker, Lauren took a moment to read the ingredients on the side of the box; "Artificial coloring and flavoring, fat free, cholesterol free; a performance-powered morning meal for kids." She looked at the package with disgust as she crossed the kitchen. "Whatever happened to Wheaties?" she said to no one.

The door to Tucker's bedroom stuck sometimes, so Lauren lifted it slightly as she pushed inside. Picking up the trail of toys and crayons that led to her son's bunk bed, she mechanically dumped the carnage in a toy chest nearby. Tucker, five years old, blond and beyond cute, was partially hidden beneath a menagerie of stuffed animals that guarded him like sentries. Lauren didn't have to wake him; he always was up as soon as the first ray of sun shone through his window. Their morning ritual had more to do with "a little loving" than the arrival of "Mom the alarm clock." Clearly, this was the best part of Lauren's day; the big Tucker hug and kiss before he stumbled into the bathroom always put everything in perspective for her.

"I have to go potty," he said every morning like it was new information.

"What do you want to wear for your last day of school?" Lauren asked as if she didn't already know.

Tucker pulled off his pajama top as he reentered his bedroom. "My cape and shorts," he said, matter-of-factly.

Lauren smiled, grabbing his Batman cape off the shelf. "You're such a fashion plate."

"Is that good?"

"If you want to get the girls it is." She loved to tease him.

"Mom, I hate girls!" He rolled his eyes at her, then charged out of the room.

Much to Tucker's chagrin, the box of pink fluff cereal had been thrown in the garbage. Nonetheless, he obediently munched on the bran cereal swimming in milk while he told his mother about the dream he had last night: "And just when I was going to fall into the dark place, and there were monsters everywhere, it got all light, like when you look into the sun and your eyes cry.

But my eyes were closed, and the light didn't hurt them. It felt warm and . . ." He paused for a moment deep in thought.

"And?"

"And then I woke up because I had to go to the bathroom."

"Dang, you were just getting to the good part," Lauren sat next to her son at the table drinking a fresh cup of coffee. "God has such a safe place for us, doesn't he?" Tucker nodded as a raisin rolled off his spoon and sploshed back into his bowl. "Good shot," Lauren noted, stealing a few flakes of his cereal. Tucker nodded again. Surely, this boy was the light of Lauren's life.

There was a brief knock at the kitchen door announcing Susan's entrance. Lauren couldn't help but think that this woman looked like some sort of haloed intruder on a coffee break as the sun backlit her shock of white hair. If the truth be known, Lauren actually considered Susan to be an angel. Yes, she knew all biblical angels were male types, but this woman fit God's qualifications, no matter how you sliced it. She had prayed for Lauren's salvation since they'd met; she'd mentored her; she was a prayer warrior for Lauren and her entire nonbelieving family; but most importantly, Susan presented herself as a godly woman who beautifully represented Christ as he lived in her heart and spirit. Susan would always say that she was just a regular person making her way through life, hopefully with a bit more style and grace than the average bear and with a lot of help from God.

"Suz," as Lauren called her, headed straight for the brewed coffee on the nearby counter, pouring herself a large mugful laced with four Sweet and Lows to flavor the river of heavy cream she religiously used in her morning upper. *So what*, Lauren thought, *if Susan is a sixty-five-year-old chubby angel with a few bad health habits.* If not for a couple of minor flaws, she'd be too perfect to be true. Lauren looked at this lovely woman and acknowledged that she too wanted to age gracefully with the same inner beauty that set Suz apart, beauty from the inside out.

"I'm starting that new herb tea diet today, right after my coffee." Suz offered light-heartedly as steam from her coffee concoction fogged her glasses. She wiped her vision clean with a sweep of a napkin, then addressed the "wee one" in the room. "Hi, Tuck," she waved her mug at the boy in a toast. Tucker practically threw his orange juice glass over his shoulder in a return gesture.

"Tea diet?" Lauren queried. "Never heard of it."

Just for fun, Tucker let loose with a random raisin that flew past Susan's left ear. She batted at it like an annoying fly, letting her wink to Tucker endorse their morning salutation before continuing her conversation with Lauren.

"It's supposed to detoxify you while it melts the fat away," Susan tried to look enthusiastic about her newest health commitment. Before Lauren could shoot her friend a response, Suz acknowledged her folly with another wink, escaping the conversation by pouncing on Tucker for her morning kid fix. She was all over him, kissing and hugging him, affectionately pulling his earlobes and tickling his neck.

It amazed Lauren that her son put up with Susan's onslaughts; she had explained her friend's behavior to Tuck, "Susan is suffering from 'empty nest' syndrome." And after Lauren clarified to her son that "empty nest" was just an expression and that Susan's kids really didn't grow up in a tree, Tucker decided to let Susan smother away.

Satisfied by her lovefest with the kid, Susan turned her attention back to Lauren. "You're a real adventurer, you know. I'm so proud of you. I'd never have the guts just to pack up and start a new life, no matter how many times I fantasized about it."

"Hey, you stuck with a not-so-perfect marriage, raised six kids and . . ." Suddenly, the sound of an emergency alarm cut through the air. Lauren responded at a dead run, sprinting out of the kitchen and across her yard to an office by the back of her house. At the audibly annoying intrusion, Bingo the cat simply crawled deeper into her fluffy nest of towels while William made a gallant but brief effort to follow his mistress before falling back into the comfort of his bed.

Familiar with the alarm routine, Susan yelled after Lauren, "I'll take Tuck to school."

"Thanks, Suz. Bye, Tuck. I'll pick you up at noon, buddy!" Lauren never looked back as she burst through the clinic's entrance.

❧

The buzzer sounded repeatedly until Lauren reached the front door and opened it, leaving her other life behind in a cloud of dust. Lauren always found it interesting that she so easily could be pulled away from her concerns when she was called to duty. She greeted an older woman accompanied by Claudette, a uniformed maid. Together they held a limp, black cat, his white point markings reminiscent of a tuxedo.

"Doctor, Oscar passed out in his water bowl!" wailed Mrs. Cramer, her frail eighty-year-old hands shaking the feline for some sort of response.

Humiliated, Oscar the cat impatiently stared at Lauren, his "lifesaver." The cat's hind end was cradled in Claudette's arms as she squeezed herself through the doorway next to Mrs. Cramer.

"Lord, Ms. Lauren, I figured it ain't that hot yet for Oscar to want to swim in his water bowl. That's what I thought when I saw him laying there," Claudette sputtered.

Lauren immediately gathered the cat up and headed for the examining room, both women following closely behind. "How long ago did you find him?" Lauren asked between strides.

"No more than twenty minutes. Thank God his little pink nose was above water. He could have drowned!" Claudette lamented. Mrs. Cramer glared at her maid. "Swimming my foot! He doesn't even like to go out when there are clouds in the sky."

"Ladies, please. Have you changed his food in any way?" Lauren checked the cat's vital signs.

"Oscar gets liver on Sundays and fish whenever it's fresh at the store," Claudette was definitely defensive.

"How about the dried food we discussed?" Lauren was clearly in her vet mode.

Mrs. Cramer jumped in proudly, "Why, yes, I've started putting dried food in his bowl at all times in case he wants to snack."

Lauren was at least happy to note a cause of illness. She exhaled on her next sentence: "It looks like he has a bladder infection. Do you remember my mentioning that male cats most often can't tolerate the ash contained in dried food? Eventually it will cause urinary tract problems." The women glanced at each other in a show of embarrassment.

"Not to worry," Lauren assured the ladies with her best bedside manner, for which she was renowned, "I'll call over to Camon Clinic, and they can put Oscar on an IV for a day or so. He'll be good as new, promise."

"I told you he didn't like that dried stuff. It ain't even good for him," Claudette muttered, hiding her relief.

In an attempt to turn the tide of recriminations, Lauren continued, "The good news is that Oscar is going to be fine. Just keep him off of dried food, and he'll outlive all of us." Lauren smiled encouragement to the scowling twosome.

Mrs. Cramer waved her hands about as if fanning away some imaginary pest. "I was really scared, I must admit."

"I'm so sorry, Mrs. Cramer. Honestly, Oscar should enjoy a long healthy life." Lauren handed her the cat while she made the call to the other clinic.

"By the way," Mrs. Cramer added, "my neighbor says her cat ran away yesterday. It's fat with kittens and expecting any day. She thought somebody might have brought her to you."

"No, I haven't seen her, but I'll keep my ears peeled," Lauren offered.

Amused, Claudette and Mrs. Cramer looked at each other.

"What?" Lauren asked, puzzled.

"Miss Lauren, I think you mean your eyes peeled. You keep your ears open and your eyes peeled," Claudette tried not to insult her.

"So noted," Lauren smiled sheepishly. "I always get sayings turned around, since I was a kid."

By the time Oscar, Mrs. Cramer, and Claudette were on their way, peace had been made by all, and the cat's future looked bright. Lauren couldn't help but smile when she thought about how many times over the years those two women had brought Oscar in for one reason or another. They fussed over him like he was their only child. Oscar seemed to have an innate sense of humor about his station in life, playing the two women against each other like a chess master. Oh boy, Lauren was really going to miss Susan and her practice.

She recalled what brought about her decision to become a veterinarian so late in life. It began with her move from New York City, which ended her career as a headhunter; all that corporate wheeling and dealing nauseated her. But the primary reason for changing her world was the pain of her first destructive marriage. And when it finally ended, she needed to begin again or else she'd simply expire from a broken heart.

Sure, it was hard going to school all day and working as a receptionist at an emergency vet clinic half the night, but she was determined to finally embrace some independence, including from her sister, Irene. It was at that point, when Lauren was bereft spiritually and stripped to her core emotionally, that she met Susan. Suz had brought a stray cat into the night clinic, and from then on, these women were instantly friends. Over the next six months, Susan helped Lauren set up shop next door to her house while she witnessed to Lauren about Jesus. Not only did Lauren have a glorious graduation day from veterinary school, but straight from that celebration, she and Susan went to the local church where Lauren was baptized. When she emerged from the water after making her public proclamation that she "was a sinner, that she needed a Savior, that Jesus was the Son of God who died on the cross for all sin, defeated death, and sits at the right hand of our Father in heaven," Lauren felt truly loved for the first time in her life. That was almost ten years ago—a decade filled with stumbles and bumbles, battles and growing pains, yet the love of God had sustained her, and his promises continued to see her through even her darkest hours. No doubt, she was a work in progress, but she wasn't a victim anymore, and for that she was eternally humbled and grateful.

Suddenly, the clinic's alarm rang again, shattering her moment of serenity. Wow, for a closed business, this sure was a busy morning. Lauren hastened to open the door to find Mr. Franks and his pit bull, Frances, glaring at her. The dog held up her front paw in obvious pain.

"Mr. Franks, what happened?" Lauren stepped back as the two plowed into the office like a title wave. "I know you've closed on us, but my girl here has a burr stuck in her foot, and she's cranky about it!"

Lauren moved toward the dog who curled her lip on cue. "She does look a little out of sorts." She paused in a moment of caution before attempting to make contact with Frances. As Lauren knelt next to the dog, she couldn't help but stare at the piece of upholstered furniture that hung around the canine's neck.

"Mr. Franks, is that some sort of new fangled collar?"

"Don't be silly, woman. She's being disciplined," Mr. Franks muttered.

"Of course." Frankly, Lauren was dying of curiosity as well as concern. At the risk of being called plain old stupid, she decided to proceed with her questioning.

"Disciplined for what, sir?"

"Chewing the furniture, of course. My wife nearly kicked me out of the house when Frances chowed down on her best chair." The man shook his head at the memory, then grabbed the hanging mass around the dog's neck and tugged on it slightly. Frances regarded her master with disdain.

"Forgive me," Lauren inquired as politely as she could, "but I'm not sure I understand how tying the chair to the dog's neck will stop her from chewing."

Mr. Franks looked at Lauren with concern. "For a pretty good doctor, you don't know a thing about raising and rearing, do you?"

"No sir, I guess I don't. You've always been an education for me, Mr. Franks." This had certainly proven true over the years. Mr. Franks had been her first client, one with a big heart and a small stipend to live on. "No charge" was an unspoken show of respect from this wet-behind-the-ears vet to a man with a wealth of knowledge and wisdom, despite his latest furniture necklace.

"An education free of charge, I might add." He cleared his throat. "Where I grew up, when one of our hounds got in the coop and ate our chickens, my daddy tied a dead one around the dog's neck for a week or so. Believe me, that hound never killed another bird." Mr. Franks looked pleased with himself as he waited for Lauren to see the light. Of course, she still didn't get the connection. After a beat, he decided to be kind to this city girl and explain his point further. "The bird carcass would rot after a day or so and turn the dog right off by the smell. Basically, it'd make the dog nauseous even to think about a chicken."

"Oh, I get it." Lauren's breakthrough lasted only a moment until logic took over. "No, I don't get it. The leg of the chair isn't going to turn rancid, so how will that stop Frances from chewing?"

Mr. Franks just shook his head, finally responding in an indulgent tone, "It's the principle that counts."

"Yes, sir, of course." Lauren knew that would be the final word on the subject, so she proceeded to examine Frances's paw. Now, this is when Mr. Franks stood back and watched with respect. "No question, you have a way with my girl."

"Thank you, Mr. Franks." Lauren gingerly pulled the last of the burr from between the dog's pad and handed the leash back to the old man. "No charge, sir. It's the least I can do for all the things you've taught me."

He winked at her as he adjusted his fishing hat to assume a more roguish angle. "Mighty kind of you, miss." Opening the door to the office, he walked toward the street, then turned to the veterinarian who was still watching them leave. The charming gentleman paused for a moment, not for the sake of drama but rather for thoughtful reflection, before he spoke: "You should remember, Ms. Lauren, you've never charged me in seven years, and Frances and I appreciate it." He tipped his hat and disappeared around the corner. Yes, she was going to miss her practice here!

Lauren heard the phone in the house ring just as she shut the clinic's door; the "closed" sign flapped in the breeze. As she made the twenty-yard dash across the lawn for the millionth time since she opened her office, Lauren had a momentary fantasy of filming her own exercise video once she hit Music City. It would be called "The working mother/veterinarian/runner/sprinter/jogger/eighteen-hundred-stairs-a-day/child shuttle service/over fifty, how-to-stay-in-shape tape."

When Lauren picked up the phone in the kitchen, her delusions of grandeur and a million bucks vanished at the sound of the voice on the other end of the line.

"Lauren, it's your mother." Margaret, a robust seventy-five- year-old, frantically pressed a collection of television remote controls pointed at the three VCR machines hooked up to various sized TV sets located around her bedroom. "Nuts! No, not you, Lauren. Your father switched all my clickers, and I'm missing two of my programs as we speak!" Her face flushed under the pressure.

"You called me? You never call me." Lauren was visibly stunned.

"I never call you because you're never available. You're either operating, driving Tucker around, shopping, cooking, taking a bath, on the other line, running out the door, in the middle of an emergency . . ."

"OK, Mom, you made your point." Remembering Susan's word about her impatience, Lauren caught the snap in her voice. "My being busy is nothing personal, Mom."

"So you say. By the way, you were a lot more fun when you weren't Doctor Dolittle, or Mother Teresa for that matter. Not that I don't love Tucker, mind you. It's just that you used to . . . oh never mind!" Margaret leaned back against a mound of pillows that surrounded her voluminous body. "I just hate talking to your answering machine. It's like talking to your father when his football is on . . . or tennis, or . . ." Margaret's face soured, "And I'm not going to stop complaining about it! After fifty-five years of marriage, I wouldn't want him to think I just rolled over on the issue. I swear, if I never saw another ball, bat, net, trap, or pulled hamstring, I would be a happy woman."

Suddenly, all three of Margaret's television sets brought up different soap operas on their screens. She settled further back into the pillows with a look of accomplishment on her face, but only for a moment. "I just called to say that the movers have left already and . . ." There was a long, awkward pause before she finally continued, "your father and I want to thank you for organizing everything and including us." Before Lauren could respond, Margaret forged ahead, "I talked to Irene. She'll be arriving in Centennial a few days after we do, so I'll cook a roast. Lamb if you like; I know it's your favorite. It will be nice to be all together again, and that's all I wanted to say."

Stunned, Lauren forced her mouth to form the words, "Great, Mom." She stared out across the yard, happy for the warm exchange. Her eyes wandered over to a horse paddock attached to an empty stall. The click of her mother hanging up brought her back to reality. "Bye, Mom," she said to the abandoned phone line. Suddenly, the lack of sleep and her list of unfinished details hit Lauren like a brick wall. She was beyond exhausted, and it was only nine in the morning.

Chapter 3

-Moving Right Along-

Tucker burst from his classroom at full throttle and headed to meet his mom who was double-parked by the exit door. He raced along with the enthusiasm of a young colt let out to romp. Throwing her arms open to greet her son, they collided in a bear hug. He held up a pile of papers and well wishes from the other kids in his class. "Look what I got!" The boy tried to put on a brave face.

Lauren knelt next to him, noting that her joints cracked as she descended. "That's great, buddy." She wiped some dirt off his forehead. "Remember, I have everyone's address so we can write to them about our move."

"Just Mark, OK?" Tuck looked away to avoid any probing questions from his mom when he dropped some of his drawings;

a small gust of wind whisked them away. Shoving the rest of his papers into Lauren's hands, Tucker ran off to collect his escaped works of art now strewn all over the school lawn.

Sometimes Lauren felt like she would literally burst with love for her son. She never realized caring for someone could bring such indescribable joy. She had questioned herself a million times as to whether Tucker was going to be happy with this move to Tennessee, but she firmly believed he needed to be close to his dad. She also believed it was the right move for her mom and dad, as well as her sister and her seventeen-year-old niece, Chelsea. Lauren was on a mission to find some mutual ground so everyone in their nutty family might begin afresh.

Thinking of Irene, Lauren's mind drifted back to some of her old haunts in New York City. She shook her head in embarrassment as she reviewed her past; it felt as if she were watching a foreign character in someone else's movie. Yes, younger Lauren was a wild child, and her older sister was always bailing her out of one mess or another. Who would ever have guessed that it would be Lauren who would radically turn her own life around, albeit in slow motion? She was still driven but not frantic; passionate for God's touch, not a man's; and she had to admit, she was a darn good mom. For a rare moment Lauren decided to give herself credit where credit was due instead of constantly dwelling on her mistakes. Yes, she had pulled herself up by the bootstraps, left her big city corporate shark career, and moved to the west coast. She recognized that few people ever throw themselves into their childhood dreams and make them come true as she had. And even though everyone, from family to friends, thought she was crazy to choose the west coast over the east coast, she forged ahead anyway.

The hardest part, though, was leaving Irene and Chelsea behind, and she was determined to rekindle all her family ties no matter how frayed. Yes, the time had come. Lauren couldn't stand the pain her sister was going through lately; she longed finally to become a port in the storm for Irene and her niece. She prayed that she could be strong for her sister—protective, as Irene had always been for her. Lauren's thoughts flashed back to her teens in the summer of '62.

Downtown New Haven's Main Street was lit up like a cake; cars cruised this mini-metropolis looking for action. A green 1959 Chevy weaved through traffic in front of a movie theater. The marquee above the long ticket line read: *To Kill A Mockingbird* starring Gregory Peck.

Tom, a hip, blond, sixteen-year-old, struck his best James Dean pose at the wheel of the Chevy. Glued to his side was Lauren, age fifteen; they both smoked cigarettes and honked at passing friends. Tom flicked his cigarette butt out the window, then put his arm around Lauren. "The Twelfth of Never" by Johnny Mathis played on the radio, encouraging Lauren to snuggle a little closer. Suddenly, she ducked down in her seat, causing Tom to swerve the car wildly. "What are you doing?" he yelled.

Lauren popped her head up to stare out the rear window. "Turn around! My parents just passed us!" Her voice cracked.

Total panic registered on Tom's face as he slid the car into a U-turn between oncoming traffic.

Sam and Margaret Patterson were in the front seat of their Dodge station wagon. Sam, a forty-five-year-old burly man dressed in a shiny blue suit, glared through the rearview mirror. Margaret, overweight at forty but still very attractive, twisted in her seat to look through the back of the car, adjusting her dress so it wouldn't wrinkle. "You're crazy, Sam."

He slammed on the brakes, throwing Margaret into the dash. "I'm telling you, it was our car!" He offered his wife no assistance as she pulled herself back into her seat.

The kids made a quick right turn down a side alley. Tom frantically looked about like a caged animal. "I thought you said they were out for the night!"

Lauren wriggled in her discomfort, "They're supposed to be at a party!"

The Pattersons' station wagon swerved through traffic, barely avoiding a collision; Margaret braced herself against the dash. "Sam, please slow down! Where are you going?"

"To check the house." Like a bloodhound, Sam did not have the personality to give up on a fresh trail.

Tom and Lauren sped down a residential street—he with a vice grip on the steering wheel; Lauren close to tears. "You don't know my dad. I'll be grounded for the rest of my life!"

"I know your dad. He's going to punch my lights out!" Tom shut his eyes at the thought. The Chevy slid into a driveway at the end of a residential block stopping in front of a small, run-down white house.

Dust surrounded the car as Tom choked the engine; Lauren was out before the car came to a full stop. "Go, go, go!" she wailed frantically waving her arms about.

Tom sprinted across the lawn, then disappeared around the corner. Meanwhile Lauren raced for her front door, stumbling over the porch steps in her haste, then burst through the door and headed straight to the back of the house. Most of the lights were out, although music could be heard coming from one of the far rooms. As Lauren zoomed through the simple, yet neatly furnished house, she screeched, "Rene!"

Her sister was sitting next to a bowl of popcorn on her bed working on some handwritten pages stuffed in a leather-bound diary. When she heard Lauren, she nearly jumped out of her skin, turning down the radio just as Lauren ran into the bedroom. "Rene! What am I going to do?" The girl could barely swallow.

Jumping to her feet, Irene's eyes widened. "What? What's wrong?"

Lauren talked a mile a minute, all the while shaking Irene by the shoulders for emphasis, "Tom and I took the car, and we passed Mom and Dad downtown, and I think they saw us! We were by the movies and . . ."

Irene pushed Lauren's hands away, holding her at bay. "What? You took the car? Are you crazy? You don't have a license!"

Now Lauren started shaking from head to toe. "I wasn't driving. We weren't going to take it for long, but they must've seen Tom when they passed us. I mean, it looked like Dad."

Irene's mouth dropped open in horror. "You let Tom drive Dad's car?"

Lauren twirled around like a top looking for an avenue of escape. "Yes! And they saw us, and I think Dad followed us. You have to help me, Rene. You have to do something! Please!" Lauren was on the verge of hysterics.

Now it was Irene's turn to grab her by the shoulders and shake her. "Calm down. I can't think!"

Margaret held fast to the door handle as Sam slid around a hidden curve. She begged her husband, "Please, Sam, slow down. You're going to kill us. Irene wouldn't take the car!"

"Lauren would." With that, Sam hit the brakes and finally swung into their driveway.

Margaret made her way out of the car with difficulty, clearly rattled by the high-speed chase. She was instantly relieved to see their other car parked in the driveway. Straightening her dress once more, she tried to adopt a casual tone in an effort to camouflage her heightened nerves. "See there, Sam. I guess it wasn't our car after all." Not to be deterred, Sam stepped over to the Chevy for a closer inspection.

Margaret positioned herself between her husband and the car, trying to route him back to their station wagon. "Come on, Sam, we're late as it is. Let's just go on to the party."

But Sam pushed past her, slamming his hands down on the Chevy's hood. "She's still hot!" Margaret stepped away, watching the back of his neck flush.

Inside the house, Lauren huddled on the bed while Irene paced back and forth. Lauren whined like a scared rabbit, "Rene, where are they?"

Suddenly Irene stood before the cowering girl with authority. "Shhh! Now let's go over it again, OK? I'm going to tell Dad I took the car and left you at home. Right? You've been here all night, and I . . ."

Before Irene could finish, their father crashed into the bedroom with Margaret close behind. Sam immediately made his way over to Lauren, pushing Irene aside. He picked his daughter up by the shirt collar, and in one fell swoop, stood her before him. "What were you doing with my car, young lady?" Sam's mouth twisted in anger.

Margaret tried to intervene, worried what he might do to Lauren. "Sam, please. Just calm down. I'm sure there's a simple explanation."

Margaret looked helplessly at her two girls when Irene stepped forward; her voice was unwavering, "I took the car, Dad. Lauren was here all night."

Now Sam focused his rage on his other daughter. "You did what?"

"I'm sorry, Dad. It was stupid. I needed more paper to work on my book."

"Did I give you permission to take my car out at night?" The vein on his forehead pulsed with anger.

Irene was quick to reply: "No, sir. I'm sorry, sir."

Again Margaret tried to diffuse the moment while pulling Lauren behind her for safety. "Sam, Irene won't do it again." She glanced at her eldest child who nodded with emphasis.

"No, sir, never again."

Tension choked the room while everyone waited for Sam's response. He finally broke the standoff with a frightening lunge toward Irene. Lauren screamed as Margaret pulled helplessly at her husband's shirt; within a brief moment it was clear what Sam's punishment was to be. With his massive hands he mercilessly attacked Irene's precious pile of writings stacked on her bed and ripped them to shreds. And with that, Irene collapsed in a river of tears. Sam stared his daughter down before pulling his wife out of the bedroom, and after the momentary calm that follows a storm, the girls heard their father's booming voice as he slammed the front door. "You're right, Margaret, she won't do it again. Irene will learn not to lie for her sister!"

When they were sure they were safe, Irene went over to Lauren who pathetically tried to match the torn, scattered papers that now covered the room. Irene took her sister in her arms, and with a soothing voice, comforted her—a voice Lauren had come to rely on. "It's OK, sweetie."

"No, it's not," Lauren wailed, "He ruined your book! I hate him!"

Irene just held her tighter. "It's OK, really."

As Lauren fast-forwarded to present day, she was visibly touched by her past review. No question, she loved Irene dearly. She was also concerned for Irene, who seemed lost and broken since her impending divorce. What was worse, Lauren didn't seem to be able to offer Irene any real comfort. Although Irene was happy for

Lauren's new life and faith, she was just not interested in being "evangelized." Clearly, there was going to be some radical adjusting to do once the family all relocated to Tennessee.

As Tucker continued to gather his artwork, Lauren's focus returned to her son and their move. She recalled as a child the times she had to attend a new school and how she tried to get into a clique before anyone discovered how absolutely petrified she was; Lauren never quite made the in crowd. And as usual, Irene tried to protect her, back then at least, when they weren't fighting with each other.

After Lauren helped Tucker with the last of the elusive wind-blown pages, they both piled into the car. She kept chatting about anything and everything she could come up with to try to distract Tuck from his obvious malaise. No matter how strong this young boy was trying to be, the intermittent quiver of his chin betrayed his true feelings.

As Lauren's jabber began to sound like a broken record, she thought, *At what point do children stop expressing their every feeling and start holding things in?* She called it the "starter package of adult baggage" carried through life just to ensure that happiness doesn't come too easily. Oooh, she hated that old negative tape that played over and over in her mind: *You're not lovable. You're invisible, you're not good enough. You'll never make it.* Or worse, *You have to earn love.* What a lie!

Tucker broke into Lauren's mental wanderings in a sad, soft tone: "Dad's coming to Tennessee with us, right?" The boy kept staring out the window while he waited for his mom's response.

Lauren wondered, *How come some of life's toughest questions come in the sweetest packages?* After a beat, Lauren fired up her best casual tone, "Daddy's going to fly there with you, but he's not going to be living there—with us, I mean."

"How come?" Tuck slowly drew a face on the dirty window with his index finger.

Lauren tried to see if the face on the window had a smile or not, but most of her son's drawing was hidden from her view. "Well, Daddy's going to take you for the weekend. You'll get to go to the circus, and you'll have so much fun! Then I'm coming out after I close up the house here. Auntie Irene and your cousin Chelsea will be arriving right behind us, and Grandmommy and Granddaddy will already be there! Cool, huh! One big happy family."

Tucker glanced at his mom with a look of trepidation, "But when you get to Tennessee, Dad is staying, right?" When Tucker shifted positions, Lauren caught a glimpse of the face he'd drawn on the window; it only had two eyes and a nose.

"You mean, staying with us? Staying in our house?" she asked when she already knew the answer.

Tucker sat a little taller, "Could he?"

Lauren was always amazed at how her son could stare at her for what felt like forever and never blink. "No, Tuck, he can't. Daddy and I will still be divorced when we move to Centennial, just like the last three years, son. But Daddy's moving nearby too, so he'll see you a lot, just like here. Everything is going to be OK, I promise. It's all for the best." She tried to encourage him with a smile.

This was the part Tucker hated. It kind of felt like the times he had to go to the doctor for a shot. Everyone would tell him it was going to be OK. That it was going to be good for him and to be brave. But the truth was, there wasn't a thing about the whole doctor deal that didn't scare him, hurt him, or make him want to throw up or cry. Tucker figured out for sure, right then and there, that he didn't much trust things that were supposed to be "for the best."

"You know that Daddy and I love you very much and we always will. You know we picked you out when we adopted you because you're so special. And what's even better than that, God loves you the most! And God has a gigantic plan for your life, so he'll look out for us no matter what."

Tucker had heard this pep talk his entire little life. "No matter what." He mechanically repeated.

Lauren tried another smile as she turned the car up their driveway. She knew what was coming on the heels of their arrival home, a Tucker escape. And, true to form, the boy was out of the car the instant the wheels came to a stop.

"Where're you going?" Lauren tried to keep her voice tender.

"My fort."

Lauren wondered if he would slow down for her approval. He did. "OK, buddy. I'll call you when dinner's ready. I'm making your favorites!" She hoped that his little mind would focus on her promise of hamburgers and apple pie and not on being scared. Thankfully, it worked.

"Hamburgers and apple pie, yeah!" Tucker sang as he disappeared around the corner. He knew his mom liked to see that skip in his walk.

Chapter 4

-Irene-

Irene knew there was no looking back for her or her daughter Chelsea; their New York high-society lifestyle was vanishing like the fading Manhattan skyline in the car's rearview mirror.

What she was finally putting behind her was painful enough, but what lay ahead frightened Irene more than any of the horror movies she admittedly was addicted to. And none of Lauren's late night marathon phone calls, words of encouragement, and prayers had eased her concerns. On top of that, moving to the Bible Belt offered Irene zero comfort since she thought all that faith stuff was just a bunch of mumbo jumbo. At least that was an area of agreement she shared with her daughter as well as both her parents. Besides, there were practical matters to face, and *amen* had never been a turnkey phrase for her.

Although the twosome were rolling out of the city in a BMW station wagon, Irene's about-to-be-finalized prenuptial divorce settlement would barely afford her a decent down payment on a small home, even in Tennessee. And the concept of moving in with Lauren and her parents was not even up for discussion. Never. Not a chance. Over her dead body.

She gasped for air; her emotional ventilator was working overtime. Irene insisted that she was in control of her circumstances. Even if her life felt like a runaway train, she merely had to calm down, take stock, and regroup. After all, she had always been the logical, together, solid-as-a-rock older sister and perfect daughter. OK, so her choice in men stank, and motherhood had always been a challenge with her willful daughter and her daughters' absentee father. But at fifty-two years old, she never imagined she'd find herself alone, lonely, broke, broken, and relocating with her relatives in Twangsville, USA, where the finest dining was called "Meat and Three." Irene wondered what the *three* was, and she was afraid she was about to find out, all too soon. How on earth did she end up in such a mess?

Before she fell into a crater of depression, she reminded herself that she still had some "giddy-up in her get-along," as Lauren would say. Yes, she was still attractive; after all, the New York press had labeled her "exquisite and sophisticated." Her long legs and dancer movements still shifted a few eyes, although there were times she'd strolled down Fifth Avenue in the past year or so that she felt totally invisible. Still, on a good hair day with some backlight for highlights, even Chelsea said her mother "rocked." Maybe this move to Tennessee was just a bump in the road, not the end of the road. She could begin again; no one could take away her talent and her drive. She'd be sought after no matter where she lived; she just wasn't sure she wanted to test her theory in a small southern town.

❧

Friends had warned Irene about the potential disaster of a prenuptial financial arrangement if something were to go awry with her marriage to Ford, but Irene was in it for the long haul, like Mom and Dad. Unfortunately her husband wasn't. And when her final divorce decree became a *fate accompli* in a couple of weeks, the reality of Irene's balance sheet would dictate that Chelsea would have to attend public school for the first time in her life. Moreover, beyond Irene's abruptly changed social status, this once-envied woman of leisure was finally going to have to attend to her broken heart in spite of her overwhelming urge to bury her head in a pillow for no less than a quarter of a century.

Thoughts flashed across her mental radar screen like a pinball game gone mad. *What about my work? My art? My heart?* Her body ached as if she'd just run a triathlon, and her once-tenacious personality seemed stalled in neutral—a sad, frozen asset staring at the biggest dilemma and despair of her life.

It was embarrassing for Irene to explain to Chelsea that her second marriage of twelve years to Ford Williams had failed at the hands of his infidelity. What made matters more untenable was that her husband's mistress turned out to be Irene's best friend. Oh well, just more fodder for the gossip columns.

As Irene wrestled to curb her thoughts, more damaging recrimi-nations echoed internally as she reviewed her relationship with her only child. She tested herself: *How could I have been a better mom? Why was there so much anger? It must be all my fault.* Irene was determined to repair her relationship with Chelsea, but how? Were they just experiencing the next round of hand-me-down generational heartache that she and Lauren experienced with their own mother? Surely the apple doesn't have to fall *that* close to the tree. Again, she took a deep breath and stared ahead, mesmerized by the oncoming headlights that illuminated what seemed to be an endless stretch of road before her.

At seventeen, Chelsea had a mega-bad attitude toward her mom; "Hey, whatever," was this beautiful-yet-rebellious girl's theme song. The only reason she was even going along on mom's "ride" was the annoying fact that she wouldn't turn eighteen for another eleven months, twenty days, and thirteen minutes—so she had no choice. Besides, she kind of liked the idea of Nashville as a springboard location for her future career; she was going to be the next shock wave in country music. Strategizing how to play her soon-to-be-found freedom to the hilt, she'd remind her mom that "the second I come of legal age, watch my dust." Irene real-ized that she didn't have much time to make a new start with her estranged daughter.

As the miles passed on their trip to Nashville, Irene silently reviewed Chelsea's past, searching for the root of her child's pain.

The first serious warning appeared when Chelsea's dad had abandoned their family when their little girl was only five. According to Chelsea, her mom didn't wait long enough for Chelsea's father to come back home before Irene moved on to another man. The little girl lashed out at her mother, and her accusations of fault festered like an open wound. All the pain paved the way for future demons of jealousy, anger, competition, and resentment to run their evil course between mother and daughter. The truth of the matter was, Irene had waited for over six months without hearing a word from Chelsea's father. He loved to call himself the "artist type," but in fact, he just simply vanished, another deadbeat dad offering no support for either Irene or his daughter. After a few more months of silence, Irene did finally decide to marry Ford.

Admittedly, their courtship was fast, but Ford was a compelling man of means who courted Irene with determination and doted on Chelsea to boot! Irene was thrilled that Ford and her daughter had taken to each other so quickly. But for the last several years, it appeared that Ford had little time or use for Chelsea. Ford's withdrawal of affection toward his stepdaughter confused Irene, and she began to complain about his cold attitude. Something was wrong, but she just couldn't put her finger on the source; tensions between Ford and Irene were observed by friends and family as well as by the New York columnists.

If that weren't enough for Irene to digest, communication between Lauren and Irene had become a challenge; it wasn't that the sisters had experienced a parting of ways, per say, nor was there a blowup, which was normal fare in the Patterson family. The conflict began when Lauren flew in from Los Angeles for Irene and Ford's third anniversary bash. Lauren, a new west coaster and an even newer believer, suddenly felt like a stranger to Irene. Her sister suggested that Irene find faith and new priorities based on God's ultimate authority and truth instead of a fat pocketbook. Irene told Lauren that she sounded like a cover story on *Star Magazine,* sporting phrases like "born again," "Jesus saves," and "unconditional love." Irene concluded that her sister was simply on another one of her tangents that should, according to past history, last about as long as her next haircut.

And so it had been with these sisters; a slow erosion of their once-close relationship had persisted over time. Nonetheless, both desired repair, and moving in closer proximity to each other was the first stepping stone toward that end.

With a background as a recognized artist, poet, and author, Irene had been the perfect package to be paraded on her husband's arm. Much to her chagrin, she eventually realized that she had unwittingly become this international businessman's trophy. She also finally had to admit that she had sold out in marriage for the sake of family and financial security. That revelation opened up her proverbial can of worms, and Irene became emotionally crippled by the layers of secrets and shames she had hidden deep within her soul. Despite hours and hours of psychotherapy, which only left Irene with head knowledge of her problems, she was caught in a vicious circle. Spending enough money in therapy to pay for her shrink's kids' and grandkids' college, it seemed there was no way to get off the couch. At three hundred dollars an hour with half of the time spent crying off her mascara, nothing was getting resolved, just more past issues to be analyzed and more meds to numb the pain. Sadly, there was also no healing in store for Irene because the unraveling of her problems never connected her mental comprehensions with the remedies of her heart. So, despite her determination and new-age, self-help thinking, all her efforts were futile.

Irene bit her lip and pushed back her tears, determined not to appear weak in front of Chelsea. Actually, at that point in time and travel, Chelsea couldn't have cared less; she was lost in her own world, buffered from her mother's hurt by blaring country rock music on her head phones and stacks of fashion magazines spilling off her lap. Irene decided to take her time of solitude as an opportunity to do a more in-depth review of her life; she needed to find some sort of solid footing, especially before the family reunion. Now that was a scary thought. She drifted back into her past, searching for some answers instead of merely rerunning her fears.

1990: Steam dripped off the beveled mirrors that framed a massive marble bathroom. Irene stood like a statue in her shower under a deluge of water, her expression vacant. As if coming out of a trance, she mechanically turned the water off, pushing her hair away from her scrubbed face. She stepped into the bathroom; her bejeweled hand rubbed the steam from the mirror like a windshield wiper, revealing her image on the other side. She stared at herself, a small smile crossed her face, and she giggled like a child. "Bette, that tickles," Irene said to the huge female German shepherd who had just entered the room.

What a bittersweet memory for Irene. She missed her dog so much. What a mean trick. The old adage, "Better to have loved and lost than never to have loved at all" did not comfort her in the least, especially when she had to put her dog to sleep at the same time she was going through her divorce. Losing Bette to cancer was almost too much to bear. Lauren said that Irene should get another dog ASAP, but Irene refused. "There will never be another dog like Bette," she insisted. Ever the persistent one, Lauren offered to share William with her until she realized she needed some four-legged companionship in her life. Too sad and too tired at that point to argue with her, Irene put Lauren off with a "We'll see."

⚜

A winter's day in 1986 was a hard one for Irene to forget. Sitting in a private alcove getting her hair styled, behind her, the salon was a flurry of activity—beauty at any cost. Irene's hairdresser teased, sprayed, and mercilessly yanked at her locks to create an inspired look while a makeup artist worked on her cheekbones.

"Will we be finished by 2:00? I still have a fitting, and I have to get my nails done." Irene queried as she watched her scalp rise from the hairstylist's relentless brushstrokes.

"She's in such a snit today." Annoyed at Irene's obvious lack of appreciation for his creative job, the hairdresser threw the barb to the makeup artist.

"It's an extremely important evening." Irene countered, aggravated at herself for even caring what he thought of her.

"Aren't they always?" The cohorts shared a snide giggle. Embarrassed, Irene avoided their eyes, glancing blankly at the magazine in her lap.

Her double-stretch limo waited at a bus stop in front of the salon. Irene pushed through the front door, holding her wet nails up to the cold wind like alien appendages; her hair held fast like a cement block in a storm.

Later that night, New York's jet set mingled at a cocktail party in a private room at the Twenty-One Club. Present but not accompanied, Irene looked uncomfortable as she sipped on her nearly empty glass of wine; she was conspicuously alone in a room full of couples. When the maitre d' approached, Irene turned to him like a child whose punishment was imminent; she chanced a fleeting smile. "Mrs. Williams, Mr. Williams just called and left a message that he'll be unable to attend."

Irene tried not to look disappointed as the maitre d' departed with a slight bow. Before Irene could gather her thoughts, an elderly woman greeted her. Irene immediately assumed the perfect-wife role. "Wonderful to see you, dear. You look delicious." The grand dame scanned Irene, then the room. "Where's Ford?"

Without skipping a beat, Irene delivered one of her most charming smiles, "He was unavoidably detained out of town.

He's terribly upset that he couldn't be here personally to accept the award."

"I see." The woman gave Irene a knowing look. And with that she moved off, leaving Irene alone to deal with the roomful of curious onlookers.

Dressed in a quilted robe later that evening, Irene sat on her bed surrounded by satin and lace pillows. Ever by her side, her dog, Bette, lay on the floor. Irene adjusted her reading glasses while she absentmindedly turned the pages of her old leather-bound notebook, her wine glass empty on the nightstand next to the clock, which read 12:03 a.m. Suddenly, the bedroom door flung open, and Irene instinctively hid her notebook beneath the bedcovers. Bette was alert in a flash but relaxed when she saw that the intruder was a family member. The shepherd did not take to Ford but obeyed Irene's repeated commands not to growl at her husband.

"You're so late." Irene removed her glasses, repositioning herself on the bed. Despite her disappointment, she couldn't help but notice how good Ford looked—tall, fit, with sharp blue eyes and slicked-back, graying blond hair. He mechanically kissed her on the forehead, then started to undo his tie. "Everyone asked for you. I said you were out of town." Irene offered in a manufactured calm tone.

"Good," was her husband's only reply. Then the phone rang. Ford grabbed it before the second chime. "Hello? . . . Yes. . . . No, no. You're not disturbing me. . . . Tomorrow . . . I see. I'll meet you for breakfast at the club, seven sharp." He hung up and headed for the bathroom; Irene followed. She stood just outside the door like a child waiting for permission to enter.

"I finished the first chapter today."

The phone rang again. Ford answered, "Hello? . . . Yes, bring him along. Goodnight." He hung up the receiver once again and turned to Irene. "Was the press there tonight?"

"AP, UPI, and CBS," Irene responded quietly. Ford emerged from the bathroom in his pajamas. Irene watched him get into bed.

"Chuck told me the PR firm did a good job. Cuomo's using them." Ford repositioned some of the pillows, then turned off his light.

His wife remained at the side of the bed for a moment before she joined him under the sheets. Lying there quietly for a few minutes, she finally asked, "Would you read it?"

"Read what?" His voice was muffled.

"I finished the first chapter of my book today."

"Of course, darling. Maybe over the weekend." He kissed her once more on the forehead and rolled over. "Oh, Guiding Eyes for the Blind called my office and asked for you to head up their walkathon. Quite an honor."

Irene was stunned, "But Ford, that's the charity Louise used to run."

"And?"

"She still uses your name. People might confuse us."

"Nonsense. She just keeps my name to get into restaurants. In New York, that's more valuable than her alimony." He grunted, then half-laughed at what he considered to be a joke.

Irene wasn't amused. "But . . ."

Before she could object further, he cut her off, "I already told them yes."

"But I won't have enough time to work on my book," she heard herself start to whine.

"I'll send you off to an island after the walkathon and you can play Hemingway to your heart's content." With that, Ford buried himself in the covers; the discussion was over. Deflated, Irene turned out her light; the dog groaned in the stillness of the darkened room, sensing her mistress' unhappiness.

Morning found Irene alone in bed, having missed her husband's departure. Annoyed, she glared at the clock. Countless nights she had fallen asleep in quiet tears after Ford's rejection of her, only to wake to an empty bed. She had developed a temporary method of pain relief for these all-too-often occasions; it was called her "plastic revenge," which meant a day of antique shopping with Ford's platinum card. She gazed around the room recalling how each blow to her femininity and marriage was soothed by the exquisite surroundings she'd attained: a handmade Tiffany style lamp she purchased the day after Ford had thrown a childish fit about her paints and canvas "cluttering" the study; a shelf of priceless first-edition books on subjects Irene could have cared less about; the custom, handmade, wrought-iron bed frame she commissioned after smelling an unfamiliar perfume on Ford's starched shirt. She had even imagined how she might scatter traces of a phantom romantic rendezvous of her own, hoping to evoke some semblance of jealousy from her increasingly estranged husband—but eventually thought better of it. Bette stood, growling at the sound of a light knock on the bedroom door.

"Come in," Irene mumbled. The butler merely opened the door a crack to announce, "Mrs. Williams, your sister is here."

Leaping to her feet, Irene was on the move. "Tell her I'll be right there. Thank you, and would you please let Bette out?"

"Of course, ma'am." Now the door swung open wide just as Irene vanished into the bathroom.

Irene dressed in record time and dashed out to greet Lauren. But before she could make it through the expansive hallway, Irene was affectionately mauled by Bette who acted like she hadn't seen her in years. Trying to avoid a run in her stocking from the dog's playful paws, Irene adopted a defensive pose, "Bette, down! . . . Stop it!" Her commands had little effect; Bette continued to lick her wildly.

"Down and stay!" a voice echoed from the next room. The dog hit the floor like a brick awaiting the next command from Lauren, who now appeared in the doorway. Although dressed in "European funky" with long, wild, curly hair, the family resemblance of these sisters still showed through their distinctly different styles.

"Wonderful. You give me a dog that only listens to you," Irene teased.

"Where have you been?" Lauren wailed like a teenager. Irene gave her a quick kiss, then pulled her back down the hall.

"Don't worry, we'll make it. Promise. I just have to put my face on."

Lauren trailed after Irene, leaving Bette on her "down" command. Frustrated, the dog whined but stayed put. After a moment, Lauren called for her to come. The dog leaped up, scrambled across the glossed marble floors, then ran down the hall, sliding into the bedroom in a Keystone Cops ballet move, taking a floor lamp down before skidding to a stop. Lauren nonchalantly picked up the lamp before jumping on Irene's bed. "A little sloppy on the landing there, Bette. I'll give you a nine."

Irene smacked her makeup on rather haphazardly while Lauren gathered herself into a cross-legged position on the bed, calling for Bette to join her there. Lauren absentmindedly played with the dog while she chided Irene, "I don't get divorced every day, you know."

"Tell Bette to get down."

Lauren ignored her sister's request, throwing an imaginary ball up in the air for Bette to catch. The dog did an airborne sunfish move before landing in a heap once again next to Lauren. "Men are never who they say they are."

Irene could hear the pity dripping off her sister's words, she responded, "No, you just invent who you want them to be."

"Like the men you write about in your books?" Lauren countered, now rolling all over the silk comforter with the gleeful dog.

Irene refused to be distracted by their playful antics, "The difference is that I write fiction. You *live* it."

"Irene, admit it, we share many a bad habit. Guess it runs in the family."

"Thank you, Dr. Ruth." Irene pulled a hot roller out of her hair. "Please get Bette off the bed. Ford doesn't like dog hair between the sheets."

"It's not worth it," Lauren replied.

"They're two-thousand-dollar sheets!"

Lauren corrected her sister with a condescending tone. "I meant men. Aren't *we* in a good mood."

"You without a man is like . . ." Irene fumbled with her blouse buttons as she tried to think of a witty comparison.

Lauren filled in the blank, "You without money."

Irene let that one pass. She moved to the mirror, watching Lauren's reflection as she spoke. "You're just running away from him so he doesn't leave you first. Lauren, you told me you were in love. You said that Steven was 'incredible, funny, brilliant, wild.' That should last more than a minute and a half, even with you."

"Why are you being so mean to me? I didn't come here to be lectured!" Lauren was about to cry.

"I'm not . . . and get my dog off the bed!" Irene yelled as she started down the hallway.

Lauren yelled after her, "Hey, I'm the one getting divorced. I'm the one who's supposed to be upset!"

Irene stormed out of the Park Avenue apartment building, Lauren close behind, flanked by Bette. They all climbed in the back of the limo; Bette claimed the jump seat. Once settled, Irene took a handful of jewelry out of her purse and started to accessorize herself, patting Bette while she hooked on some bracelets. As the car took off into traffic, Lauren was deep in thought. Concerned, Irene scrutinized her. "I think you should see Dr. Stern."

"Hey," Lauren bristled, "if I'm such a mess, what does your shrink say about you?"

"I'm not happy. I just think I am."

"Admit it. After two years with Ford, the perks aren't worth the price."

"I married Ford because I love him."

"No, you married him because you didn't get published. You love the lifestyle, not Ford. Where's the excitement? Don't you know that your prime time is now?"

"What you really mean is, it's over."

"What I really mean is, if you're going to make a move, do it while you can enjoy it, while it's still exciting, before you wrinkle. Remember, don't cut your nose off to spite your profile."

"Lauren, don't you know that what you want out of life doesn't exist?"

"Yes, it does."

"Of course. That's why you're so happy all the time."

"Isn't that the kettle calling the coffee black?" Lauren glared at her sister who suddenly started to laugh. "What?" Lauren asked.

"It's, 'don't cut your nose off to spite your *face,* and isn't that the pot calling the kettle *black,*' Lauren."

"OK, OK, you know what I mean." Lauren changed the subject. "So, where's Chelsea? I checked her room out to say hi, and her bed was already made."

"What do you care, Columbo?"

"Because I'm her auntie, that's why. What's the matter with you, anyway? Are you nurturing your bad mood so you can grow it into a bigger one?"

"No. Chelsea stayed at a girlfriend's for the night," Irene stated with authority. "We had an engagement last night, and it was the nanny's day off."

"*We* who? Did Ford grace you with his presence, or did you have to hold down the fort for him, yet again? And why didn't you call me? I love to watch Chelsea."

Irene powdered her nose in annoyance, "Because you're in your drama mode about your divorce. I didn't want to intrude on your soap opera!"

"That was mean, Irene. Not cute—mean! You know I always have time for Chelsea—unlike you." Lauren once again quickly changed the subject. "And why do you always cross-examine me?" she demanded.

"Because I'm worried about you! Because . . ."

Again, Lauren finished Irene's thought for her: ". . . my life is a mess. I failed one more time, OK. On top of that, I don't have any money because Shapiro won't pay the Preston commission."

"Who's Preston?"

"He's my client, for the Shapiro placement I've been working on forever! I was counting on that money to get me through the next couple of months. I'm making some major changes."

"What changes?"

"I don't know." Lauren waffled, "But it will be really big, you'll see."

Suddenly flooded with compassion, Irene put her arm around her little sister in a familiar hug. "Everything's going to be OK, sweetie."

Lauren could only return a disbelieving expression of hopelessness.

Now it was Irene's turn to reroute the conversation. She clapped her hands as if calling a court to order, "OK, here's something to curl Shapiro's hair." She gave Lauren a sly smile, "Tell him that you deal directly with his primary bank and his biggest retail customer, and you're sure they'd be interested to learn that he doesn't keep his word, or pay his commissions, so it would behoove him to make right the placement monies you've worked so hard for, or you'll pick up the phone."

Instead of a show of inspired direction, Lauren's shoulders dropped as she started to sob. Irene quickly gathered her up again in her arms. "You're going to be OK. I'll see to it."

Lauren devoured her in a bear hug, messing Irene's hair and neatly arranged jewelry. "Thanks for coming with me, Rene. I won't ask you to do anything for me ever again." Irene held her little sister for a moment longer, then pulled out her compact and started to powder Lauren's red nose. Catching her image in the mirror, Lauren fell back into her whine mode, "I look like the lead in *The Phantom of the Opera*—and I'm not talking about the pretty girl."

The limo pulled up in front of the federal courthouse in lower Manhattan. Lauren's countenance was one of a convicted criminal on death row. "Endings make space for new beginnings, don't you think, Rene?" she asked like a child.

"Absolutely." She gave Lauren another hug of encouragement as Irene's flashback faded into the blackness of night.

⁂

"Wow," Irene mumbled, pulling herself into the present. She shook her head, recounting Lauren's radical decisions immediately following her divorce ten years ago. First, she called a family summit, flying their mom and dad into Manhattan for the weekend. She even insisted that Chelsea attend the discussions, sure that Ford would be a no-show. (She was right on that count.) Irene pointed out that Chelsea would probably rather have a playdate than attend a Patterson debate, but Lauren argued that she wanted Chelsea to understand why she had to leave town.

No matter how envious Irene might have been about Lauren's relationship with Chelsea, she loved them both above and beyond her pangs of jealousy. Even though the two of them spent endless hours walking Lauren's herd of dogs in Central Park, shopping, going to the Plaza Hotel for tea, taking carriage rides, going to the movies, spending afternoons at the zoo, and catching every Radio City Music Hall show, Irene was happy for them—wasn't she? Actually, that's why Irene accepted Lauren's gift of Bette, thinking that she and her daughter might share a common interest in the dog. Ironically, the shepherd bonded to Irene instead of Chelsea, so the girl continued to spend more time with her Aunt Lauren rather than with her mom.

But then, a little more than a decade ago, Lauren left Manhattan to attend veterinary college on the west coast. Instead of her absence making more room for Irene and Chelsea's relationship to grow, it seemed to have had an opposite effect. Irene knew it sounded insane, but there was an indescribable sense of competition and tension between her and Chelsea starting when her daughter was as young as six years old. Granted, Irene was never the play-type mom, preferring to take Chelsea to fancy restaurants with a good wine list rather than the circus or ice skating. Still, she always made sure her daughter was well cared for, loved, and exposed to all the stuff kids adored, indulging her at every turn.

Maybe that was why Irene was particularly pleased when her Chelsea took such a shine to Ford; they used to play cards and do magic tricks till all hours of the night. She loved the fact that her daughter would finally have a supportive and affectionate male figure in her life since her natural father was never in the picture. Then again, if Irene forced herself to make an honest evaluation, she was also an absentee parent much of the time between her charitable commitments and wifely duties to attend to, not to mention fulfilling her art and writing aspirations. Irene painted portraits that brilliantly captured the soul and essence of her subjects. And her novels, although nary a one had been published, allowed Irene to live vicariously through the passionate story lines of her leading ladies. No doubt, Irene was talented yet, for the most part, undiscovered.

Checking some road signs to confirm that she was steadily making progress along the highway due south toward Nashville, Irene's mind worked overtime while her daughter now slumbered, headphones still torqued to high decibel levels.

As her thoughts wandered again, Irene offered herself some solace. No, she wasn't nuts when she suspected that her best friend since college was acting strangely every time she got within Ford's proximity. But the cut went deeper than her concerns.

In response, her husband always played on his wife's insecurities and neediness, reminding her that she had a bit of an issue with jealousy and abandonment. Ford was also quick to point out that the emotional baggage from her first marriage was wreaking havoc on their relationship, and that was something he simply would not accept. It was no secret to most that this dominant man could, and would, easily badger his wife into the corner, then simply leave her there at a loss for words.

Speechless was a new condition for Irene; she had always been a strong conveyer of her beliefs. No one would have dared describe Irene as a mealy-mouthed individual. But Ford had so many manipulative control tricks up his sleeve, not the least of which was to play on Irene's hormone levels. He'd swap at will between accusations of monthly PMS irrational behavior on her part, to the big demon called menopause madness. And with Irene locking horns more and more with Chelsea as she grew into her teens, Ford sarcastically labeled their battles the "hormone-horror time." Bottom line, he told Irene that she was out of control and demanded that her paranoia, exacerbated by her heightened sense of neediness, must be addressed. He spoke to her like a child, then let her work out the details of her depression with her shrink, Dr. Stern, whom Irene later found out was in Ford's pocket. That meant there was no doctor-patient confidentiality when it came to Ford's access to his wife's innermost feelings. Betrayal consumed her.

Ford was a master at his insidious forms of verbal abuse and battering designed to erode Irene's confidence. Although he never hit her, in a way it would have been better if he had; at least then people could have seen Irene's bruises and understood her pain more easily. As it was, Irene had been badgered into thinking that she was losing her mind. Little did she know the extent of her husband's twisted behaviors; those deep, dark discoveries were yet to be made. What did become devastatingly clear was, as far as her closest friend and her husband were concerned, Irene's worst nightmares had been playing out for years right under her nose (as well as between her sheets).

⁂

Cigarette smoke billowed out of the BMW as they traveled at breakneck speed toward Nashville, Irene chain-smoking all the way. She remembered Lauren's worn-out remark, "Where there's smoke, there's my sister." Although Irene would constantly admonish herself for putting herself in harm's way with the threat of ill health, smoking was Irene's way to appease her anger. After all, it did calm her nerves and curb her sweet tooth.

She dragged at the last vestige of her cigarette, then pulled some perfume from her bag, spraying a layer of airborne camouflage. Slowing her car, she gingerly opened the window and stuck her head out sideways to suck in some fresh air. Next came the gum and lipstick ritual. Catching a glimpse of herself in the rearview mirror, she wondered if this stupid hide-and-lie game of hers was actually getting over on Chelsea. Whether it was or wasn't, Irene simply did not want to flaunt her bad habits on her already-too-grown-up daughter. She glanced over at Chelsea who, thankfully, remained sound asleep, snoring.

The road sign read: Nashville, 107 miles.

Chapter 5

-Eleanor-

Eleanor purposefully moved among a group of young adults in the social hall after church as she did each week when they gathered to hear her speak. No, she was not the pastor's wife or even a regular Sunday school teacher. She was just "Ms. Eleanor," the local high school nurse and second mother to any and all who might be in need of advice or comfort.

It was easy to see why people of all ages were drawn to Eleanor, forgoing an hour or so of their Sunday afternoon relaxation time just to sit at her feet and immerse themselves in her unpretentious style of delivering God's messages. There was never condemnation in her voice, never, although she never compromised the Word of God. There was also no bitterness or anger in this forty-seven-year-old African-American woman who had seen and heard of the indignities the Old South had subjected her family to for generations. There was only the love of God and her life's calling to share that gift with anyone who wished to hear.

From her earliest memory, Eleanor had been a born-again Christian and an integral part of the church's extended family. With a melodic voice that could raise the roof in song or sermon, she began today's lesson with a probing challenge: "Have you ever looked up at the mornin' sun and felt its warmth envelope you like a toasty comforter on a cold winter's night? Or rallied after bein' protected and comforted, held fast in your parents' arms when someone mistreated you at school? Perhaps you've experienced the safety nets loyal friends offer durin' personal crises or advanced your aspirations with the confidence that comes from having family members watch your back, no matter what. The embrace of unconditional love; there's nothin' quite like it, and as children of God, we are called to love one another in Jesus' name and in Jesus' way. This is not a request; it is a commandment, and God never asks us to do anythin' he does not empower us to do.

"Consider a newborn baby, or new life unfoldin' as flowers do in springtime. Or the joy you felt when your mom would bring to school the homework you'd forgotten. What about weddin' rings worn as symbols of commitment that remain pure between spouses, sure of one another as best friends and lovers?"

Eleanor paused briefly, allowing the images she'd painted to achieve their full impact before continuing; her audience was enthralled.

"Don't you just adore the natural high of a vision that soars in the sky with the perspective of an eagle, glidin' through rarified air while explorin' the terrain below, steadfast, like a dream that won't die.

"What about the exhilaratin' relief of healin' and wellness that returns after you've recovered from an illness? Just think for a moment about the sense of accomplishment derived when people dare to put their aspirations down on paper, then labor diligently until each comes to fruition.

"Could *you* be the one to ignite the essence of someone's spirit with expressions of encouragement? Words found on lips of the courageous, those who do not give up or cry unless to cry out to God Almighty in thanksgivin'—not only for their many blessin's but also for the 'thorns in their sides'. Who of us has sidestepped those worldly thorns that keep us humble and reliant on God yet alive, as Christ lives in and through us? Oh yes, my brothers and sisters, God's grace is sufficient."

On the heels of that biblical truth, Eleanor offered a quiet smile to every eye in the room, allowing the message to sink even deeper into their quickened hearts. Then she filled the silence with Scripture from the New International Version: "He who has ears, let him hear" (Matt. 13:9).

Her sense of timing was flawless, her eyes gleaming as she began again with the wisdom held fast and deep within her spirit.

"Have you ever wondered when you arise in the mornin', how you made it through the night? Did you order your breathin' or command your heart to beat with life-givin' blood and oxygen? Who supported the life in your body while you slept unaware? Surely, you have marveled as first mornin' light revealed the glory of God's creation before you, the canvas of life he crafted in six days.

"Have you fully received God's gift of imagination that allows us to see through windows with no views? A photographer's eye may share his frame of mind as he captures the basic colors in an explosive kaleidoscope of rainbows. While music soars, lifting us to higher dimensions by arrangin' variations of a handful of simple notes of which symphonies are made.

"God wants us to trust that his love for us is unconditional and that all answers are found in him who is the livin' Word. When we can put on our résumé that our joy, love, and peace are unswayable and God's economy becomes our priority, we know his promises are everlastin' and his grace is truly amazin'."

After another long beat of silence, Eleanor bowed her head, and all said the Lord's Prayer in unison.

⁂

Now one might attribute this wonderful woman's impact on others to be the result of a good upbringing, higher education, and unique talents born of a compelling personality. But Eleanor would be the first to tell you that, left to her own devices, she's as lethal as a snake and as trustworthy as a scorpion. The only good in her comes from a personal relationship with Jesus Christ. Her husband, Hamilton, called "Ham" by those who love him, concludes that Eleanor's statement is true about everyone, but his wife is the only one who is willing to admit it. Married for thirty years, theirs is a union any couple would desire to emulate. As the basketball coach at the local high school, where Eleanor was the nurse, Ham always teased his wife that he'd never let the love of his life out of his sight, even during the work day.

Fall was coming soon; Eleanor could feel it in her bones and see it on her over-crammed school calendar. But for the moment, she sat quietly on a corner chair by an open window in her doctor's office. She was fixed on some wind chimes hanging in a nearby tree, encouraged by a light breeze to play comforting tones. Although the office was bustling with patients waiting their turn, Eleanor was calm, lost in her own world as she cradled her worn, leather Bible to her chest.

Her thoughts turned to her husband; she always smiled whenever she thought about her man who called himself the "smartest nobody you'd ever run into." Oh, how she loved Hamilton Walton Robert James III. The fact was, Ham had forgotten more than most people ever knew, as Eleanor would constantly remind her beloved. Then a warmth came over her when she considered their greatest success and joy—Mark, their only child, now practicing law in Washington, D.C. At twenty-eight, tall and strapping, this accomplished young man had a quick wit matched only by his generous heart.

Eleanor's sweet thoughts of her boy were cut short, "Mrs. James?"

Lifting her head, she stood at attention; although startled by the invasion of her peace, she recovered instantly. "Present," she said, realizing by her response that she'd spent way too many years in a school setting. Eleanor smiled sweetly at the young nurse as the two disappeared into a back hallway.

Waiting to greet his next patient, Dr. Ned Logan, an African-American man of great distinction with kind eyes weathered from years of office hours and community work, paced behind his mahogany desk. When Eleanor entered the office, she immediately took a seat. The smile on the doctor's face indicated that these two shared a long relationship, and Eleanor's relaxed posture exhibited the confidence she had in her health and welfare overseer.

"How are you, my friend?" he began in a warm tone.

She nodded graciously, "Absent from the body, present with the Lord, I always remind myself." At that, a slight expression of discomfort crossed the doctor's face, just enough to sow another seed of concern in Eleanor. She cleared her voice, refusing to release her smile as she drew her Bible once more to her chest. "Well, Ned, I imagine you have not called me here for a chitchat and a cup of tea."

He finally settled into his high-back desk chair. Crossing his hands over a folder before him, he stared at it as if he were surrounding an enemy camp. Finally, he forged ahead, "Eleanor, I'm afraid that your biopsy was positive."

Although Eleanor had experienced her unfair share of hard times while dodging life's slings and arrows, this woman always remained a blessing to others in spite of her circumstances. But now it appeared that her circumstance was breast cancer.

Her friend and fellow believer in Jesus offered his hands out to this patient. After a beat, Eleanor released her vice grip on her Bible and extended her right hand into his. "Eleanor, we have fantastic success rates at beating this and more options than ever about how to approach your care."

Now it was her turn to nod before she responded, "You do realize that if it were any other doctor telling me this, I'd be off and running to get a few hundred second opinions. But I trust you, Ned, and I trust the Lord." She took a deep breath, "So I'm in your hands. But I'll bet ya' pork loin to pig's snout that when I pray in the name of Jesus, this demon of cancer will jump out of my body and head right back to the pit of hell where it belongs! I'm givin' you fair warnin'; don't be too embarrassed if, before you do all your fancy medical footsteps, you'll be callin' me with a clean bill of health."

Although her doctor couldn't help but laugh, he remained cautious. "You do your do-diligence, Ms. Eleanor, and I'll do mine. But believe me, I hope you win your bet. Now I'll remind you as you get into your warrior mode, God designed medicine as well as prayer."

Eleanor agreed. "Amen and Amen!"

"Alright then," Ned continued, "where's that handsome husband of yours?"

Eleanor glanced away for a moment. "He'll be here for the next round. I didn't want to make a big ordeal out of this if it turned out to be nothin'. Now that it's 'somethin', I'll be havin' him with me, you can be sure of that."

"Alright then," Dr. Logan stood, "I'll see you both in my office on Monday, four sharp."

Eleanor saluted, "Yes, sir." *Oh*, she thought, *how awful for those who have to face frightening times alone. Yes, I am a lucky woman.* "Thank you, Lord," she sighed in relief.

They hadn't had pork chops in years. Since Eleanor had read the Old and New Testament too many times to count and believed all of God's Word to be true, she finally had to address his directives when it came to an appropriate diet. Much to her chagrin and Ham's disdain, pork was out of their diet as well as lobster, clams, any crawling shellfish, and bottom feeders. Oh, it went on and on. But the one thing Eleanor didn't mind giving up was snake; she was never thrilled with the prospect of dining on the devil's disguise. Her dietary commitments had nothing to do with the law of the Old Testament versus the grace of the New Testament, but rather with the Great Physician, God, letting his children know exactly how he designed them so as to stay healthy and prosperous in all avenues of life.

"Be all that as it may," Eleanor rationalized, tonight she desired a feast, and pork was her pick. The chops sizzling on the stove were Ham's first hint that something was up. And then there were all the candles strategically placed around their simple home where they had lived their entire married life. Yes, Eleanor and Ham still lived in the 'hood, just off Main, where they had raised their son and knew their neighbors. Financially they could have moved "on up to the East Side," so to speak, after they put Mark through law school, but they both felt they would be of greater service to the community where they were. In 1996 the South was all about ongoing change and hopes of reconciliation ignited in the sixties, and it was their calling to see that dream come to pass.

❦

Centennial was a small, affluent town located thirty minutes out-side of Nashville, Tennessee. This postcard-perfect suburb cen-tered itself around a historic town square with carved statues of Civil War heroes, highbrow shops, impressive steepled churches, old battlegrounds and cemeteries, good-ole-boy politics, south-ern charm, and lethal southern gossip. Corporate industry had moved in, and subdivisions were sprouting like weeds.

On the surface, all looked fine and dandy in Eleanor and Ham's hometown, but in reality Centennial was a town with a split personality. Turn one way off of Main Street, and you'd be in a neighborhood of $500,000 to $5,000,000 homes; turn the other way, and you're in an area the residents call "The Bucket of Blood," where families were barely surviving in low-income hous-ing projects and dilapidated dwellings.

Yes, Centennial was indeed a town of contradictions. Gracious hospitality and profound faith contrasted by prejudice and mistrust: opportunity versus lost hope, black and white, rich and poor, old and new collided in Centennial with a shower of sparks on a daily basis.

❦

After leaving the doctor's office, Eleanor didn't go straight home; she didn't know where to go for a while. She just drove around aimlessly through town, gazing at the expensive antique shops that she always felt were somehow out of her reach. *The devil is a liar,* she told herself; although, bottom line, she was content with her lot in life.

Cruising down the road past the Dairy Queen, she wavered; she considered the two and a half pounds she'd lost at such great sacrifice over the last month, determined not to give in to the inevitable thickness of age. But this time she didn't care to call on enough discipline to pass her favorite treat spot. She didn't want to engage the whole scenario of her wisdom having control over her fleshy body. She wasn't going to go that deep. It was simple; she was merely going to get the biggest vanilla cone dipped in chocolate on the menu, and she was going to enjoy it as long as she could before unavoidable guilt set in.

The post-Dairy Queen chocolate on her white blouse as she entered her home suddenly became an amusing telltale sign marking her return to adolescent thinking. *Well, if I want it, I need to have it. I need to have it now because I'm stressed. I deserve it. I want it. Give me my ice cream!* She giggled, decided not to change her blouse, and headed straight to the kitchen with her bags of groceries, but not before she paused at the piano where she had spent so many precious hours teaching her son to play and sing along with others from church.

For years Eleanor secretly wrote her own songs, storing them away until she was bold enough to play them for Ham. When her husband heard her sing in her glorious voice the music the Lord had given her, his eyes expressed all the audience approval she would need for a lifetime. Clearly Eleanor was a spiritual sparkplug, and God used her myriad of talents for his glory.

Not at the beginning of their meal but rather at the end, well after she and Ham had laughed and talked a bit, Eleanor shared with her husband the doctor's findings. Ham acted surprised, even though he had a strong suspicion that his bride of so many years had been wrestling with some serious issue—a "thorn in her side," as she had addressed last Sunday.

Fighting back an urge to ask Eleanor why she would exclude him from such a turn in their lives, Hamilton let her take her time, as he always did. Because he loved her, he allowed her to come to what she needed to say in her way and at her pace. "So," Eleanor began quietly, hesitantly, her words picking up as she went on, "Ham, I went to Dr. Logan last week for my annual checkup, and he sent me on to some more detail people." Ham felt like his feet were falling out from under him, unaccustomed to not being there for every moment of his wife's experiences.

"I just needed to see what was going on. There was concern, and I didn't want to bother you with that. It's just so deeply personal." They looked at each other for a long moment, their years as a couple framing their desire to share whatever the future held together.

"Ham, the doctor found a lump on my breast. I went in for another ultrasound and biopsy." She suddenly became visibly tense; he held her close. She relaxed a little, "The doctors say I have cancer." Then, surprisingly, a slight smile emerged, her eyes clear with a vision. "So that's what the doctors say, but I haven't confirmed it with God yet. I'd like to do that with you, Ham.

But first, Dr. Logan says there are some things we need to decide as far as medications and therapy, and—I just need a breath—I need to be with you so we can pray about this together."

Affection for his wife overwhelmed him, "You're going to be perfect, better than alright."

No more words were necessary for Ham. He simply gathered her in his arms, lifted her up in his heart, and immediately started praying over her in the Spirit. When she rested her cheek flush against the crook in Ham's neck, she could feel the pulse of his heartbeat. She felt safe there, easily fitting between his arms that held her in an embrace she knew would last for a lifetime. And it was just that position that she needed tonight.

Chapter 6

-Pam-

The moonlight danced through Pam's waist-long, blonde hair in stark contrast to the gloomy buildings that surrounded her. Deep shadows cut across homes pieced together with spit and glue, set against brick barrier-type, government units that left nothing to the imagination except a feeling of hopelessness. Even the corner bus stop promised a trip to nowhere.

If wisdom only comes with age, Pam Elliot would be the exception to the rule. For a hometown girl who'd never set foot outside a hundred-mile radius of Centennial, this thirty-year-old ball of fire had the vision of a world traveler with her finger on the pulse of humanitarian issues that continued to challenge her elders.

Pam would be lying if she boasted total ease as she made her rounds through "The Bucket of Blood." This low-income housing, occupied mainly by the black community, was the boil that festered in the shadows of southern pageantry and polish. Seemingly, no one could be more out of place in this part of town than this five-foot woman who weighed barely a hundred pounds soaking wet. Her soft features were belied by her personal strength; her cobalt blue eyes sparkled with promise. Who would imagine that this fair-skinned, freckled young lady was on a mission with heart and determination to turn her hometown upside down? Pam had hope, and that was exactly the name that she, Ham, and Eleanor had decided to call their project—the Hope School.

Pam had grown up on the better side of the tracks, graduating from Greystone High with honors. While there, she met Ham and Eleanor, as did most of her classmates. The girl found solace and advice from the older black couple. It didn't matter if Pam went to Eleanor privately to discuss her concerns when all the other girls had gotten their period and she still had not, or when it was an appropriate time to wear a bra even if she didn't need one; she could always count on Eleanor's candor and understanding. But more important, Ham and Eleanor offered Pam endless measures of inspiration and encouragement, urging her to color in the details of her wildest dreams and aspirations. Ham would say, "You can't right your course if you never set sail. Don't be double minded; God wants our hearts, not just our heads. He did not give us a spirit of fear but of a sound mind, so make yours up, and God will pave the way if it is his will!"

Prompted by Ham's insights, "Choose first and charge ahead!" became Pam's motto.

Although she was reared in a church-going family, over time it became clear to Pam that she was the only true believer in her household. Richard, her older brother, went through the motions in Sunday school and attended church with the family by rote, but he rebelled against organized religion as he reached puberty and, much to her parent's chagrin, resurfaced as one of the bad boys in town. Unfortunately, the family unit was not solid enough to reel Richard back into alignment. In frustration and embarrassment following two arrests, the boy was shipped off to military school.

Resentment coursed through Richard's veins, and on those rare occasions when he was home on vacation from school, Pam caught most of his wrath. He vented his jealousy toward his sister in the form of scathing comments that devastated her, often sending Pam to Eleanor's shoulder for a cry. She missed the brother she'd known as a child, and although Pam loved Richard, she hated his cruel behavior.

Competition ruled their relationship, spawned by the deep need both brother and sister shared for parental guidance and affection. Sadly, their mother, Sarah, was too involved with the local bridge team and flower club to be sensitive to nurturing her children. As Pam grew older, she realized that her mother's apparent lack of interest was probably part of her survival mode since her husband traveled extensively and was rarely home to deal with the family or provide emotional support for his wife. No question, Sarah was one bitter woman who candy-coated her private pain behind the mask of a serene smile.

Family appearances were kept up as best they could in an effort to silence the inferno of southern gossip—most assumed that the Elliots' marriage was not made in heaven. In addition, most of the town's "busybodies" agreed that it was a good decision that Richard was sent away to school before the family's dirty laundry was aired in even more extensive public displays.

Pam's stability and steadfastness were obviously gleaned outside the influence of her brother and parents. From early on, she spent most of her time at church and with her youth group. She felt safe there, loving the Lord deeply and profoundly as a child. At thirteen, after being invited to a Wednesday evening service at Eleanor and Ham's church to enjoy soulful praise music, Pam stepped forward during their altar call to receive Christ as her Lord and Savior. Since that time, Eleanor and Ham had filled in as surrogate parents, her church group becoming Pam's only real family. It was also during that time that her spirit began to soar, drinking in Ham's constant references to God's words from the book of Proverbs, "Without vision, God's people will perish." He loved Pam like the daughter he never had and adored watching her faith mature.

Pam decided at the age of eighteen to move out of her parent's home into an apartment behind her church so she could attend a local community college. This motivated teenager made ends meet by starting an after-school children's group for two- to five-year-olds, that soon blossomed into a summer Bible camp, and teaching the youth group. Yes, Pam had found her niche and moved stealthily ahead with God's plan for her life but, as Eleanor and Ham would point out, not without some major bumps in the road. Nonetheless, each one of those experiences gave Pam a more personal platform from which to help others in need.

Although she had sidestepped the entanglements of unsuccessful relationships as well as premarital sex, Pam had experienced her share of tragedies. At the tender age of sixteen, she lost her brother at the hands of suicide. Richard hanged himself on his graduation day at the military school, leaving behind tormented accusations pointed squarely at his parents as well as noting Pam at the top of his hate list. It took her years of wrestling with guilt and internal review to realize that suicide is not only a cry for help; it is the ultimate selfish act, often meant to punish others with whom the victim felt in conflict. It took a lot of counseling with Eleanor, Ham, and her pastor, for Pam to realize that she was not responsible for her brother's anguish. Still, she wondered how two kids so close in age, born of the same parents, could turn out so differently.

Frustrated, Pam stared at the receiver of the pay phone on the corner of Forest Drive and Griffin. She checked her watch, then listened for the beep after hearing the message on Ham and Eleanor's answering machine: "You can run out of time, you can run out of money, you can run out of things to say, but you can never run out of love. Leave us a message at the beep! Ham and Eleanor." *Beep!*

"Hey guys, it's Pam. Well, I must have lost my twinkies. I thought we were supposed to meet on the corner about seven on Friday. Oh well, just calling to make sure you're OK. Anyway, I'm going over to Tonya's and hope I can find Shooter. He'd better be jazzed for the first day of school come Monday. Class of '97 made in heaven! Go, go, go!"

Before Pam had an opportunity to say any more, she spotted three silhouetted major machos in the distance, sauntering down the sidewalk toward her with the look and attitude of "get out of our way." To most, this vision would indicate an ominous intrusion, but Pam was used to the turf and had learned long ago not to show any fear or trepidation while in the projects.

Outwardly, she remained cool as a cucumber, but inwardly Pam Elliot sighed in relief when she recognized Shooter through the shafts of light as one of the approaching trio. "Hey, Shooter," she offered with a slight waver in her voice; abruptly hanging up the phone, she stepped out from the booth. Her breath showed in the unseasonably cold night air as she buttoned her sweater up to the top. Billy, the shortest of the three boys, pursed his lips at the sight of Pam, ready to whistle his approval at her foxy looks.

But before he had a chance to make a sound, Shooter slapped his enormous hand over Billy's mouth, "Chill, man." As the eldest at eighteen, and head and shoulders over his buddies, Shooter demanded respect; his cohorts stepped back in silence.

Pam's shoulders eased, thankful for her friend's recognition. "Hey, I was just coming over to see Tonya and you. She home?"

"Don't know. I'm making my way there in a while. You can tell her."

"Sure," Pam nodded, glancing at each of the other boys before looking back at Shooter. "Can you believe school starts

Monday?" All three boys groaned in unison, sounding more like five-year-olds than overgrown teens.

Ever the optimist, Pam continued, "It's gonna be a great year, Shooter. Your year to shine, right?"

Slightly embarrassed, Shooter dropped his eyes as he kicked a rock out of his path. "Right on." He was determined to get picked up by the college scouts; a basketball scholarship was his way out of Centennial, and he wanted it, big time.

Pam recognized Shooter's friends, "How 'bout you, Billy? You've got pretty fast hands."

The other boy, called Robert Jack, piped in, "He got the hands, but I got the legs."

"Yeah, and together they make one. They'd look pretty stupid tied together on the boards." Shooter threw them a good-natured wink, then locked hands with Pam in an elaborate handshake known only to those in the 'hood. With more moves than a ballet, the greeting took on the appearance of a game of patty-cake.

Pam's petite frame barely reached above Shooter's elbow as he patted her on the head in a surprising show of affection. Billy and Robert shuffled back another step or two to observe the ritual of these two unlikely friends.

"Ms. Pam, you get on with yourself, now. I can't be covering for you, no matter how long you've been walkin' where you don't belong." Pam took no offense, accepting Shooter's protection with gratitude.

"I was supposed to meet up with Ham and Ms. Eleanor."

His eyes lit up like a Christmas tree at the sound of their names, "Tell Ms. E I'm gonna be in for my B-12 shots as soon as school opens." Shooter grinned wide, "Alright, big sister." He patted her on the head again, then about-faced as if in a military band. Flanked by his buddies, they all headed down the darkened street.

As Pam watched them go, a sudden choir of snarling dogs blanketed the neighborhood like a wave taking the shore in a storm. Yes, there was something eerie and dangerous about this part of town; nonetheless, this angel of the night moved through the 'hood as if she were heaven protected, which is exactly what Pam was.

No one had lungs like Tonya and Shooter's four-year-old son, Bobbie. The boy was in the final stages of a late bath when Tonya answered Pam's knock on the door. If there was ever a chunk of a child, it was Bobbie. Woeful yet loving, he was the spitting image of his dad. With formidable thighs and forearms, even as a four-year-old, Bobbie was born with the body of a middle linebacker.

Tonya, on the other hand, was tall and lanky; her legs seemed to extend for miles. With skin bronzed in color, her gray-blue eyes hinted at an interrupted line of heritage. No doubt she was a beauty—a beauty who's future had the potential of being rerouted by early motherhood and her single status. But not so, according to Tonya. "Looks are deceiving," this twenty-year old would tell anyone who'd listen. She was absolutely determined not to be defined by her past; Tonya was some feisty female.

Bobbie was among Pam's afternoon wards in her children's program, allowing Tonya to attend local college classes. Tonya didn't have a mother or family to watch over her son as was so often the arrangement in the 'hood. Both her parents had left Centennial for parts unknown before Bobbie was born. Thankfully, the church stepped in, along with the local crisis pregnancy center, in support of the young mother, and during that time Tonya and Pam met. Although ten years apart in age, their friendship was forged on shared losses and big dreams, spending much of their time with their church family.

Tonya was adamant about getting her teaching credentials and especially dedicated to the notion that Bobbie would be one of the first students attending the Hope School. Although still in the planning stages, the school would offer top-notch education to all, regardless of economics or race. In the late nineties, this educational concept continued to be an arguable idea in the South. Still, Pam was convinced that reconciliation was available through Christ, who was an equal opportunity Savior. And although taking on the Herculean task of fund raising for the Hope School earmarked to open in the fall of 1997 was a noble cause, her faith would be sorely tested.

Shooter and Tonya had been an item since they were kids. Although Shooter was waiting to make it big time in the basketball league so he could do right by Tonya and Bobbie, he, in fact, was doing better than most when it came to fatherhood and being Tonya's loyal man. Oh yes, Ham and Eleanor had more than a thing or two to say about Shooter not marrying Tonya as yet, but the young man was still on "God's milk" when it came to doing things his way and in his time. Nonetheless, this young couple's love was holding fast.

Tonya fumbled in an effort to keep her wiggling wild child inside his towel as she leaned over to give Pam a quick peck on the cheek. "Hey, girl, what's up?"

Before Pam could answer, Bobbie squealed, "Hi, Miss Pam. I had a bath and washed my hair all by myself!"

Pam gave him an affectionate pat on his chubby shoulder, "Good job, Bobbie boy. You're up kind of late, aren't you?"

The child waved his arms about, excited at the opportunity to tell his favorite friend about his evening's escapades. "Mama took me for pizza, and I dropped it in the car coming home."

Tonya groaned, "He threw it all over the car is more like it. He was in such a hurry to stuff his fat little face, we had to peel cheese and sauce off the windows."

The boy nodded as his eyes widened. "And the cheese burned me on my lips."

Pam cringed at the thought as they all moved into the living room. The apartment was modest, to say the least, but it was also neat and clean. Tonya referred to her humble abode as "better than a kick in the head." Pictures of the baby and Shooter were all over the walls, and although Shooter didn't live with Tonya, he was clearly recognized as the man of the house. "Ya' wanna Coke?" Tonya offered, setting her son on the couch so she could put on his pajamas.

"No thanks, I'm sugared out for the day."

Tonya laughed at her friend, "Girl, you're gonna blow away if you don't put something on those bones. Want some half-mangled pizza with a little window tint on the side? I've got some leftovers in the fridge."

"No thanks, I've already had my stomachache for the day." Pam feigned a dramatic look of pain, then made herself comfortable on a nearby rocker while Tonya struggled to stuff Bobbie's Flintstone-shaped feet into his pajama bottoms.

"Hey, I thought Ham and Eleanor were coming over with you."

Pam curled up in the chair like a kitten, "They were supposed to meet me on the corner at seven. I called, but their machine picked up. They're probably out on a hot date. You know those two."

Tonya yelped, "I just hope I feel like that with Shooter after thirty something years together."

"Tonya, you can't get to your diamond anniversary if you never get married." Pam wagged her finger.

"Don't start with me, girl. He's not getting me again until I get that ring. The rest is up to him. I ain't begging no man, no how. As long as he's good to Bobbie and treats me with respect, I'll leave the rest up to God and him. He'll come around."

"Yes, he will, and on that note, he said he'd be over later. I met up with him on the street. Oh, and I just found out that the abstinence classes start next week, not in two weeks."

"I heard. I'll be there. I moved one of my classes to the evening so I could make it. Can you watch Bobbie for me?"

"Sure." Pam adored her time with her godson. Bobbie squealed again as his head popped through his pajama top; this boy was such a delightful bundle of noise and nonsense.

Thrusting a pillow behind her back, Pam wiggled out of her shoes, clearly at ease in her best friend's home. "I know it's going to be an even better program this year. Apparently, there's a lot more curriculum and a lot more buzz on the street about the idea of 'waiting.'" Her expression suddenly hardened. "Can you believe President Clinton's veto of the partial birth abortion ban! What is that man thinking?"

Tonya sighed in agreement. "It's beyond comprehention. I have to admit, when you first asked me to lead the abstinence program, I thought, *How am I gonna sit there bouncing Bobbie on one hip all the time tellin' the girls to respect themselves, that they don't have to keep their man by doing whatever he wants sexually or any other way.* Girl, I was still fuzzy on the idea that God sees me 'white as snow' after gettin messed up early on." Tonya gathered her son in her arms, offering him a sip of juice that was sitting on the kitchen counter. Hugging him a little tighter, she added, "But, I'd be lost without this little man." She shook her head, almost in tears. "When I think of how close I came to making the wrong choice—goose bumps!"

"That's the point. You made the right decision after making a wrong decision. You've been there, done that, and didn't get a T-shirt for the sex part. But you've got Bobbie. Who else are the girls going to listen to?"

Pam's T-shirt image cracked Tonya up, "Sure ain't goin' to be you, Miss Priss!" Thirty years old and never even messed around. Never engaged. Never hooked up. Aren't you even curious, living in never-never land?"

Pam gave Tonya a look of consternation, "Of course, I'm curious. I'm not dead—I'm just waiting. I'm also lucky because I don't think I could stand the disappointment of falling in love and ending up alone. Listen, I gathered all my hormones and put them way back on a shelf. I'm just trusting God that he is going to bring me Mr. Wonderful in his time, before I shrivel up like a prune and no one wants me. And by the way, I have messed around, at least enough to know that if I kept messing around I'd be in humongous trouble."

"My, my, my. And there I thought I knew 'bout all your stuff, girl!" These two loved to tease each other.

Pam threw her shoe at Tonya for a direct hit, "I'll whoop you!"

"OK, uncle! But I have to say, I'm glad you ain't no perfect ten Snow White." Tonya headed for the bedroom door rubbing her bottom. "Be right back. I'm gonna put Bobbie down, and then we can tell each other dirty stories." Bobbie waved to Pam, then yawned wider than an alligator. Tonya kissed her sleepy boy on the head. "Don't you ever waver, Pam! You're the one that keeps me strong. We're gonna show 'em all how it's done right."

Pam nodded to her friend as she disappeared into the bedroom. "That's right," she mumbled to herself. "Lord, give me strength."

Chapter 7

-Stephanie-

J ust as every snowflake is unique in design, Stephanie is a one-of-a-kind, wonderful woman. Between her sharp sense of humor and her down-to-earth good looks, this forty-one-year-old is a standout in any crowd, which, by the way, is usually where she can be found, serving all three jammed shifts at the local diner.

The restaurant is called Norros after it's owner, the ex-sheriff of Centennial and the manager of the twelve-unit EZ-Rest Motel on Route 96. The only topics hotter than the local gossip about the motel are the business and political shenanigans consummated in room number 6.

Norro has had his eye on Stephanie ever since she moved in to Centennial with her son two years ago from a pinprick town in Alabama. Boss or no boss, Norro was not on Stephanie's hit parade, and, as she shared with Eleanor one day over coffee, "He's a slippery slope heading down to the under belly of life." Her description of Norro amused Ms. Eleanor who agreed whole-heartedly that the man was a slug.

Starting at six a.m. every morning except Sunday, Stephanie served early to truckers and the laborers who kept Centennial on the historic renovation trail, much to the delight of sightseers and potential transplants to Tennessee. Her next shift was the lunch crowd, where she would wait on a variety of patrons from businessmen to women out on ladies' day stuffed into the private booths that wrapped around the extensive fifties flashback of a restaurant. The evening crowd had become a bit more upscale ever since Stephanie had insisted on sporting candles and cloths on the tables for the dinner service.

As hard as Stephanie worked and as much as she cared about every little detail, patrons might assume she was the owner of the establishment, but that was just Stephanie. She'd always told her teenage son, Trace, "There's nothing worse than mediocrity," a saying the boy scoffed at, reminding his mother, "If that's the truth, you wouldn't have to work in a diner." But despite his naïve argument, Stephanie always won him over with one of her ever-optimistic looks that rarely left her pretty face. And no matter what her circumstances, including Trace's renegade take on life, the respect he held for his mom would prove unchallengeable at the end of the day.

Transitions are trying at best, even for those experienced in the adversities of life, but for a still sprouting young man of formidable size and potential, Trace had adopted an attitude to match his massive feet. At seventeen, he was not really thrilled about entering his senior year at Greystone High. Having moved into the Nashville area with his mom to find a better life, Trace's athletic goal was to play ball for one of the sports elite universities where pro scouts might notice him. College was also not in the cards for this boy without a scholarship, and for two years now he and Shooter had become arch-enemies while competing for the star position on the basketball team.

As coach and mentor to both these guys, Ham considered their being slammed against each other in unhealthy competition a shame for such talented young men with similar goals. Ham offered what he believed to be a reasonable concept, that all parts of the body of a team were stars. But jealousy made team efforts hard for these two aspiring athletes.

With Trace's good looks, one would have thought he'd have the world by the tail; instead, he harbored a lot of anger at being labeled "white trash" by some of the kids at school. No matter how high his points totaled on the scoreboard, Trace remained an outcast who provoked too much envy to be liked by his male peers. Now, the girls were another story. In retaliation to his reception by his male schoolmates, Trace was determined to date all the girls from the highbrow side of the town and then dump them as fast as he trophied them. *After all, they should know what it feels like to want something they can't have,* he told himself as he checked himself out in the mirror. But despite Trace's efforts to remain cruel, somewhere underneath all that bravado, he basically was a good young man with a protective, caring heart.

"Have you ever seen a sunrise moments before it bursts forth into the dawn of a new day?" That's how Stephanie described her son. "Trace Lee Paul Parker, you're one of the good guys; you just don't know it yet." He merely shrugged in response to his mother's assessment of his life. Then he was quick to point out that 1996 was a lot harder to grow up in than the seventies. "No way, baby," Stephanie argued. "We thought, 'Love the one you're with,' would bring nirvana; but it only led to nervous breakdowns, addictions, abortions, and extended families. My entire generation should have 'Do as I say, not as I did' tattooed on their foreheads."

But beneath her light-hearted approach, Stephanie understood Trace's anger. The change in her son had been radical since his Dad was killed during a road accident on a truck-run three years ago. That's why he and Stephanie had moved to Centennial—in hopes of a more genteel place to live. Unfortunately, the town had turned out to be exactly the opposite for them. Continuing racial tensions whitewashed by false advertising made the "Welcome to Centennial, Where Hospitality Abounds" sign misleading at best.

Since their move, Trace had become especially protective of his mom, and if the real deal be known, he wished she'd been dealt an easier hand when it came to loving and living. In the reserves of his heart, this boy worried about his "mama" working at the diner. He privately swore that when he got out of college, he'd take her away from all the stress and strain—including two-faced suitors.

Yes, Trace did have sweetheart moments, but he also could flair into a rank attitude with a shutdown mode faster than his mouth. "I'm pressing the pause button!" Stephanie would bellow when confrontations with Trace occasionally spun out of control. The boy had learned the hard way that when he heard "pause button," he was about to evoke his mother's formidable wrath, so he'd invariably back down from the argument. Not with an apology, mind you; that was too radical for Trace. Still, he respected his mom for sometimes being right and always being there for him.

Stephanie also had been particularly protective as well as worried about Trace ever since they'd moved to Centennial. He hadn't made any friends, and he'd been in more than his share of trouble. Trouble that had sent him not only to the principal's office on a regular basis but frequently to the nurse's office as well. Eleanor had patched Trace up more than once following schoolyard brawls with the locals, and she'd had many a late-night chat with Ham about this troubled young man who insisted on fighting the world at every turn.

Reluctantly, Stephanie finally confided her concerns about Trace to the school nurse, and since then, Stephanie and Eleanor had become joined at the hip with a common goal of straightening Trace out. They began to knit together a circle of friends, and before you could bounce a penny on a pregnant woman's tummy, Pam and Tonya joined this unusual sorority of sisters in Christ. The foursome had turned more than a few heads in Centennial, a conservative town full of bigots and forked tongues. The ladies were a new breed, sidestepping color, economics, and upbringings by meeting each other's needs, not going for the jugular. Instead, they embraced the uniqueness found in each other in friendship and trust. What a sweet scent this circle of friends were to God.

Beyond the myriad of shared concerns within these ladies' lives, all were delighted and blessed by Eleanor and Stephanie's passionate love of music. To have a fancy turn of phrase and the command of notes that take one to a completely different dimension through song is a true gift that divides those who have and those who have not—and Eleanor and Stephanie were definitely in the "have" category.

One Sunday after church, the two were yammering over a cup of coffee at Norros when they started humming a hymn together. Before you knew it, the crowd at the diner were on their feet in lofty applause as they listened to Stephanie and Eleanor harmonize an awesome rendition of *Amazing Grace*. Since then the two traveled on Wednesday nights to various local churches to sing for the glory of God. The buzz around town, even from those working on Music Row, was that Stephanie and Eleanor could easily have their own record deal. Although humbled by all the compliments, these two ladies of grace were content to remain at their respective stations in life; fame and fortune would just have to wait because they had kids to raise, schools to start, and lives to change. Still, when pressed, Stephanie was quick to admit that she'd like to rewrite one minor detail in her life; she'd love to meet a good man like Ham. In fact, all three of the single circle of friends were secretly waiting for the proverbial loves of their lives to arrive on white steeds—or at least with paid-off student loans, houses, and/or cars. But for now, and forever more, Jesus was the lover of their souls.

It was a typical Friday night at the diner—too many customers and not enough help. Nonetheless, Stephanie thanked God every day for her good fortune of having a reliable cook on board to "wow" the patrons. "Saint Multi-task," as Stephanie called the 250-pound seasoned evening chef Zarr, kept the customers coming back with his amazing southern cooking as well as his imagination. "Bubba's" little sprigs of decoration and surprise morsels adorned every plate, turning great food into a visual and taste delight at no extra charge. Supporting the chef's talents was a working machine of a backup crew; and, due to collective efforts, all breakfast, lunch, and both evening seatings at the diner were packed with patrons.

Although Stephanie was run off her feet daily as the only server at Norros, she was also thankful that she was the only one getting all the tips. Her goal was to buy a home for Trace and herself in order to give him a sense of stability and roots before he went off to college. It was a big dream, one she was not going to let go of easily. When Eleanor would remind her, "There is nothing worse than the death of a dream," these friends would stand together in agreement in prayer, then house hunt just to tire kick, and thank God in advance for his favor.

As Stephanie hoisted a huge platter of food up on her shoulder like the pro she was, ready to deliver Bubba's steaming works of art, Trace bound through the back kitchen door. "Hey, Mama!" he bellowed, giving high fives to some of the kitchen help as he made his way over to Stephanie. This compelling kid never stepped into a room without changing its temperature and grabbing everyone's focus merely by his presence.

Always beyond pleased to see her son, Stephanie stood like the Statue of Liberty, balancing the food tray while she waited for Trace's inevitable request. "Kenny Simms is playing at the Java, so," he slammed her with his best smile, "I'm gonna catch the late show."

Stephanie was never good at hiding her motherly concern whenever Trace was fixing to step out of her watch, but she tried to be cool, having learned some time ago that letting go brought young ones back quicker than bacon or designer sneakers. She had also made a definite choice to be Trace's disciplinarian rather than trying to be his best friend, which was what she secretly longed to become after his rearing was accomplished. "What time will you be home?"

"Midnight, maybe earlier." He gave his mother a quick kiss on the cheek, then started to take off before getting her permission.

"Whoa there, earlier is better than later—11:30." She squared him with a look. Turning back in his tracks, Trace had no time to negotiate, "Deal." Trace threw an "I love you, Mama" over his shoulder as he jogged out of the kitchen.

Stephanie stared after him as if it were the last time she'd ever see him; but then again, that's always how she felt. So she stopped and prayed once again, then and there, "Father God, I give my child to you because I know you are only loaning him to me. You know everywhere he goes and everything he does, thinks, says, and aspires to. Cover him with your mightiest angels and soften his heart, by the power of the Holy Spirit, to want to know you, please, so my son can become great in your name and will! Amen and Amen in Jesus' mighty name!" Once Stephanie had completed her prayer, she made her way through the revolving doors into the dining area.

❦

A cacophony of sound hit her as she flew past the second seating for Friday's special: fried chicken, grits, collard greens, and corn puree, with double mashed potatoes. The clientele at Norros were all adults at dinnertime, while afternoons following school would bring in a mixed group of kids for sodas and burgers.

Ham and Eleanor were the exception to the ethnic balance of white folk in the room that night, ensconced in the corner booth chosen for privacy and always a little romance. They were just opening their dinner napkins when Stephanie locked eyes with Eleanor, indicating that she'd be right over to take their order.

Stephanie's bobbed thick auburn hair swept across her eyes like a horsetail going after a fly as she passed her ravenous customers, throwing verbal assurances, "Food's on the way! The wait's worth it because the waitress is rockin'!"

After delivering a tray full of table delights to the other customers, Stephanie bent over for quick hugs and hellos with Ham and Eleanor before she pulled out her order pad. Ham piped in, "We're here for dessert, if that's OK?"

Stephanie giggled. "Are you guys playing hooky or what? I gotta call from Pam and Tonya a while back checking to see if you were stuffing your faces here on Bubba calories."

A quick flash of guilt crossed Eleanor's face as Ham shook his head. "Can I use the kitchen phone?" Stephanie nodded.

When he left, she sat with Eleanor and leaned over in an excited whisper, "OK, what's the scoop? Another romantic rendezvous, or . . ."

Before she could finish, Eleanor's expression told a different story than the words she was about to speak, "No, no, Ham and I just forgot, that's all."

Stephanie's eyes narrowed, "Bunk. Fess up. Are you alright?"

Eleanor uncharacteristically snapped, "I'm fine!" then glanced out of the window to escape Stephanie's gaze. The tension of the moment was broken when Ham returned with an insincere look of "I'm OK, you're OK" on his face. And, once again, he and Stephanie shuffled places.

Clearing his throat, Ham grabbed Eleanor's hand, "I caught Pam and apologized." He glanced good-naturedly at Stephanie, "Just another senior moment for us, I suppose. Hey, I heard a good one the other day: 'The alternative to Alzheimer's is when you remember things that never happened.'" Without waiting for his joke to settle or give way for further conversation, he ordered: "I'd like a double portion of everything that's good, and don't tell my wife about the cholesterol." With that, Ham laughed at his own joke, in an effort to let Stephanie know that he and his wife were just fine.

Unconvinced, Stephanie just stared at the two until Norro's booming voice cut across the room. "Stephanie! People are waiting!" This overweight, middle-aged, greasy-haired, balding lug bitterly tapped his foot on the floor in annoyance.

At that, Stephanie was off and running, but not without an, "I'll be right back, and I'm calling you tomorrow, Eleanor," over her shoulder to her friend. Eleanor waved her on, adopting the best look of serenity she could muster.

❧

The Java Coffee Club in downtown Nashville was jammed to the seams as people listened attentively to the old time artist with a forever list of number-one hits and the fastest fingers on guitar that Trace had ever seen. The boy leaned against the brick wall with keen attention, taking in this seasoned performer's every joke, every smooth vocal turn, and every musical lick.

At six-feet-three inches, blond, with a build a bull rider would envy, Trace also had music in his heart. If he hadn't grown up in such a practical world with a dad on the road all the time and a mom working triple time, Trace would have allowed himself a bigger share of his fantasies; those of becoming a country music star. His aspirations weren't based on fluff—with a haunting voice and a range that was the envy of those who had occasion to hear him sing a solo at church years before, Trace was blessed with more than his share of promise in all areas of his life.

Stephanie was the only one with whom Trace shared his career dreams, having kept his desires a secret from his dad who'd been focused only on the boy's sports career. But again, all that changed when his dad died; and since then, Trace had seriously taken on the roll of man of the house. Frankly, he couldn't stand the idea of his mother being with anyone else besides his dad, so he tried to make up for the void in her life, proving to be as protective of Stephanie as his dad had been. And, although she appreciated her son's attention, Stephanie didn't want them to step into some kind of role-reversal scenario. She also didn't want her boy shackled with responsibilities that weren't intended to be his. She was the mom and he was the child—she'd remind herself.

Her husband's name was Frankie, and he and Stephanie were childhood sweethearts since grade school. They went to every dance, prom, party, and sports event together in between ice skating, bowling, and chowing down on hamburgers and malts. Although Frankie was not outwardly the most romantic man, he made Stephanie feel safe. Not only that, he never failed to bring her flowers every single time he came off the road, regardless of whether or not they were fighting. Surely theirs was not a perfect marriage, but it was a sincere one. It was sealed with the knowledge that they were going to spend an eternity together in heaven with all other believers in Christ, no matter how much time any of them had here on earth. Even though she kidded about not liking the role of a single mom, Stephanie was alone—but not lonely.

As the music floated through the room, Trace leaned back and took a big swig of coffee. There was no question that all eyes were not on the performer; clusters of females of various ages flirted with Trace, offering their best body language and come-hither glances. This was nothing new for this older-looking teenager—not that he was necessarily cavalier about the attention he commanded, he was just used to it.

The irony of it all was that, despite the flurry Trace always made, he always felt alone. It didn't seem to matter how many girlfriends he had, there was an emptiness in the pit of his stomach and the center of his heart that he couldn't shake. And at the worst of those times, he liked to sneak into the woods and drink some beer so he could forget that there was an outside world swirling around, waiting to devour him. But tonight was not going to be one of those nights; he'd promised his mom that he'd be home, and no matter what the voices in his head said, he was not up to disappointing her. On the heels of that thought, he remembered a little saying his mom most always quoted before he'd head out for an evening, "Few of us are fast enough to keep up with our best intentions. Be careful, son." Then she'd blow him a kiss just as she did when he was a little kid.

Chapter 8

-Home Run-

Lauren's almost nonstop haul across the country from L.A. to Centennial was filled with pit stops, dog walks, kitty-litter changes, bad directions, and long phone conversations with her equally road-weary sister, Irene. And then there were her morning chats with Susan in lieu of caffeine to keep Lauren awake on her seemingly endless trek. Oh, how she missed her buddy Susan, always overflowing with encouragement and sidebar remarks that offered recipes for laughter in what otherwise was beginning to feel like a journey straight into a war zone.

Lauren had also regularly checked on her mom and dad to make sure the realtor had left the keys to her new house, that the electricity was turned on, that the gas was flowing—details galore. And then Lauren's cell phone went dead.

Every so often Lauren would glance back in the rearview mirror of her truck as if looking at a ghost, expecting to see her horse trailer that usually tagged along behind her Ford 250 as "Gracie, nasty horse" incessantly fussed. Lauren kept telling herself that it was not the right time, economically or practically, to bring her fantastic-yet-frustrating mare to Tennessee. And with that realization, she had donated her horse Amazing Grace to a college that would take great care of her and deal with the winning horse's particularly arrogant attitude.

Lauren had bred Gracie out of her old show mare, knowing that it was impractical to entertain the thought that she might ever be able to afford the hundred- to two-hundred-thousand dollar price tag required to buy a winning show horse. And winning was what Lauren was all about. Never satisfied with second place, Lauren knew that she'd have to dive in and raise a foal to see if she'd get a chance at competing in the National finals she'd missed as a junior rider (broken body parts had been so annoying). Unfortunately, despite all her best intentions and expertise, Lauren couldn't seem to make her desires come true with Gracie, considering the horse's endless lameness problems and high-strung demeanor.

Never one to say die, Lauren consoled herself with the fact that, until her limbs fell off from old age, she was bound and determined to fulfill her equestrian aspirations as soon as she hit the lottery and found a more amiable animal for a partner. Besides, at the moment, Lauren was consumed with the task of getting Tucker securely settled into his new life. Beyond that, she was on a mission to ensure that her entire family would—she

A FALL TOGETHER

hoped—be able to happily share close proximity to one another. The truth was, that became an overloaded concept to Lauren given the volatile-yet-fascinating personality mix of her immediate family. Still, she held fast to her vision; Lauren looked forward to her son enjoying the nearness of his relatives regardless of the daunting reality of their miles of emotional fences yet to mend and lifestyles to meld. She was absolutely convinced restoration was promised to all, but that promise came with a choice.

Lauren had learned long ago, after coming to her faith, that the operative word for healing was forgiveness, and the release valve to that process was her choice to take off the cheap coat of excuses filled with finger pointing and pain that she'd worn her entire life. It was her call to choose the better way. *What a marvelous thing grace is,* she thought as she zoomed down the highway.

The last sputtering conversation on her failing cell phone was with her mother, Margaret, to confirm her late, yet imminent Friday night arrival at their new house. Margaret somehow felt that if she spoke louder into the phone, it would help the waning cell connection; she did get in a last word that the lamb dinner would be waiting for Irene and that she had made chicken for Lauren's arrival. Lauren couldn't help but think, *What's up with that?* But being cross-eyed with exhaustion, she let it go. And then finally, with her last gasp of strength, she turned into the tree-lined driveway, making her way up to the illuminated home before her with the sudden anticipation of a child; she was actually pleased that this new chapter in her life ignited her heart to beat a little faster, since all she'd experienced of late was tension bordering on uncontrolled anxiety.

103

Sitting tall in her seat, Lauren cleared her throat, then announced to William the dog and Bingo the cat that they were about to arrive. William was alert enough to express a look of longing after the endless hours in the car, but Bingo just curled deeper into her cave of a kennel, clearly having made her mind up that nothing was going to motivate a happy expression on her furry face until she figured out where the heck she was going. Lauren already had scolded her kitty cat for such an attitude, "How feline of you," but the cat didn't seem to care. During the long days of the trip, Lauren recalled the fun and frolicking times she'd shared with Miss Kitty Bingo, despite the fact that they surfaced more infrequently as the cat had aged. Nonetheless, when Bingo decided to be outrageous, no one could top her. Lauren was just hoping that the move across the country hadn't taken the last frolic out of her wonderful friend.

The brick home, typical of Tennessee architecture, was not Lauren's favorite style. Nonetheless, there were things about her new house that she'd been drawn to from the jump-start, beginning with the fact that prices in Tennessee were a fraction of what homes cost on the west coast. And with that extra cash in hand, she'd looked forward to expanding her new digs to accommodate her parents, herself, and Tucker, as well as leaving a sizable deposit in her checking account to make the move to a new life as easy as possible. With all the details she had to take care of, Lauren had decided she was going to treat herself to professional movers and packers and only worry about people travel plans. And now, there she was, parked in front of the house that sat on a hill; no one could ever say that Lauren wasn't bold or brave. She had actually bought this home from photographs with the sign-off of a good house inspector who checked out its true condition.

I'm really here. Thank you Lord! she said to herself as she sat in the driveway, *I don't believe I bought a house sight unseen. I don't believe I'm about to move in with my parents. No! I believe that this will be a good thing.* "OK," she took a deep breath, "Here we go, guys!"

Lauren turned off the engine, opened the back door for William, and grabbed the cat's cage, knowing full well that it would take several days for Bingo to check out her new environment without fleeing into the night in terror. She reminded herself that the first thing she had to do was put up signs on every door, KEEP CLOSED! FRANTIC CAT WILL BITE.

After she gave William some good sniff-around time, Lauren ascended the steps; she was actually shaking in anticipation. Lusty aromas from a home-cooked meal floated out through the windows, and for the first time Lauren realized how blessed she was to have her parents staying with her. No matter how debilitating their past clashes had been, she loved Margaret and Sam deeply and wanted more than anything in the world for them to know the peace she had found in her faith. She wanted her parents to know that it was an honor to have them in her home, and that all of the details everyone collectively worried about would all work out as long as they remained on course without falling into the clutches of past scenarios. She also knew that she needed help from God with every breath she took, with every move she made, every word she said, and every thought she thought, because she also knew that she was the only believer in her family.

Before Lauren tried to turn the knob on the front door to see if it was open, she thought of her sister and how difficult her ongoing passage was. And even though the realization was comforting that Tucker, Chelsea, Irene, Margaret, Sam, William, and Bingo would all be under the same roof by tomorrow night, the idea of house hunting for Irene and unpacking the mountains of boxes she was sure awaited her made Lauren nauseous.

"Lauren?" Sam's voice boomed from inside. Lauren stiffened like a little child about to be chastised. But when the door swung open and her dad's rosy face broke into an explosive smile, Lauren melted.

Margaret was right behind her husband, arms wide open as if never a harsh word had ever been said between them. "Hello, darling!" Margaret offered with enthusiasm. As greetings were exchanged, William practically knocked Sam over in his exuberant entry into new territory. And then came the first sound heard from Bingo in the last three days, a wail of a meow in protest of all the confusion surrounding her cage.

Lauren stood in the doorway, mesmerized by her new surroundings. She couldn't believe the amount of work her parents had done to make her homecoming a welcome and warm experience. She thought, *When they're good, they're very, very good.*

And when they're bad, they're horrid. She giggled to herself as she recalled the poem about the little girl with the curl in the middle of her forehead.

"Thanks, Mom and Dad, everything looks incredible!" Daughter and mother hadn't seen each other this excited in years.

"Well, darling, we've worked the packers to the bone. Of course, your father and I couldn't do it all, but we oversaw everything, and we're pretty well-organized in our apartment as well. We have your bedroom all set up, and dinner is ready." By the time her mom had finished, Lauren was flat out crying; tears rolling down her face in gratitude.

Unfortunately, the sweet and fuzzy moment came abruptly to a halt once Bingo was put in Lauren's bedroom and the troops entered Sam and Margaret's apartment—Sam slammed the door on William's nose. Lauren immediately objected, "Dad! He wants to come in. He's been in the car for days. He won't hurt anything!"

Margaret piped up, she being the one least comfortable with animals, "Lauren, you know that I get nervous with your pets hanging about. I know you put the cat away, but I'm just not comfortable."

Well, there it started: Lauren was in her own home, and she couldn't even let her dog inside for dinner. She quickly had to remind herself that this was not her "own home," her parents' apartment was their apartment and under their rule and authority, even though it took up half the house's main floor.

Lauren hated her internal complaining. *Lord, teach me how to handle all of this stuff!* she quickly prayed to herself before she opened her mouth again. As she stood in the apartment doorway, she reviewed her past pain. OK, her parents never understood how she felt about animals, but by this time one would think that they would finally let go of their stiff attitude. Miffed again, Lauren decided to offer a wee bit of an argument before she gave in on the ancient battlefield of family wills, "Mom, you know my dog. You've been with him in my home tons of times. I feel like I'm stuck between a rock and a hard heart."

Before she could continue, Margaret cut in, "Lauren, he makes rude noises and smells that clear a room faster than an elephant."

Lauren couldn't really argue that point other than to say, "OK, but that doesn't happen all the time." Sam quickly avoided the conflict by pouring himself and Margaret a vodka on the rocks while William was held at bay in the doorway.

"Once is too much for me, Lauren. I just need to know that I can call my own shots here."

Lauren bristled for a moment, then once again she caught herself, "Well, I'm confused, Mom. Why is it that you let Irene smoke in your apartment, and I can't bring my dog in? Smoke stinks." With that said, Lauren suddenly realized she distinctly sounded like a little girl comparing herself to her sister in sibling rivalry. Lauren offered a truce. "Sorry, Mom. You're right. It's your apartment. Once William settles in and has a consistent digestive track with the new food I've ordered him, I'll give him a flea bath, Frontline, and tick collar him, send him to the cleaners for a good starch and pressing, and then, maybe, I'll be able to broach this subject again, if I may!"

Despite Lauren's increasingly sarcastic tone, Margaret threw her arms wide open again, burying her daughter's head in her voluminous chest. "Oh darling, it's alright, let him in. But if he makes a rude noise, he's out!"

"Thanks, Mom." Lauren heard herself exhale in exhaustion.

William lay sprawled across the middle of the rather small apartment yelping at, one could only assume, imaginary rabbits in chase as his paws wiggled during his vicarious dream. Candles were lit about the room, and a spectacular dinner by Lauren's one and only mom, the best cook in the world, was spread out on the dining room table, a feast for the eye and the palate. "Oh, home sweet . . ."

The phone rang just before dessert was served, something that was never missed in the Patterson family. It was Irene calling from the road. She asked to speak with Lauren first but was allowed to only after she was ordered to give detailed map points to her dad who insisted on navigating his eldest daughter's last day of travel on an entirely different path than previously planned.

After hi's to mom, Lauren finally got on the phone; Irene sounded deflated from the weariness of road travel. "What time do you think you'll be in tomorrow?" Lauren asked with enthusiasm inspired by a good meal.

"Well, given the new route Dad demands we take, who knows?"

Lauren intervened, "Hey, are you OK?"

"No," Irene came back like a gun. "But who cares. So, according to my former calculations, we'll be there yesterday."

Lauren couldn't help but giggle at her sister's humor. "I can't wait to see you and Chelsea! Just pull yourself up by your toenails, painted and all! I'm going to explode, I'm soooo excited! I get Tucker in the afternoon. He's spending his last day at the circus with his dad. I wanted to unpack a few of his things first so he feels like he's home when he gets here. I want to do the same for you and Chelsea. What can I get you? What do you need?"

Irene relaxed ever so slightly at the sound of her sister's excitement, then glanced back across the coffee shop to consider her daughter who still had her earphones on and was chowing down a double cheeseburger and shake. "How about a big bottle of scotch?" Irene puffed on the cigarette that she'd been manipulating between her fingers like a poker chip.

Lauren didn't skip a beat, figuring that her sister was at her wits' end. "How about the fantastic lamb dinner Mom's cooking for you. Rene, Mom and Dad have really worked hard with the packers. The house looks great! You're going to love it! There are so many beautiful places here in Centennial. We'll start looking for your own house as soon as you're ready. I love you, Rene."

Suddenly numbed again, Irene inhaled more deeply on her cigarette, her nerves unraveling at the thought of reestablishing a new residence and family ties. "Bottom line, Lauren, I'm ready to go back to New York, but I know New York is not ready for me."

Lauren noted her sister's pain, "Come on. You're the toast of the town anywhere you go. Everything will be better than good, just like you've always told me. Hang in there, OK? Be safe and you'll see. We're moving on to a better chapter in our lives. Promise."

Lauren heard a vague "OK," and then the click of the receiver was Irene's final edit of Lauren's rein of sisterly love.

Prior to the arrival in their new town, Irene had taken care of registering Chelsea as a senior in Greystone High School. Still, the timing seemed way too intense for Chelsea, who wasn't particularly thrilled at the notion of having only a weekend at Auntie Lauren's before starting school the next Monday. But despite the lack of comfort zone, all agreed to stay on schedule if not on track. Anyway, if Tucker could acclimate at age five, Chelsea should be able to at age seventeen, right? At least that was the general family consensus, until everyone thought about the difference between ages seventeen and five; youngsters are resilient, but teenagers are amazingly fragile, stuck between their body changes and awkward identity crises that so often direct them to a time of hating their parents so they can finally chart their own courses. Bottom line, everyone was going to have to chill for a while and adjust as best they could.

"Oooooh," Lauren ooozed, as she laid her head down on her pillow for the first night in her new home. She chuckled as she glanced over her still bare bedroom walls. "So what if there are no pictures up, and there's no particular personality to the room yet. The sheets are mine, the comforter molds to my body, my dog is lying at the foot of my bed, and my cat continues to stare maliciously from her open cage. All's right with the world." Suddenly, Lauren felt better.

After a moment of relaxation, Lauren considered Bingo's timidness and decided one more time to try to draw her kitty near her for comfort. Lauren dragged herself out of her cozy bed, picked up the cat cage, and put it on the other side of her as she lay back down. After a beat, she decided to pile pillows around Miss Kitty Grump, then coax the cat far enough out of her cage so her nose was finally in view. And as she spoke to her animals softly, comforting them with one hand on William's head and the other on Bingo's schnoz, she finally heard Bingo's first purr!

Morning took the room with a rush. The sun streaming in through the bare windows coaxed Lauren to rise; jumping to her feet, she was unsure of where she landed for a moment until she got her bearings. Interestingly, she had slept right through the two-hour time difference of west coast and central time without even blinking, as did her animals; exhaustion is a great sleeping pill.

While Lauren dressed, Bingo showed early morning courage as she cautiously perused every corner and facet of the bedroom. William, typical of his good-natured self, just stood grinning at his mistress, wagging his tail and whining in anticipation of being let out for his morning jaunt. Yes, it absolutely seemed that all was well with the world that morning for Lauren. "Thank you, Lord. What a blessing!"

As Lauren brewed the first pot of fresh coffee in her new kitchen, she could hear her mom and dad rustling about in their attached apartment and was grateful beyond words for their remembering to buy her heavy whipping cream "a la Suz" for her coffee, a necessity for her launch into every day's purpose. And after a little while, a photographic moment occurred as the sun broke over the higher hill's treetops now filling the kitchen with its warmth. Bingo actually decided to escort Lauren and William onto the screened back porch. The three sat in the middle of the unfurnished room for a time; then Lauren opened the back door as an invitation for her pets to patrol the uncharted realm of the yard. William was outside in a flash. Not to be outdone, Bingo strolled forth on the heels of William as if following the Pied Piper. Before long the cat's concerns eased, and not much else could have lightened Lauren's heart more than seeing her two pets, not quite frolicking as yet, but investigating their new surroundings without a raised claw or fur up on the back of their necks or tails.

Lauren bathed in the morning sun as she finished her coffee, then returned quickly to her bedroom to grab her Bible and a jacket. And then again, much to her delight, William and Bingo accompanied her as she walked the one-plus acre property, dedicating it to God in Jesus' name. What a treasured time of peace surrounded Lauren that early morning, albeit only for a brief respite.

Bobbie and Tucker met for the first time that Saturday at the circus. As it so happened, Tucker and his dad were seated in the front row of the spectacular Canadian circus troupe performance. Next to them were Tonya and Bobbie, their tickets a gift from Miss Pam who couldn't make the show because of preschool obligations. Both four-year-old Bobbie and five-year-old Tucker were raised on the toes of their high-top sneakers in delight, transfixed as they watched the horses and riders perform an awesome equestrian ballet; not only were the kids attending the show delighted, so were the parents.

During the spectacular figure-eight event, Tucker's dad, Brian, and Tonya struck up a light conversation. Realizing that Brian and Tucker were new in town, Tonya was quick to welcome the two; she loved giving "transplants" the real skinny about Centennial; and, of course, that also included a hard sell on the Hope School for Tucker next year.

When Brian and Tonya exchanged numbers, he shared that he was a single parent and would love to get the kids together. At the same time, Brian was trying to catalog the attraction he felt for this young woman. He quickly reviewed the inadvisability of pursuing any kind of personal relationship with this very beautiful yet *very* young woman and thought it best to bring his ex into the conversation. "I bet Tucker's mom would like the kids to play, too. She's also new in town, and I'm sure she'll be looking for a good church and new friends for Tuck."

Tonya considered this charming man and wondered what could have possibly happened to break up his family as Brian appeared to be such an attentive father to Tucker. But first appearances can be deceiving, she told herself. There must be a darker side to this seemingly pleasant man sitting next to her at the circus. She caught herself staring at him for more than a brief moment before responding, "Please give Tucker's mom my number. What's her name again?"

"Lauren Patterson." He hesitated, "Thanks, I'll do that." The two smiled politely at each other. A twinge of discomfort pulled her attention to her commitment with Shooter, but then her thoughts wandered once more to this more mature man. *Ah, just a fleeting fantasy,* she told herself as she regarded their two boys knee-deep in sawdust and balloons. Yes, it had been a special time.

Tucker was wound as tight as a drum when his dad finally navigated his way along the unfamiliar streets to find Lauren's house at the end of a cul-de-sac. If a child could jump out of his skin, Tuck would have done so when he saw Lauren at the top of the steps by the front door; William and Bingo charged down the entrance to greet their boy and escort him up to his mom.

Few words were exchanged between Brian and Lauren; after smothering Tucker in hugs and kisses, Lauren's main interest was to get him in the house to say hello to his grandparents. With a quick "Bye, Dad," from Tuck to Brian, Lauren grabbed her son's duffle bag full of toys and clothes that would supply him with a comfort zone for his first night home; and she was off.

Lauren had to admit, as she closed the door and glanced out at her retreating ex-husband, it was never easy seeing him go. She always loved the cowlick on the back of his neck, his broad shoulders, his kindness when he was in the mood. Then, as quickly as that image enthralled her, she rejected it, calling forth vivid memories of verbal abuse and endless deception amidst their relatively short marriage.

The stereo blasted forth famous Sara Vaughn and Frank Sinatra classics that permeated not only the interior house but the entire general vicinity outdoors as well. Oh yes, the Pattersons were at play while they waited for Irene's arrival and celebrated Tucker's tent, which he single-handedly pitched in the backyard—his own private sanctuary. Lauren couldn't remember another time as rich as the one she now was experiencing. And, despite the dog's rude noises, the cat's intermittent rude attitude, and Tucker's exuberance as he spilled his milk all over the hors d'oeuvres, nothing watered down the unequaled happiness of the evening. And then Irene and Chelsea arrived.

Tucker was the first to trumpet their entrance. William followed on course, barking diligently at the unfamiliar car's arrival while Bingo scooted under the back porch. The BMW station wagon remained at the bottom of the driveway for a moment as if wary of proceeding. But the entourage of family and animals soon prompted Irene to gun the engine up the hill, stopping the vehicle just outside the front entrance. Despite herself, Irene was excited to see her welcoming family. Chelsea, on the other hand, was fast asleep in the back of the car, her earphones maxed out as usual. Irene opted to say hello to everyone before awakening Chelsea, cautious of what kind of mood her daughter might be in.

The long anticipated coming together of Lauren, Irene, Sam, Margaret, Tucker, Chelsea, and pets was unique to this family who had never been particularly effusive in their affections for one another. The usual tone of the Pattersons was one of reserve until their gatherings most always took off down an alcoholic path, leading to dramatic expressions ranging anywhere from arguments to adoration. And usually at that point Sam, if he was in a good mood, would break into a ditty by Mike Konstant called "Natty Man":

> There was a natty man with a thousand dollar
> tan bought a week ago tomorrow and he's glad he has
> the bread.
>
> It's a very cozy bed that he sleeps in it at the
> top, but he wouldn't want to stop, he remembers cold
> despair, and the times he didn't care. So we cut out
> of the race, but he couldn't find a face he would like
> to wear, though he wore important airs. He had no
> peace of mind, and he wasn't very kind to the people
> that he loved. Even though he tried, he couldn't stop
> the ride, and so many good things died.
>
> And he's sorry for the dead, but he's happy for
> the head that he carries on his shoulders, and his
> arms that now unfold . . .
>
> A very special part of life that he cut out of with
> a knife, made of years of looking at, until he discov-
> ered that . . .
>
> There ain't no heaven this side of heaven.

Lauren had always been curious as to her father's fascination with that particular ditty since it seemed to describe many of the chinks in his own armor. Maybe, just perhaps, Sam was experiencing a moment of enlightenment about his personal M.O. Naaah, what a silly thought.

Chelsea's behavior upon her awakening was as predicted; she did the teen whine-thing and went to her room feigning a lack of interest in Tucker, Lauren, her grandparents, and the whole new "Nashville 'thang'." But, on the other side of her bedroom door, where no one could see her gleefully rolling around on the floor with William and Bingo, Chelsea was just happy to be a child for a moment instead of who she thought everyone expected her to be.

What didn't surprise anyone later that evening was William passing gas and Irene insisting on smoking in Sam and Margaret's apartment. The dog, of course, got shut out as if he'd broken all the Ten Commandments, while Irene continued to suck on her cigarette as if her sanity depended on it, which at that point it did.

It was hard for Lauren to be around the carousing Pattersons and Irene drinking and smoking because, the truth was, Lauren wanted to indulge more than any of them. Her libations had dwindled down over the years to some wine with dinner. Still there was the ever-present "Moon Lady" lurking inside her, ready to throw all caution to the wind and join the party. Thankfully, the smoking part was easier for Lauren to resist since she had given it up about five years before. Now, that was not to say that stopping the dastardly habit was a piece of cake for her—quite the contrary. With great trepidation and wrongful thinking, Lauren believed she would lose her real identity if she couldn't inhale cigarettes whenever she spoke on the phone, finished a meal, or, oh my, made love. It was only when Lauren finally stopped feeling sorry for herself when she couldn't have a cigarette that quitting became a possibility. She decided she'd rather be whole and healthy for Tucker than stay skinny and hooked. But at the end of the day, it was only by the grace of God that she found the strength to give up the nasty, stinky, lousy habit. *Nope, I'm not going back there,* she'd tell herself every day since she'd tossed her last pack of Marlboros in the trash.

Lauren prayed that her family's passage to a better dynamic would come sooner than later, for the sake and salvation of all.

Chapter 9

-Coming Together-

I rene and Lauren decided over coffee to swap kids; Lauren was going to take Chelsea to the local theater to see *Braveheart,* and Irene was going to be wild and crazy and go bowling with the "Tuck-meister" (the biggest kept secret was that Irene absolutely adored her nephew). Lauren believed that a film, a little lunch, and a lot of shopping might be a good start at rekindling the communication she used to share with her niece. Irene, on the other hand, simply wanted to avoid making a fool of herself while attempting to bowl, a sport she had tried only once when she was eleven.

Tucker flew into the kitchen, talking a mile a minute with excitement as he greeted his aunt and mom. "Auntie Rene says she's going to take me school shopping after we go bowling! Mom, can I get a new Spiderman backpack? Please, please, please!"

"Sure," Lauren winked at her son as she pulled out her wallet, handing a fifty-dollar bill to her sister.

Irene pushed it away, "Nope! My treat. I haven't seen Tuck since he was a tot." The two sisters haggled for a moment, passing the bill back and forth when Tucker lunged at the loot and stuffed it in his shirt.

"Touch that, you die," Lauren warned her son, then without skipping a beat, she retrieved the money and stuffed it into Irene's shirt pocket. "I'm just glad you guys get to spend some time together. Now, please."

Irene removed the bill, carefully folded and flattened it, then replaced it in her pocket so she didn't look like she had a lopsided chest. Then, grabbing her purse from under the table, she handed Lauren a twenty-dollar bill. "Fair is fair, you pay for Tuck, I pay for Chelsea's movie. And watch out for the shopping; she can spend money faster than Ivana Trump. Remember, neither of us is rolling in dough."

"That would be true," Lauren concurred. As the three headed for the kitchen door, an annoying honking blared from outside. "Are you guys coming or what?" Chelsea boomed from the driver's side of Lauren's truck. Tucker disappeared through the door when Irene pulled Lauren aside.

"Are you sure you want Chelsea to drive? We take cabs in Manhattan, in case you've forgotten. Chelsea only had two driver's ed lessons before we left town."

Lauren grabbed Tucker's tiny bicycle helmet off the stand and plunked it on the top of her head for emphasis. "We'll be fine."

"You don't know what you're taking on," Irene cautioned. "That girl flat out does not listen, and that's an understatement."

"It's all in the approach, Rene. Like when I couldn't get my horse into the stall. A bunch of us tried everything from carrots to whacking her on the rump, but the mare wouldn't budge because the stall was dark and scary to her. And then this old groom sauntered over, turned my horse around, and simply backed her into the stall. Then he wagged his finger at all of us and walked away. Boy, did I feel stupid. 'You can lead a horse to water, but you can't make her think.'"

Irene shook her head, "What on earth does a horse have to do with Chelsea?"

"I'm going to try different approaches until I figure out what she responds to, starting with letting her drive. The kids get their licenses here at sixteen, and she's gonna feel like a total nerd if she doesn't have wheels."

Irene whipped Tucker's helmet off of Lauren's head, "What's with 'nerd' and 'wheels?'"

"OK, I confess," Lauren straightened her mussed hair, "I bought *Glamour* magazine so I could bridge the lingo gap with Chelsea."

"I wish it were as simple as a few phrases de jour." Irene was clearly frustrated. "If you haven't noticed, Chelsea hasn't said word one to anyone since she got here other than yelling at us to hurry up."

Lauren seemed unphased, "It's called being a teen, Irene."

"Fine. You've always had the magic touch with Chelsea. I hope you can turn her around." Irene rummaged through her purse to check for her cigarettes. "I can't seem to make any headway. Her behavior is just flat out rude, and I don't care if she has raging hormones!"

"Just tell her that your hormones are bigger than hers, and your hot flashes are bigger than her mood swings." Lauren jabbed her sister in the ribs, "Lighten up, Irene. You know what they say about women in menopause. We're Dobermans with lipstick."

Chelsea impatiently honked yet again. Lauren screamed, "We're coming. Hold your horn!"

Heading down the driveway, Irene corrected Lauren, "It's 'hold your horses.'"

Lauren sweetly smiled, "You know what they say, 'Don't look a gift horse in the nose; it might sneeze on you!'"

Irene slammed her car door, "Oh, you're so ridiculous."

Lauren bowed at her sister, "No, Irene. I'm fun, fun! Remember fun? You should try it on for size."

Before joining Chelsea, Lauren ran over to the other side of Irene's BMW and stuck her head in through the open window, kissing Tucker on his forehead. "Did you put your armor on yet?"

Tucker shook his head, "I forgot."

With that, the two began in unison, "We put on the belt of truth, the breastplate of righteousness, the helmet of salvation, the shield of faith, the sword of the Spirit which is the Word of God, and our feet planted firmly in the gospel of peace ready to go in Jesus' name!" By the end of the prayer, Tucker was at a high-pitch squeal, wiggling his feet and thrusting himself about as he played soldier. Lauren checked to see if his seat belt was tight. "And, why does God have all the armor on the front of you?"

Tucker saluted, "Because he's got my back!"

"Right!" Lauren nodded at Irene who regarded her sister as if she had lost at least most of her mind.

Eleanor and Stephanie sat at the back booth at Norros sharing afternoon coffee and doughnuts while taking advantage of one of the rare occasions the diner was empty.

Having cried most of the night, Eleanor's eyes and face were so swollen, she looked like she'd gone twenty rounds with Evander Holyfield. Despite her husband's comforting prayers and loving arms, the devastating realization that she had breast cancer invaded her sleep with a vengeance. Stephanie held her friend's hands as she listened intently. "And that's all I know 'til we see the doctor Monday afternoon. Great way to start the new school year, huh? You know how my face swells when I cry. Everyone's goin' to think I got mugged."

"Who cares, Elle. Cry away. Don't hold it in, or you'll explode." Stephanie tried to look chipper. "It's all going to be just fine, I'm sure of it. Does anyone else know? Tonya or Pam?"

Eleanor took a deep breath: "Not yet. I'll tell 'em when we all get together Tuesday. I'll know more from the doctor by then. Then I want their prayers!" She violently shook her head as if fighting off an unseen enemy. "Durin' the day I'm able to keep my thoughts under wraps, but last night . . . I believe it was the worst night I've spent in my entire life. There was so much spiritual warfare goin' on over me, I couldn't figure out which way was up. Made myself wake up at least ten times just to get my bearings, pray, rebuke Satan, then try to get back to sleep. Woke up this mornin' and felt like I'd been rode hard and put away wet. Satan and his stinkin' demons just love to steal our peace, and I gotta admit, they're givin' me a run for my money!"

Stephanie squeezed her hands so hard, Eleanor winced with pain. "Sorry," she released her grip, "You know we'll all be praying like crazy and believing for your healing."

Eleanor nodded in appreciation, "I know, I know. It's just that I can't help fearin' the worst. What if they didn't catch it in time? What if I have'ta have a mastectomy? What if? What if? What if? I feel like a scared little girl. I know that fear's not of God. He's got it covered, and he's in control, but I'm still shakin'. Oh Lord, I hate feelin' this way."

Stephanie could commiserate with Eleanor. That's how she felt when she lost her husband, totally out of control with grief and pain with only the desire to fold up and quit. "You're going to be alright, Elle, no matter what. But you've got to let others help you for once. Don't expect to hear that kind of scary news one day and be on top of the world the next. God never said that we wouldn't ever be afraid; he just wants us to know he'll help us go through it while we're afraid. There's no shame in the feelings. Just don't let the tail wag the dog. That's what I kept telling myself when I lost Frankie. You're not even allowing yourself time to digest it all, let alone grieve."

"I ain't grievin' somethin' I haven't lost yet!" Eleanor whipped a half-eaten doughnut off Stephanie's plate. "And I don't feel like bein' in control; I feel like screamin'. So I think I'm gonna eat the rest of your doughnut to keep my mouth busy for a spell. And after I stuff my face, I'll be enjoyin' an incredible sugar rush, which'll lay me out flat in 'bout an hour. But I don't care nothin' about an hour from now . . . I just care 'bout this minute." With that she slammed half of the remaining doughnut in her mouth and began to chew with an expression of petulant satisfaction on her puffy face.

Stephanie giggled, "Go, Elle! Hey, do you want me to get you that chocolate éclair staring at you from the end of the counter? It's got your name on it."

Muffled with a mouthful of sugar-glazed doughnut, Eleanor shook her head. "No, ma'am. No . . . no more! When I first heard 'bout this cancer nonsense, I went home and made 'bout five thousand pork chops for Ham and me, and that was after scarfin' down a giant Dairy Queen. I haven't stopped eatin' since. Ha! I might just explode before those surgeons can take a knife to me. No! I've gotta catch myself and stop speakin' this thing into bein'. I already made a bet with my doctor that I'm gonna get a clean bill of health no matter what the ole radiologist say."

Both ladies raised their hands in victory as Stephanie exclaimed, "Praise the Lord! . . . But, Elle, if you do need a little help on the medical side, you're going to do what they say, right? You know God sometimes uses doctor's hands to deliver miracles."

"Yes, you sound like my doctor. But, I'm a nurse, remember?" Eleanor took a moment. "And it's because I'm a nurse that

I know how serious all this could be. I've never been real good at 'hurry up and wait.' I just wish I knew how they intend to attack this thing. There's a boatload of difference between surgery, chemotherapy, and radiation. I happen to know that chemotherapy can kill your good parts as fast as it is killin' the cancer. And what's really got me worried is if the monster's spread." Eleanor gazed out the window, watching a leaf fall nonchalantly from a nearby tree.

"What's the first step?" Stephanie's tone was soothing.

"Surgically assess what's goin' on." Eleanor suddenly sounded exhausted. "They have to find out if the cancer—oh, there I go again!—if the possible cancer has spread to my lymph nodes, or worse."

Stephanie softly took her hands once more. "One step at a time, Ms. Eleanor."

A slight breeze rushed through the empty restaurant as the front door opened, admitting Lauren and Chelsea, who was carrying a half-eaten bag of popcorn under her arm. Stephanie and Eleanor watched the two take the first booth. "Wonder if they're new in town or just passin' through?" Eleanor queried, grateful for the change of focus.

"I've never seen them before. Pretty girl though, huh?" Stephanie noted.

She wasn't the only one that noticed Chelsea's good looks. While the girl was scanning the menu, Trace came into the restaurant through the kitchen entrance. He locked eyes with Chelsea's for a fleeting moment before moving on to talk to his mom. Chelsea blushed slightly, then looked out the window to appear aloof.

Approaching Stephanie with a triple burger clutched in his hand, Trace greeted the women with a wide grin. "Hey, Ms. Eleanor." She smiled back at the boy, happy to see him looking so "up." "Trace, that hamburger's bigger than you are."

"Yes, ma'am. It's one of Bubba's specials." He stared at Eleanor's disfigured face, not sure whether to say, "I'm sorry," or, "What's the matter?"

Eleanor saved him the trouble. "Allergies."

"Wow." After closer inspection of Eleanor, Trace finally turned his attention to his mom, "I gotta get some school stuff, so Bubba said I could work in the kitchen this afternoon to make some extra money." Stephanie nodded, "I'll be thanking him for that. Just get everything you need to start the year off right."

Exiting, he waved his hamburger, splattering some of its juice on the floor. Trace bent to clean it up when his mom shooed him on. "I'll get it, I have to take care of those folks in front anyway."

"Thanks. Bye, Ms. Eleanor. I hope you feel better." And with that he was off, but not without checking Chelsea out again before disappearing behind the kitchen doors.

Stephanie straightened her apron, regarding Eleanor who was finishing the last vestiges of the doughnut. "I'll be right back, I just gotta take their order. Do you have time to sit for a while?"

Eleanor nodded, holding her hands over her eyes as if she could simply wish away her bloating. "Lord, I don't have bags under my eyes; I have suitcases! Yes," she sighed in frustration,

"I have some time, Ham's over at the school doin' inventory of the team's uniforms. He's comin' to get me in about a half hour." Stephanie gave her a thumbs up.

As she approached Lauren and Chelsea, Stephanie offered a welcoming smile. "Hello, ladies. How's the day treating you?"

"What a nice thought. Just fine, thank you." Lauren returned the smile; predictably, Chelsea didn't bother to respond.

Stephanie pulled out her order pad, "Well, good then. What can I get ya?" Chelsea instantly rattled off, "Double cheeseburger and fries with a Diet Coke."

"That's sort of an oxymoron, isn't it?" Lauren teased her niece, "A Diet Coke and fries?" Stephanie laughed, but Chelsea didn't find the comment the least bit amusing, stuffing some more popcorn in her mouth for effect.

"I've got a son 'bout her age with a bottomless pit for a stomach, too." Stephanie chatted. "Don't you just hate that kids can eat anything they want and never gain an ounce?"

Lauren looked at Stephanie, taking an immediate liking to this woman, "Obviously, they haven't heard about mad cow disease. I have to admit, I'm scared to death to eat hamburger."

"Oh, I can promise you, ma'am, our meat is good." Stephanie quickly assured her, "That was my boy going through here a minute ago slamming down a triple 'Bubba Burger.' But, if you prefer, our southern fried chicken sandwich is real tasty."

"Perfect. And I'll have a real Coca-Cola for good measure."

"Be up in a jiffy." Stephanie wheeled about and headed toward the kitchen.

Lauren noted her niece's distant gaze, realizing she'd made zero headway as far as rejuvenating their friendship. Still, she was not about to give up. "How'd you like *Braveheart?* I thought it was an amazing movie."

Chelsea mumbled, "I liked *Sling Blade* better."

After a moment of silence, Lauren tried again. "You drove really well. And don't you worry about the fender. It was just a tap."

"Sorry," Chelsea offered unconvincingly. "Don't tell Mom, OK?"

"OK, why not?" No response. "So, what's your favorite music these days?"

The girl crumpled her popcorn bag, then wiped away some butter from her mouth with the back of her hand. "Seal." Lauren looked at her, waiting for a bit more information. Finally Chelsea relented, filling in the gap, "Seal is the singer's name. The song's 'Kiss from a Rose.' It's number one."

"Oh. Will you play it for me sometime?"

"Sure," Chelsea grunted.

Undaunted, Lauren continued, "So, the other day I read that Janet Jackson got the biggest record deal ever. Eighty million bucks. Isn't that amazing?"

"That's rad." Chelsea's interest perked slightly. "Eighty million." She gazed off, "When I'm a country star, I'm going to make more than that."

"Gee, I knew you had a sweet voice." *Wrong word,* Lauren thought. *Powerful. Maybe not powerful. Kids don't have powerful voices.* "I just didn't know you had those kinds of aspirations."

Chelsea looked out the window again, nonplussed, "Well, we haven't talked in a while, ya know."

"Yeah," Lauren responded, embarrassed. "Time flies when you're not having fun, huh? Hey, do you think milk comes out of a cow's nose when it laughs?"

Chelsea scrunched her face up, "That's gross."

Lauren became slightly defensive, "It was just a joke."

"Yeah, maybe for a five-year-old. Don't forget, I'm seventeen."

"Sorry. You're right, I'm kind of used to hanging out with Tucker. You'll just have to bring me up to speed with what interests you. I really do care."

After another moment of silence, Chelsea decided to grace her aunt with a response. "Yeah, well I'm not interested much in being here in this stupid town. Mom knows I'm moving into Nashville to do my music the minute I'm eighteen."

Lauren tried not to look shocked. "What do you mean? You're going to finish high school first, right?"

"All I know is that I'm going to be doing my music." Chelsea's attention was drawn to the window once more in avoidance of Lauren's stare.

❧

With a sprinkle of donut powder still on her chin, Eleanor made her way over to greet Chelsea and Lauren, "Excuse me. My name is Eleanor James. I'm the high school nurse, and I was wonderin' if y'all are new in town?"

Lauren offered her hand in greeting. "Yes, we arrived yesterday as a matter of fact. I'm Lauren Patterson, and this is Chelsea Williams, my niece. She'll be going to Greystone High School."

Eleanor turned her attention to the girl, "You look to be about sixteen or seventeen."

Chelsea cut in, "Seventeen, and I'm going to be a senior."

She stared at Eleanor, who matter-of-factly pointed at her face in regard to her deformed swelling, "Inherited from my mother's side of the family." With that said, she changed the subject, "You'll like our school. It's got lots to offer. Where ya'll from?"

"I'm from the west coast, and Chelsea is from New York City. We decided to meet halfway, and . . . I'm a veterinarian, by the way, and I'll be opening a practice with Dr. Burke on Route 96 just outside of town."

Eleanor thought for a moment, "Dr. Burke, don't believe I know of the gentleman."

Lauren couldn't help but be a bit disappointed, "I think he's relatively new in town, but I'm told he has a good reputation and a big practice. It was hard to find an office that was already set up and willing to take on a second doctor."

"You should do just fine. The well-off in these parts are mindful of their pets. Although, I can't say much good 'bout the local pound."

Lauren stiffened, "I heard about that place on the news. I can't fathom that they have chutes that people can just drive by and drop down animals they don't want into some holding pen—cats, dogs, birds, whatever, all together. Believe me, I plan on making some noise about that as soon as I get settled in. It's just pitiful to do that to any animal."

"We're a mixed bag 'round these parts, Ms. Lauren. We got good ole boys, corporate transplants, old money, old poverty, nouveau riche, music stars, farmers, rednecks, and animal abusers." Eleanor smiled good-naturedly. "But we also got a church on just 'bout every corner and God's mighty hand over us."

Chelsea rolled her eyes, then turned her attention toward Stephanie, who was on her way from the kitchen with their lunches. "Here you go, young lady. Just what the doctor ordered." She set the drink and a huge plate of food in front of the girl, then delivered Lauren's order.

"Oh my, that looks good." Eleanor's appetite peaked again. Turning to Stephanie, "I'll have one of both of those." She laughed out loud, flailing her hands in reaction to her own silliness. "Just a joshin'. Listen here, Chelsea is Trace's age, and she's goin' to be a senior at Greystone. Ms. Lauren is a veterinarian. Ya'll, this is Stephanie. We call her 'Steph,' not like the infection that . . ."

Stephanie smacked Eleanor on the arm, "She's had one too many Benadryls."

"Pleased to meet you both." Stephanie wiped her hands on her apron, then gave them a little wave. "And like I said, that was my boy who walked by before—Trace." Stephanie boasted.

Chelsea was about to decimate her hamburger when Lauren motioned her to wait, bowing her head. "Thank you, Lord, for this food and sanctify it for your use, in Jesus' name." Annoyed,

Chelsea chomped down on her burger while the other two women joined in with an "Amen."

Eleanor reached for Stephanie's order pad and pen. "Lauren, here are our phone numbers. You call anytime. We'd love to have ya come and visit our church and meet some folks soon as you're settled in. Now, if you need any help with anythin', you just holler."

Lauren appreciated the hospitality of this lovely lady. "Thanks, I'll sure do that."

"Now, sweetie cakes, just wave me down when you're ready for some dessert or coffee. We have the best chess pie in the South," Stephanie offered as she and Eleanor returned to the back booth.

Chelsea was most of the way through her hamburger before Lauren enjoyed the first bite of her sandwich. "Well, they were nice, weren't they? A little different from New York City. The people here seem really friendly."

"Yeah, and really slow," Chelsea spoke in between bites.

"What do you mean, slow?"

"I don't know, they just kind of talk slow and look a little frumpy, ya know?"

"'Frumpy'? Well, I guess all middle-aged women look frumpy to you." Lauren unconsciously straightened her shoulders.

Chelsea looked up with a fleeting grin. "Yeah."

"Well then, let's go shopping, and you can 'defrump' me, and I'll buy you whatever's 'in and cool.' But, in return, you have to help me on your computer. I hear you're a whiz, and I can't even do e-mail. I'm going to need to learn just the basics before I start at my new office."

"OK, you teach me to drive a car, and I'll teach you to drive a computer."

"Deal." Lauren smiled, relieved to see even a slight glimmer of excitement from her long-lost niece.

Chapter 10

-Settling In-

Lauren was going to call Eleanor to find out where her church was for Sunday's service, but she quickly found that she was the only one in the household who intended to go, so she didn't bother. Even Tucker showed little enthusiasm; he was not interested in meeting new kids at church on Sunday and then meeting new kids at school on Monday. Frankly, he was having a little "too much new" overload for his five-year-old mind.

Lauren decided to give in, at least for this first Sunday; she'd stay home with the rest of the family for brunch and get some more never-ending unpacking accomplished. She'd learned long ago that her spiritual mission was to boldly deliver God's invitation of salvation to others, but it was up to the Holy Spirit to soften their hearts and convict them of the truth that everyone needs a Savior, and then it was up to them to choose eternal life.

Given Lauren's inherent overachiever personality, it was excruciating to her when someone, especially her nearest and dearest, heard the Word of God and chose to reject his sacrificial offer of forgiveness, healing, and grace. Often she would take that rejection as a personal failure, which she had finally come to recognize as a product of her own pride. Lauren knew full well that she couldn't force her faith on anyone, including those she loved deeply. She could, however, continue to pray for their salvation, walk her talk, and go to church—alone if need be—to share in the fellowship she sorely missed.

Bacon and sausage sizzled on the grill while Mom's famous array of omelets, muffins, breads, fresh orange juice, and cinnamon buns were already on the table. Lauren thought she'd died and gone to heaven. What a marvelous way to start the day.

Ever watchful of her figure, Irene picked at her food while the rest of the family dove in, voraciously consuming the spread. Irene perched herself on a section of her chair with one hip hanging off; she had a look of discomfort on her face. "Are you, OK?" Lauren couldn't ignore her sister's odd expression.

Tucker giggled, "She fell on her bottom, Mom!" All eyes focused on Irene who just shrugged, "I guess I forgot to let go of the bowling ball. I went halfway down the alley before landing in the gutter in a heap, ball and all. It was truly embarrassing. I smashed my bum, and what's worse, I'm probably the talk of the town, and I've only just arrived." Irene was surprisingly good-natured about her mishaps. Clearly spending some time with the 'Tuck-meister' was just what she needed to lighten up. Then Irene suddenly turned an accusing finger toward her nephew, feigning betrayal. "You promised you weren't going to tell on me!"

"But you were sitting funny." The boy cringed.

Irene softened, letting him off the hook with a smile, "I don't blame you. I blame the bowling ball with a mind of its own!" Irene managed to amuse the entire family, which was quite a coup for her.

Tucker went on with his meal while Bingo batted at William's nose when the dog tried to invade her space under the table; there was no question that Miss Kitty got first dibs on any food that fell during meals. Knowing their routine, Lauren slipped a bite of her goodies to William so he wouldn't lose his mind out of frustration, and then she looked around the table at her family, finally altogether. She was overcome with love, savoring the sweet moment for future reference.

In between petite mouthfuls, Irene glanced at her daughter, "Are you going to take the bus in the morning, or do you want me to drive you to school?"

Chelsea whined, "Mom, I have to get a car, ya know. It's so dorky to be driven to school by your mother, and I don't know what kind of kids ride the bus."

"Well, dorky or not, you won't have a car by tomorrow, you know." There was noticeable sarcasm in Irene's voice. "You don't even have a license yet, Chelsea. So which will it be?"

Chelsea gulped her juice down in disdain, "The bus, I guess."

Lauren changed the focus of conversation to her son in an effort to divert the building tension between Irene and Chelsea. "Hey, Tuck. What about you? Do you want me to drive you to school on the first day, or do you want to take the bus? It'll be a different bus from Chelsea's because you're going to a different school. I'd love to take you for the first day if you want me to." As she stuttered along, she was praying her little boy would say yes, more for her sake than for his.

"I want you to take me." Tucker adopted a lower register in his voice.

"Great!" Lauren was visibly relieved. "I've got the next week or two off while you settle into school before I start work at the clinic. So you can just let me know when you're ready to take the bus." He glanced at her with concern. "Don't worry, buddy, you're going to have a great time. You'll see. You'll have tons of new friends before you can say cheese. This is a wonderful town to live in, don't you think?"

"I don't like cheese, but I like the bowling alley. And McDonald's has a playground behind it with a really, really big slide, and you jump into this net thing with balls at the bottom of it, and you bounce around! It's really cool!"

Lauren's eyes got as big as her son's, "Wow, that sounds exciting!"

Irene moaned as she shifted in her seat, "I can attest to the height of the slide and the bouncing around part. That's when the other side of my bum got bruised."

Margaret looked at her eldest daughter in utter disbelief, "You went down a slide?"

"Yes, I did, Mom. I'm not the stick-in-the-mud you all apparently think I am."

"Bravo, Rene!" Lauren clapped.

"And, Mom," Tucker burst in, "we saw some horses in big, green fields, and I want to go riding!"

Irene winced at the thought, "I was going to leave that one up to you, Lauren. The idea of sitting on anything but a pillow at the moment makes me want to eat highly salted buttered popcorn."

Lauren gazed off dreamily, "I can't wait to ride again. Hey, Tuck, we'll find some place that has ponies and maybe something that I can ride on a trail with you."

Finishing his eggs in record time, Sam spoke for the first time since he began his daily feast. "I thought you only liked to show horses."

"I do, Dad, but I don't have anything to show right now." There was so much sorrow built into Lauren's quick response, she had to do a U-turn just to stay in the conversation. "I'll just have to get to that part of my life when I can."

Margaret poured herself another cup of coffee. "It still sends shivers up my spine when you do that jumping bit."

"Don't scare Tuck, Mom. The only time I ever hurt myself on horses was when I was riding something I had no business being on. Like trying to jump a five-hundred-dollar halfhearted dressage horse that had no idea what I wanted her to do."

Irene added, "Or race that boy from across the street on his bicycle while you were riding the neighbor's mule."

Instead of addressing the conversation, Lauren once again became starry-eyed. "Oh, I just loved that mule."

"No," Irene teased, "you loved the boy from across the street, and you were trying to get his attention."

"Well, it would have worked if it weren't for that stupid car that ran the stop sign and knocked me clear off Miguel onto the hood of a truck!" Lauren couldn't help but laugh at the memory, "That mule was indestructible. A veritable tank. Any other animal would've been crippled, but not Miguel. He just walked away from the whole thing like Mr. Clean, and I was the one that ended up with the broken leg."

"And oh, I remember how you stuck out like a sore thumb at those Pony Club events with that silly animal," Irene recollected. "Everyone going around in circles on their horses playing mounted musical chairs, and there you were on Miguel with his ears flopping in the breeze every which way like antennas gone mad. And you didn't even care. You just sat up there, proud as punch, like you were riding Secretariat."

"I loved that mule!" Lauren always embraced her fond memories with enthusiasm, especially since there weren't that many good ones to recall.

Eventhough a cold front had moved in, it was an absolutely exquisite day outside as the sun shone through the windows like shards of light. Lauren knew that her mom and dad were ensconced in their apartment with an afternoon's worth of taped soap operas and ball games to watch. Tucker was with his dad at the movies for the afternoon, and Chelsea had hitched a ride with them so she could hang out at the mall. With everyone's dance card full, Lauren was grateful she was going to have a window of opportunity to spend time alone with Irene; she was so looking forward to catching up and getting the real deal about how her sister was doing during her trying time of transition.

Irene surrounded herself with mounds of pillows as she ever so carefully positioned herself on the couch in the living room so as to not aggravate her bruised posterior. Lauren was at the fireplace building a teepee of wood and newspaper for the season's first fire. As she lit the newspaper, flames leapt up into the chimney, and before she knew it, the room started to fill with smoke. Forgetting to open the flue, Lauren had managed to foil the glorious moment. Yes, she was feeling quite dumb.

Irene was in hysterics as she watched her sister fly about the house grabbing kitchen mitts and a pitcher of water, then practically singeing her eyebrows off as she lunged for the closed flue. Livid, she shouted over her shoulder at Irene, "Stop laughing at me and help!"

"What do you want me to do? We can't both fit up the chimney at the same time, sweetie." Irene exploded in another gale of laughter.

"You could open the windows and turn on the fans for starters. I'm burning up here!" Lauren pulled back, gasping for air.

"I need a wheelchair. I can only move an inch at a time. It'll take me five years to hobble over to those windows." Irene tried to control her silliness but to no avail.

"Never mind, I'll do it!" Lauren screeched, emerging from the fireplace victorious as the smoke began to take its normal route up the chimney.

Irene quickly grabbed her nearby pack of cigarettes and lit up. Lauren glared at her sister, but she just waved her off. "Now, you can't complain, the room is full of smoke. You won't even notice my cigarette."

"I hate that you smoke." Lauren thought better of initiating a fight. "But you're a big girl, I guess."

"Yes, I am, so please don't start in on me. I'm coveting immediate satisfaction lately."

"I hope that's not a theory that you espouse to your daughter." Like lightning, Lauren threw two of the living room windows open, then turned on the fans, and within minutes, the air started to clear.

But just as the mayhem began to settle, all of the house smoke alarms started blaring, and with that Sam and Margaret flew out of their apartment door. By then Bingo was hanging onto the window screen like a bat, petrified and hissing while William bayed woefully in tune with the incessant smoke alarms.

Ever ready, Sam had a hatchet in one hand and a fire extinguisher in the other while Margaret dialed 911 on her portable phone; her frantic pleas into the mouthpiece were muffled by the red bandana she had tied around her nose and mouth for protection.

Lauren and Irene remained frozen in place for a beat, watching the out-of-control gathering before them. Finally, Irene took a deep drag off her cigarette and exhaled as she screamed, "Hello, everyone, we're not on fire!"

Lauren grabbed the phone from her mother. "Sorry, we're fine. Mom, Dad, false alarm." She pulled her mother's bandana down around her neck and held Margaret's head in her hands, "Mom, I forgot to open the flue in the fireplace."

"Well, that was stupid!" Sam scoffed.

Hurt, Lauren turned to her dad, "It was a mistake, Dad. We're fine, OK?" She pushed her singed bangs out of her eyes.

When the room finally cleared of smoke, the alarms ceased, the animals scurried outside, Sam and Margaret retreated to their apartment, and peace reigned once more. That was until the buzzer from the oven rang out; as if released by the gates at Santa Anita racetrack, Lauren made a mad dash to the kitchen before another panic ensued. Silencing the buzzer with a smash of her fist, she took a gulp of now fresh air. Once recovered, Lauren instantly was back on course with her original plan. "I'm so hungry I could eat a horsefly. You want some pizza, Rene?"

"Are you crazy? We practically just finished brunch, Miss Piggy."

"Two hours, thirty-six and a half minutes ago." Lauren pulled the pizza out of the oven with glee.

"Go on with yourself. Wear the cheese on your hips, but not I." Irene sucked on her cigarette.

"Pizza is the greatest thing since crumbs in my bed, and I'm not about to give it up." Lauren balanced the steaming concoction on a plate, then plunked down on the couch next to her sister giving Irene a smothering bear hug, "Hey, doesn't this feel like the good ole times?"

Pulling back, Irene grimaced, "You smell like burned hair."

"You smell like an ashtray, but I still love you." Lauren gave her a kiss on the cheek.

Irene softened, "I love you, too, sweetie." The two women just sat there for a moment enjoying each other's company like they used to as kids. Finally, Irene broke the silence, "So did you get through any of the barbed wire my daughter has wrapped around her pretty little self?"

"Watch Mom, no hands!" Lauren cascaded a masterful cheese twirl into her mouth, swallowing the mass in one easy gulp. "I must admit, you could catch more flies without your daughter's personality in the vicinity. She seems really angry, Rene. Every time she'd open up even the slightest bit, she'd instantly shut down."

"That's what I've been trying to tell you!" Irene stubbed her cigarette out in frustration. "I just don't know what to do. I can't imagine that every teenage girl goes through such an ugly stage. We didn't."

Lauren hooted, "Dad and Mom would have remapped our lives if we gave them even a hint of attitude. As a matter of fact, I can't believe they've been putting up with Chelsea as well as they have. Although, I did have a long talk with Mom about not feeling like we all have to walk on eggshells when we're together."

"Agreed," Irene went for another cigarette; Lauren grimaced, and after a beat, Irene reluctantly stuffed it back into the pack, sticking her tongue out at her sister like a child. "Frankly, I wish Dad would give Chelsea a piece of his mind. The more everyone placates her, the worse her attitude gets," Irene fidgeted. "I just pray that she either likes school or has a lobotomy."

Lauren dove into her pizza again, dangling the gooey cheese over her mouth like a baby bird in the nest waiting to be fed. Irene finally relented, grabbing a slice off the tray. "Oh, I can't stand it! It's one thing to control myself when it's not sitting right in front of my schnoz. I don't think I've had a pizza in at least fifty years."

"Rene, you're a rail. Just enjoy the grease. It's good for your hair. With your habit of not eating, I'm surprised Chelsea isn't dealing with some kind of disorder like so many kids her age. The impossible perfect size one is turning her generation into bulimic junkies. Thank God your girl can eat me under the table."

"Until she turns into a two-hundred-pound porker, then she'll really become hateful."

"Rene, you have to start thinking positively."

"You think positively all the time, and here we both sit in Nowheresville, Tennessee, both veterans of dual divorces and quadruple broken hearts. How exactly will positive thinking reroute our circumstances? Shall we simply lie ourselves into believing everything is fine?"

"Minus the 'lie' part, yes. Let me tell you about two farmers."

"No, please not one of your stories." Irene put a pillow over head in dismay, but Lauren ignored her, clearly enjoying the sound of her own voice. "There were two farmers. One was always a positive thinker, and the other was always a negative thinker. The positive farmer would look out on a rainy day and be thankful his crops were being watered, while his negative friend would respond to the same rain by complaining that his crops were going to wash away. On a sunny day the positive farmer would look out and be thankful for the nourishing rays of the sun, while the negative farmer would see the same day and curse because the sun was going to dry up his plants. Well, these two friends decided to go duck hunting one day and . . ."

Growing impatient, Irene cut in, "Hold it. I thought you hated hunting?"

"That's not the point, and if you interrupt me again, I will tell the whole story from the top." Irene moaned, knowing nothing could stop Lauren when she was on a roll. "OK, now where was I? Oh yes, the positive-thinking farmer took his negative friend hunting and brought along his brand-new bird dog." Lauren winked at Irene for effect, then continued. "Now, this dog was supposed to be the finest duck retriever in the county, and the positive farmer couldn't wait to show him off to his negative friend. So, when the first duck was . . . well, you know, when the poor duck hit the water, the dog jumped from the blind and walked across the top of the water, picked up the duck, walked back across the top of the water, and plunked it down in front of his master."

Irene resisted asking if the duck was dead or all bloody or some such comment that she knew would launch her sister's rockets.

Lauren continued, "The positive farmer was beaming with pride as he boasted, 'Great dog, eh?' His negative friend simply responded . . ." Lauren paused for another beat of dramatic emphasis, "'I hope you didn't pay much for that mutt, that dog can't even swim!'" Lauren buried herself with pillows, hysterically giggling at her punch line.

As usual, Irene just shook her head at her sister, "Oh, you are so ridiculous."

Chapter 11

-Meeting Up-

At the frozen yogurt stand in the mall, Trace ran into Chelsea. Although she recognized him from the diner the day before, she pretended to ignore him even while he stood smack-dab behind her in the line. Her standoffish attitude was starting to amuse Trace, but he waited until she walked away with her double vanilla cone dipped in sprinkles to tap her lightly on the shoulder. When she turned, he flattened her with his most alluring smile, "Hey, I'm Trace. I think I saw you at Norros yesterday."

Chelsea responded by batting her eyes, putting forth her best doe-eyed look of innocence. "Norros?" she said slowly.

He was mesmerized, "Yeah, Norros diner. You were there with some lady."

Now it was Chelsea's turn to smile, as if just recognizing him for the first time. "Oh right, I think I remember." Now her eyes didn't flicker until she glanced back at the yogurt stand. "You lost your place."

He shifted his weight, suddenly uncomfortable as he searched for his next "come on" line. "Maybe you'll share yours?"

His question caught Chelsea off guard. *Wham!* she thought, *Ball's in my court.*

But before she could respond, he was off in a new direction. "So did you just move here?"

They were clearly attracted to each other; their body language told their story while their conversation was merely a formality. "I'm from New York City. I'm starting at Greystone High tomorrow."

Trace nodded, then pointed at her cone; the ice cream was starting to drip down her hand. Feeling awkward, she started to walk away once more, but he seized the moment, "I'm a senior there," he offered, not wanting to lose their connection.

Without turning around, she paused in her retreat, then smiled slightly, knowing he couldn't see her expression. "Me, too." And with that, she was off again.

"So I'll see you tomorrow, I guess." He hated that it sounded like he yelled after her.

"Maybe, I guess," she coolly responded as she was about to be swept away into the crowded mall.

But before she disappeared entirely down an escalator, he called out once more, "Hey, what's your name?"

Now it was finally time for one of her dramatic Hollywood turns, taking a lick off her cone just for good measure, "Chelsea."

He was slain, noting each of her innuendos. "I'm Trace."

"I know. You already told me. And so did your mom." He followed her down the escalator like a puppy, speaking over the heads of people in front of him. "My mom?" There was a catch in his throat.

"Yeah, at Norros." *Match point*, she thought. Hesitating, she was careful to gracefully maneuver the end of the moving escalator steps as he miraculously found himself back by her side without making a total idiot of himself.

He had no choice but to pull out his big guns. "Hey, Chelsea, so, do you have wheels? How are you getting to school?"

By then Trace had caught up with her sparring pace and she knew it. "I guess I'm riding the bus. I don't have a car yet. I'm from New York City, remember?"

Quick to take advantage of the slightest opening, Trace set his snare, "OK, so where do you live?"

"Why?" she said flatly, unaccustomed to giving out her address in New York—dangers of city living. Her reaction was foreign to him; he just stared at her not knowing how to proceed. Finally Chelsea decided she needed this guy more than she needed to be coy. She remembered her mom mooning about "love at first sight," and she remembered thinking it was all a bunch of lies. Sure, she had good reasons to doubt, to be scared, to be angry, to be afraid, not to believe, to leave and hide.

No one knew how hurt she was. But then she heard herself say to this nice looking boy on a Sunday afternoon at the mall, "We're in some—what do they call it here?—um, cul-de-sac thing off 96. Oh yeah, Linden Drive."

Trace lit up, "I go right by there on my way to school. I could pick you up if you want."

Holding her answer back, she suddenly offered him her cone. "I don't want any more." Again, she put him off his game as he stood there, ice cream now melting down into his sleeve.

"Yeah, you could do that—pick me up—for school that is." She giggled slightly, blowing her "tough stuff cover" for an instant. "So, here's my number. I have a cell phone." She pulled a piece of paper out of her small pink shoulder bag and jotted it down, then handed it to Trace.

He looked at the paper, manipulating it through his fingers like a silk ribbon before finally responding, "Cool." And then slowly, after a major eye lock with her, he threw the cone in a trash can next to him, focusing entirely on the beautiful girl before him. "OK, I'll be there tomorrow morning at 7:05." She nodded in slow motion, suddenly at a loss for words again. "Out front, OK?"

Chelsea nodded again; then they both stepped back from each other, neither wanting to be the first to walk away. Finally, she made her move, "I gotta go. I gotta meet my ride home . . . my step, ex-step-uncle, whatever." And with that, she was gone, leaving Trace to fantasize about the possibilities with this new girl from a completely different world, a world he'd never known before.

His black VW convertible pulled into the driveway of Stephanie's home situated at the center of a mobile park. Although it was permanent in structure having been placed on cinder blocks with a planting design along the front walkway, it was still a mobile home, a fact Trace was not particularly proud of. Still, it was the neighborhood he had lived in for two years, and everyone within close proximity knew him by name.

Heading toward the front door, Trace's arms were loaded down with bags of school supplies as well as a couple of new shirts smashed under his chin. He bounded up the stairs as the entrance swung open. Stephanie greeted him with her usual hug, then grabbed some of the bags before they spilled out onto the walkway. "Looks like Christmas, son. Did ya' get everything?"

Trace headed toward the back of the house where his bedroom was tucked away. "All set, Mom." He glanced at his posters of Garth Brooks and Alan Jackson before dumping his packages on his bed in a room surprisingly neat for a boy his age. In fact, the whole trailer was concise and well organized with Stephanie's feminine touches adorning every nook.

Returning from his bedroom, Trace made a beeline for the kitchen table where he claimed his chair at the head while reaching across the small dining expanse to grab a Coke out of the refrigerator. As he popped the top of the can, Stephanie deposited his extra shopping bags by the hallway and started to serve her dinner that was cooking on the stovetop. "Spaghetti and meatballs tonight." She loved pleasing her son, knowing that pasta was his favorite meal.

"Thanks, Mom." They shared a moment of silence with no overtones of discomfort or stress, more like a miniature sabbatical for both, before Trace decided to speak. "I met that girl at the mall that was in the diner. Her name's Chelsea."

Stephanie could sense the grin on her son's face without even turning around from the stove. "Oh, you mean the pretty blonde one?"

"Yeah, she's alright. I'm gonna give her a ride to school tomorrow. She doesn't have a license yet. She's from New York City."

"Did you ask her mom, Trace?"

"She wasn't with anyone. Besides, I just asked her if she wanted a ride to school and she said OK. She only lives on Linden. It's on my way."

Stephanie knew her son better than that. "If it were in Texas, you'd make it on your way." She stirred her sauce as she gathered her thoughts. "I'd feel a lot better if I could check with her mom, them being new in town and all. I think it's the proper thing to do, but her aunt didn't know their number."

Trace took a beat to assess his feelings about his mom treating him like a two-year-old. He chilled out after downing the entire can of Coke in one chug, deciding then and there that he needed to stop telling his mom all of his future plans. But for now he had to play ball; Trace pulled Chelsea's now wrinkled piece of paper out of his pocket. "I got her cell number right here, Mom."

Stephanie filled his plate to overflowing with spaghetti and meatballs, then sat down with him at the table with her pittance of a meal. "Let's go ahead and eat, and we'll call her after dinner." They bowed their heads in thanksgiving, something his mom insisted on their doing together as far back as he could remember. Still, Trace did not want to push the envelope about his growing independence that night, so he prayed. And Stephanie took her usual sneak-a-peek at her son as he prayed, hoping to see a sincere gesture of faith. She'd been waiting for a sign for a long time.

❧

Lauren set William's food down on the back porch when the phone rang. She grabbed it just before the machine picked up. "Hello? Hey, Suz! No, we're not eating. Tucker's out with his dad, Rene's taking a nap, and I was just feeding the animals. How are you?"

Susan was sitting in her porch swing at the back of her house with one of her infamous cups of coffee. She smiled, just happy to be speaking with her friend. "Lovely, simply lovely. So how is it there? I don't want to snarl, but you were supposed to call me when you got in, you dog!"

Lauren jumped up on the kitchen counter, settling in for a good, long chat. "Ah, I am a dog. I forgot. It's just been nonstop here. Shoot me, squirrel me, send me to the pound. School starts in the morning. Unpacking, blah, blah, blah, but everything's fine. William and Bingo have settled in. Irene got here the day after I did. Mom and Dad are amazingly content. The biggest ruffle so far was when I smoked the house out because I forgot to open the stupid fireplace flue. And I miss you so much!"

"I miss you, too!" Susan gulped down her coffee. "If I start chattering, it's because I'm having my not allowed third cup of coffee for the day. Geez, ever since I went through menopause, my mind and my mouth get out of sync after one cup, and that's before I've had sex. And yes, *we* still indulge. Ha!"

"What's sex?" Lauren adopted her best Miss Scarlet accent, "I can't even remember." Lauren fiddled with the phone cord.

"Practice doesn't make perfect; it just used to make babies, who, of course, are perfect, until they begin to grow up. Speaking of babies, do you miss Gracie?"

"Ah! Like crazy. I can't believe she was my last foal. I keep thinking I've got my trailer behind my truck." Lauren adopted an odd lilt to her head, "I keep telling myself that dreams don't really matter. But at the end of the day, I think they're all we have." Lauren almost fell off the counter. "It's so depressing to know that I can't just stroll outside and get on my horse for a ride. I still want the blue ribbons, Suz."

"You'll ride again. It'll work itself out."

"Yeah, I know. The good news is that Tuck seems to be doing OK. His dad took him to the circus on Friday, and Rene took him bowling Saturday. And today he's been at the movies, so he hasn't had much time to get homesick."

Susan sat up in surprise, "Irene took him bowling?"

"Can you believe it?" Lauren giggled at the thought.

Warming her hands on her still steaming cup of coffee, Susan continued to probe, "And how's your niece?"

"Chelsea's a real piece of work, I'm sorry to say. She was the sweetest cutie on the face of the earth when she was little, but now she's turned into that Angelica character off one of Tucker's cartoon shows. Bottom line, she has the personality of a doorknob. I sure hope it's not a permanent condition, just the 'teen thing.' I'm trying to get a relationship going with her, but so far I'm at the short end of the log." Susan laughed at yet another of Lauren's goofy sayings. "You mean the 'short end of the stick'?"

"Sure, that's what I meant."

"Do you know where that saying came from?"

"What? 'Short end of the stick'?"

"When farming people had to carry water from a well, they'd put the heavy bucket on a stick that two would support on their shoulders. The problem came when one person was shorter than the other. The water bucket would move down the stick requiring the shorter of the two to carry the bigger weight of the load. And that's where the 'short end of the stick' saying came from."

"Why, Suz, you're just a fountain of information. I thought it meant getting beaten by someone who walked silently and carried a big board. Either way, it's a stupid saying, like 'unequally yoked.' What are we, a bunch of eggs?"

"I trust you are kidding. 'Unequally yoked' is out of the Bible. When someone is a believer, he or she shouldn't be married to someone who is not a believer because . . ."

Lauren cut in, ". . . I know, I know. 'Been there,' as you so often remind me."

"A little loving reminder isn't rubbing your nose in it, my friend."

"Believe me, I'm not about to jump from the frying pan into the dishwasher! On the other hand, I did follow 'Brian Brickhead' to Tennessee. I must be nuts."

Susan repositioned herself in her chair and resumed rocking. "Hello? We've been through this a million times. You didn't want Tucker that far away from his father. And rightly so, I might add."

Lauren bristled, "I just think it's ridiculous that Brian would move away when Tucker is so young. And why would he say all those things he didn't mean when we were married, all the promises of forever that never happened. Why did he initiate the idea of adopting Tuck when I had finally made peace with the fact that my biological clock had run out?"

Susan mused, "And aren't you so glad he did? You and Tucker are more fun than Christmas."

"True," Lauren relaxed slightly, "He's better than a double-dip sundae, isn't he? And Brian is a good dad, just a lousy husband. And, OK, I confess, I resent having to follow him around while he finds a midlife career, and I have to uproot mine! I . . . "

Suz refused to let her get negative, "We prayed about this move more than a lot, Lauren. Aside from keeping Tuck close to Brian, you have a mission to accomplish with your family. No one said it would be easy, or even successful right off, but reconciliation only comes in Christ, and you're the only one in your family who's signed up for the job of 'healing hostess.' Just keep praying, and God will take care of the rest."

Lauren groaned, "I know, but the spiritual crossfire here is like being in a firefight in Vietnam. It's not easy to be the only believer in the household."

Susan wished she could give her friend a hug over the phone. "You're going to be fine."

Lauren pushed off the counter and started pacing. "I hate this molding-shaping stuff, I swear. When I got here, I felt like I was in bed with an infestation of fleas. I was about to jump out of my skin. But it's getting a little better every day. Maybe I can make a meatball bounce." She swung around, wrapping herself in the phone cord. "Suz! I haven't even been over to the vet office yet. I'm so worried about that."

"How so?"

"Ah, " she twisted out of her entanglement, "I'm just having a wee battle with insecurity. New place, new surroundings. I was just getting my bearings where I was and bam!"

Susan was quick to reroute her focus. "Lauren, don't get caught in that 'perfect' trap. Time can be our best friend or our worst enemy. Growing old is mandatory; growing up is optional. We're only perfect in Christ. Remember what I always say, 'Jesus hung on a cross for me, knowing I could never be perfect as he.'"

"I hate it when you're always right," Lauren lifted her leg for a good stretch on the countertop. "I sound like a broken recorder. I'm going to change my tune here. For my whole life, 'I've been looking for love in all the wrong places.' Now that we're in Music City, I'm writing a new line that I think should be a country hit, 'If you ever leave me, I'm going with you.'"

Susan had to think for a moment before the phrase tickled her fancy, "Just remember, you don't need a sailor, you need a Savior."

"Gosh, I don't know how I lived one day without the Lord at the center of my world. When I think back on my crazy life! I watch Chelsea flail around, and my heart aches for her. I've never been around such an angry spirit." As an afterthought she added, "Other than my own, that is."

"You hit it on the head, Lauren. It's a spirit on her, and that's what you have to pray over and rebuke. Details of why, where, and how will reveal themselves. Right now look at her anger as a spirit surrounding her like a python. The snake of anger will slither down and surround her, and with every breath she takes to escape, the serpent tightens its vice grip on her heart until it strangles the literal breath out of her. If you don't think you all moved there for a good reason, think again, my friend. And I'm not just talking about Irene and your parents."

Lauren acquiesced slightly, still struggling with her internal issues. "Yes, oh prophetic one. I have to admit and confess that I am having daily battles, but I guess that's the way the cookie bounces. And this cookie needs a 'Suz' fix. When are you going to come and visit?"

"As soon as my husband gives me the go-ahead, I'll hop on a plane. Well, maybe I'll mosey onto a plane. My hopping days seem a distant memory lately."

Lauren threw her a barb. "Even with all your wild, crazy sex . . . huh?"

"I'll ignore that for the moment. Any way, I can't wait to see you and your new house. I do miss you."

"Miss you, too."

"Give the big Tuckster a big envelope of love from me sealed with a kiss."

"Always. And then I'll smother him because he's missing your hugs, and so am I!" Surprised at her audible gasp of emotion, Lauren held the phone away in an effort to gain control of her runaway feelings.

Susan knew it was time to hang up, "I've got to run. Bye for now!"

"I'll call you tomorrow with Tuck so he can tell you about school! Love you." She blew a kiss in the phone before hanging up like she used to as a little girl.

⚜

Tucker blasted through the front door with Chelsea sauntering behind at her usual nonclip. Tuck ran up to his mom, gave her a big hug, and started to tell her every detail of the movie he saw while Chelsea vanished like an illusion down the hall, heading toward the privacy of her bedroom.

What followed was the usual regular of William greeting Tucker, howling and crashing through the kitchen furniture to get to his boy while Miss Aloof Bingo Cat objected vocally to the flurry around her private little world, which she obviously preferred to remain calm. Lauren glanced out the window, observing Brian as he got into the car. Once again, he never failed to inspire her thoughts of longing, which were immediately curbed. Lauren thought, *If that man could ever harness his rage to something righteous, instead of insidious . . . oh, never mind.* She turned to her son who was riding William like a pony.

"Tuck, go on and get into the bath, buddy, and I'll be right with you. We've got to get a good night's sleep for your first day of school, OK?"

Amiable as always, the little boy trotted off down the hall passing Chelsea on the way; she held her cell phone out to Lauren, sour as ever. "A lady from the diner wants to talk to you. Actually, she wants to talk to Mom but she's . . . what? Sleeping probably."

"Chelsea, she's resting. She was pretty banged up from her fall." The girl just shrugged. With that, Lauren grabbed the phone. "Hello . . . "

"Yes, Stephanie, of course I remember you. Oh, and by the way, let me give you my number. It's 852-3997. Right. Yes, I was about to call you. . . . Oh, I see. . . . Trace is going to take her to school? I'm sure that's fine, but as I mentioned, I'm her aunt. Let me go get her mom and make sure that's OK."

Chelsea stood in the corner of the kitchen cringing and jumping up and down, mouthing, "Please, please, please!"

Lauren couldn't help but laugh at her drama, "Hey, Stephanie, may I call you right back? Yes, I have your number. OK, bye-bye."

Chelsea exploded, "Please say yes! Don't ask Mom. She'll just say no, and I really don't want to go to school on the bus."

Lauren regarded her niece. "I can't speak for your mother. By the way, how old is this boy?"

"You saw him. He's seventeen like me!" Chelsea fidgeted, "He's a senior and cute! He's just going to give me a ride."

Lauren headed down the hall, "Hold your tacos. I still have to ask your mom."

Irene was awake and reading a magazine when a knock came on her bedroom door. "Come in." Lauren poked her head inside.

"Hey, Chelsea just got home, and she met that boy from the diner. Remember, I told you about the ladies I met?" Before Irene could answer, Lauren continued, "All very nice. I saw the boy, and he seems really nice, and his mom . . . "

Irene put her magazine down and regarded her sister, "You're babbling. What's going on?"

"Well, Stephanie called because her son was going to give Chelsea a ride in the morning—to school, on the first day—and I think it's fine. But it's entirely up to you. He seemed like a nice young man, and his mom is a nice lady. I think it would be a good thing to let Chelsea go with a cool boy for the first day of school, don't you, Mom?"

Peeved, Irene shook her head, "What does 'nice' mean? 'Nice' is a vacation. I don't even know these people. I can't let her go in a car with some boy I've never even met."

Lauren broke in, "Oh, just let her go. I met them, and they're nice—pleasant, polite, nice! Trust me, I think it'll be just fine. Plus it'll give her a good start at school. It's only one ride. I'll tell them you'll pick her up."

After a beat, Irene reluctantly gave her permission, at which point both women could hear Chelsea squeal like a stuck pig out in the hall, "Yes!"

Chapter 12

-School Belles-

The first day of school was announced by the most glorious early fall weather Lauren could remember. Having lived on the east coast most of her life, she had yearned for the distinct colors that are only displayed in areas of the country that have dense foliage and rolling hills. She recalled the times as a child that she made her way to school through the back paths that were surrounded with the same kind of intensity of hues she was observing now. *I am thankful for the cold, wet weather that has preceeded my arrival to Centennial, turning the lush greenery into a kaleidoscope virtually overnight—just for me,* Lauren told herself.

Yes everything looked different because there was something expectant about this day. All the new beginnings that Tucker had worried about and she, as a mom, had held in great concern were finally facing them. All the nights that Lauren stayed up tossing and turning, wondering what this day would be like, how it would look, how it would smell and feel was now before her. Her endless questions of how she and Tucker would take on the challenges of new directions and attitudes were about to be answered. Yes, suddenly it was all there, like every child's Christmas morning after a year's worth of fantasies. What would be under the tree? What delight might they see or receive? In Lauren's case, how was the first day of school going to go for Tucker and Chelsea?

Chelsea was out the door just as everyone was arriving in the kitchen for some cereal and good-morning hugs. No one could be more surprised at Chelsea's early departure than her mother, since Irene had spent Chelsea's first seventeen years dragging her out of bed for whatever occasion awaited her. But for some reason—named Trace, Irene reasoned—this morning her daughter was up and gone without any prompting. Only a fleeting glimpse of her could be seen as she made her way down the steep driveway in what seemed to Irene to be an inappropriately short skirt and a way-too-tight blouse.

Irene was about to tear out after her daughter with a sweater when Lauren grabbed her by the arm. "Let her go. She'll be OK. I have binoculars, by the way."

"Where?" Irene searched the room with her eyes.

Lauren shook her sister for a moment to get her attention. "Just kidding! Calm down, will you? You're making me a nervous wreck! She'll be fine!"

Irene reluctantly retreated back into the kitchen, giving Tuck a hug before placing him up on the kitchen stool for his cereal.

"I just want to go on record, Lauren, that if anything happens to Chelsea, I will personally pull every hair out of your head one at a time." Tucker glanced at his aunt with a look of concern.

"So noted," Lauren seemed unphased.

Lauren fed Bingo who impatiently waited on the pantry countertop, then William, his tail beating her leg in enthusiasm as she opened his can of food. Tucker put on his armor of God with grand gusto, and surprisingly, Margaret and Sam made their way into the kitchen with hugs and kisses for Tuck to send him off on his great new adventure. And when Irene finally settled back with a cup of coffee, this was the second time Lauren looked around at her family, inspired by the possibilities, amazed by the changes already in progress.

An antique bowl full of ice cubes and aloe vera cream with cotton pads floating about as if on a lily pond sat on the bathroom countertop. Eleanor dipped her entire face into the medicated concoction specifically designed to shrink her increasingly swollen face while she listened to her husband in the kitchen clamoring about making coffee. Eleanor's gaze rose to the mirror before her, and an expression of excruciating dismay crossed her face as she observed her reflection.

"If I could wind the clock back, it still wouldn't make us any more on time!" Ham said with a chuckle in his voice as he entered the bathroom. What normally would have been a fun jab at Eleanor's perpetual tardiness, this morning raised her hackles.

"You go without me. I'm gettin' ready as fast as I can!"

Holding two cups of steaming coffee, Ham observed his wife leaning over the bathroom sink; their eyes met in the mirror. She only had a slip on, her makeup was strewn all across the closed toilet seat and vanity top, and her hair was still in curlers. He couldn't help but think that in all the years he'd known this lovely woman, he'd never seen her quite so out of sorts. His smile indicated the deep and profound love he had for her; his inimitable sense of humor was not to be tamed by circumstances, no matter how threatening. "You look lovely this morning, my dear. New dress?"

Although she threw a wet facecloth at him, his staunch presence and big grin brought Eleanor to laughter instead of tears. "Oh, Ham. I'm such a mess! I can't go."

He nodded knowingly. "Just take your time, sweetheart. You are my angel, no matter what you look like. I'll just wait for you outside." He left a cup of coffee next to her mound of makeup, kissed her on the back of her right shoulder, and left with a fleeting sweep of his hand down her body—her form so familiar to him, his touch so needed by her.

Centennial was esthetically compelling as a town, especially on such a crisp and sparkling fall morning. The energy in the air was kinetic as the youngsters began to gather for their first day of school. Brightly colored buses, beyond normal yellow it seemed, contrasted the fall colors as the sun streaked across the tall antique building windows in patterns of strobe-like illumination.

Down Main Street, the traffic was heavy for 7:15 on a Monday morning, but then all the students of legal driving age were sporting their cars, new haircuts, clothes, and dates as they made a slow right off of Main toward the entrance of Greystone High School. Short of the first football game of the year, the excitement was unequaled. Despite the fact that most of the teenagers had grown up with one another, every year brought new possibilities and a few new students along with it just to add spice to the soup. And although there was a definite nip in the air, any car that was a convertible had its top down, all car windows were wide open, music was blaring, and not a single student wore a jacket, even if their moms made them drag them along.

The public school was brick in structure, relatively large, and well-maintained, yet clearly not the most modern of establishments like the myriad of private schools that were scattered about the perimeter of Centennial. Chelsea tried to put on her too-cool-to-be-true attitude as she arrived at the high school, but despite herself she was nervous as well as excited about what the day might bring. One thing was for sure, she was particularly happy to have been brought to school by Trace, someone she already considered to be quite the catch.

As the slow procession of cars made its way into the high school parking lot, the lighted sign in front of the school read:

GREYSTONE HIGH SCHOOL WELCOMES
THE SENIOR CLASS OF 1997!
REMEMBER, WHEN YOU'RE TALKING, YOU'RE NOT LEARNING!—HAM

Chelsea let herself out of Trace's VW and looked up at the quote. "What's a 'Ham'?"

Trace assimilated the message on the sign, "Ham's our basketball coach. He's a real good guy. Every day he leaves some saying in front of the school. Don't know how he gets away with it 'cause it's a public school and all, but everybody loves 'em. He's got these 'Tidbits of Wisdom,' as he calls them. His wife, Ms. Eleanor, is pretty cool, too. She's the school nurse."

"I met her at the diner. Don't you think she's kind of weird looking?"

Trace laughed, "You mean her face? She's got allergies."

"Really? She told us it was 'from her mother's side of the family.' How weird."

Trace's attention was momentarily diverted when he noticed Shooter approaching with a bunch of his friends, but they all veered off into the school before close proximity between the rivals occurred. The air of tension didn't go unnoticed by Chelsea, but she decided to lay low this first day and try to get a feel for her surroundings, as well as her potential competition. She was well aware that new kids in school better have thick skin to ward off all the gossip and staring their classmates put them through. But she was ready; she was tough. She had been through much more than anything these kids could dish out or even imagine. "First days" for Chelsea were peanuts compared to her past.

"They want how much?" Pam looked incredulously at her real estate agent, Kathy. Middle-aged, robust, and dressed to the nines, she smiled at Pam reminiscent of a plastic Stepford wife, "Two sixty-nine ninety."

Pam's eyes widened, "Two hundred and sixty-nine thousand dollars and ninety cents?"

Kathy laughed, "The woman who owns the property is superstitious or something. She picked those numbers out, but I bet you could nab this beauty for two fifty."

"Two hundred and fifty thousand dollars?" Pam just stepped back and stared at the vacant, dilapidated, two-story building erected in 1910. *Or was it 1710?* she thought. The structure barely had enough left of its original style to recognize that in it's heyday, it had been quite a pretty home. But now it just looked like it needed to be dozed under and forgotten like some ugly relative.

"I can't believe that the house could possibly cost that much. I agree, it's the correct size for the school, but it's such a mess!"

Kathy seemed a tad perturbed with Pam's attitude. "Dear, it's all in the eye of the beholder. Now we've been doing this for over a year." Her tone became more placating with every passing word. "Each time you get near town, the prices skyrocket. Just the land here alone is worth a fortune. So you're either going to have to accept in-town prices or make up your mind that you're going to build your school farther out in the country."

Pam had had it with this woman. "I can't. The school has to be close to the projects! I'll never get the kids to come if their parents have to drive them. Most of the families from this side of town don't have cars."

Kathy tightened her coat around herself in a gesture of frustration. "Have you ever heard of busing?" Suddenly, the agent blushed. "Pardon me, Pam. It just hit me when I said that. Bussing. Segregated schools. It would be like turning back the clock. I know your idea for a certain kind of school is ground-breaking, but it also has to be realistic. I've been through this with you, Ham, and Eleanor. The best thing I can suggest is that you get somebody to donate a building and then start having fund-raisers. I know you have your curriculum ready, but you still have no place to teach it."

Pam was steaming; she looked like she had just spent a day at the beach with no sunscreen, "I'll have a place. There'll be a way. We're opening next fall, and that's all there is to it! So if you can't come up with something better than what you've just offered me, perhaps I need to work with another broker." As the words came out of her mouth, Pam was astounded by her sharp tone; nonetheless, this woman didn't seem to understand the importance of finding the right location for the Hope School. Then and there Pam decided that she'd get a bigger bang for her buck if she advertised herself to find just the right property for the school. What was especially sweet was that her decision was confirmed in her spirit, and a peace fell over her like chocolate coating on an Easter bunny.

Kathy huffed, "Well, I'm sorry you feel that way. I will keep you posted if I hear of anything else that might suit your real estate needs." She started to march off when she spied Irene's approaching BMW. Waving wildly to make sure Pam saw her new client, Kathy put on her most delicious welcoming smile for her next prospective homebuyer. "I'm going to have to go now, Pam, but I'll call you if anything comes up."

Irene maneuvered her car to the curbside, getting out to greet the agent. Lauren quickly sidled up to her sister as the ladies gathered on the sidewalk. Both Lauren and Irene were introduced to Pam when Irene observed the dilapidated house before them, "I hope this isn't one of the homes we'll be looking at."

"Of course not!" Kathy incessantly giggled while she spoke. I just wanted to meet you here because Pam was looking at this property." Kathy introduced all the ladies before continuing. "Pam is going to be opening a school and wanted something in town." Both Irene and Lauren couldn't imagine the dilapidated house ever being a school. Pam was quick to pick up on their expressions of disbelief. "By way of clarification," Pam cleared her throat, "the 'something in town' part is correct. This property is not correct, just in case you were thinking I have the vision of a gnat."

Everyone laughed except Kathy, who now turned to Irene. "I'm sure you'll be looking for a home in one of our lovely gated communities."

Lauren was quick to step in, "Actually, I just bought a home on Linden. It's a nice area, and since Irene and I are sisters, it would be super if she were to find something close by me."

"Yes, ma'am." Kathy nodded. Pam politely excused herself as she made her way back to her office at the church on the corner.

Barely acknowledging Pam's exit, Kathy fluttered about, excited to impress her new clients. "Why don't we just go to the coffee shop over there." She pulled an embroidered hankie from her purse and waved it in front of Irene's face like a matador. "They have lovely biscuits and pies, and we could have some tea if ya'll like while we talk about your wishing-well home."

Suddenly, Irene looked defeated before she even began. "Kathy, is it?" After affirmation from the real estate agent, Irene continued, "Kathy, I don't think I'm going to find a three-coins-in-the-fountain home. I don't think it exists in my price range. So what we need to talk about is my this-will-have-to-do house."

Lauren was disturbed by her sister's negative attitude. "Irene is from New York City, and she's always lived in the city, so, this is all very new to her, and the idea of a house is also new to her."

Kathy started nodding again, "Well, toward Nashville, we do have townhouses, if you prefer."

"No, no. My daughter is going to Greystone High, so I would like to stay in the area, as my sister mentioned. The whole family is here, in fact, so we want to live relatively close to one another. Let's just see what you have other than what we're standing in front of. Out of curiosity, what's the price tag on that one?"

Kathy hesitated slightly, "Two sixty-nine ninety." Lauren and Irene responded accordingly. Kathy countered, "Please, let me assure you, it's the location of the property that makes the price skyrocket."

"Well, I'm not looking for anything in this area, and my price range is around $200,000, tops."

Kathy visibly deflated. "I see. Well, how large a home are you looking for?"

Irene thought for a moment, "Small, very small. And easy to take care of since it's just my daughter and me. And who knows how long that will last once she turns eighteen."

"Well, let's go get that cup of tea, and we'll go over some listings. May I ask what church you attend? That might make a difference about which area of town you'd like."

Irene stiffened, "I don't . . . "

Lauren stepped in once again. "We literally just got into town, so we haven't visited any churches as yet. So, if we could take a peek at some homes in the area of where my house is, that would be a super start. Something small, simple, affordable, and charming."

"Yes, ma'am." Kathy muttered as she herded them off toward her favorite grazing spot.

⁂

"I didn't really mean to slam the door, it just slipped out of my hand," Pam told herself as she entered her office/classroom at the back of the church with a resounding bang. "I didn't mean to be rude to Kathy. Ooh, I was so rude," she muttered to herself.

Tonya had been watching the children during her lunch break from school so Pam could go over and look at some real estate, but she could tell immediately by Pam's demeanor that it was not a good "go see."

"Hey, 'Frosty the Snowman,'" Tonya teased, "Guess you didn't have a good showing."

Pam plunked herself down in the seat behind her desk, burying her head in her hands. "I am so frustrated! My knees are raw! I've prayed and prayed and prayed and prayed."

Pam and Tonya continued in unison, "and we prayed some more!"

Pam was beyond road weary, "I just don't understand what the heck is blocking finding the school's location! It's God's school; it's God's idea! We don't have a dollar ninety-eight God. Why is it so difficult to raise money? To get people to understand how crucial this program is? Why isn't God opening doors? Why isn't everything falling into place? Where's my miracle?"

"Time out, sister." Tonya patted her friend on the back. "It'll happen. God loves to show up at the last minute, just to make sure we know it's his gig."

Pam looked at her friend woefully. "Yes, but this is past the last second. If we're going to open next year, we have to break ground now. We have to get fund-raisers going, and I can't even find any reasonable property to present! How am I supposed to go to somebody and say, 'Here! Wouldn't you like your children to go to school in this dump? And, by the way, why don't you just fork over a quarter of a million dollars to buy it and then another quarter of a million dollars so we can fix it up! And all of your hard-earned money will go to a new concept of integrating children for reconciliation and education. Let me spell it out for you,'" putting on her best Martin Luther King Jr. voice, "'I have a dream.' And right about that time the door slams in my face." Pam buried her head in her hands again, close to tears, "I've got to talk to Eleanor and Ham. I'm at my wit's end, and you know that doesn't happen very often, but something's got to give here."

"Look," Tonya headed towards the door, "I gotta get to my class, but we're all getting together tomorrow as usual, right? 4:30 at Norros?" Pam grunted her affirmation.

"Well, we'll talk about it then. You're the one that's always telling me not to give up. Practice what you preach, girlfriend." Pam knew she was right; blowing her a kiss, Tonya gave Bobbie a quick hug before leaving the room.

Numb, Pam just sat there for a moment, then glanced at all of her kids at play. She could see the future; they were right there in front of her. *OK,* she thought. *This isn't a real classroom yet! But I can see how these kids blend together, the ones that need to be watched after so their moms can go to work or school and the other moms who leave their kids so they can go shop or decorate their homes. It doesn't matter. The point is, the kids are all from different types of families and backgrounds, economically and ethnically, yet they all have one thing in common; parents that love them and love the Lord.* "Yes," she whispered to herself, "Thank you, God, that you're color-blind." Pam stared at her little flock in awe while they played together, content and secure. She thought about all the pain from the past and the struggles between blacks and whites and the atrocities that had been handed down from generation to generation. "Sin. What an ugly thing to inherit," she muttered. Pam had asked God about that issue many times, but all of a sudden, it became clear to her while watching the kids, as if God had written a play for her to attend, not so much for entertainment but for some answers to eternal questions.

Pam repeated, "Sin nature." She observed her toddlers to four-year-olds, noting how the bigger ones at times pushed the littler ones aside. How they took their toys, seemingly unaware of whatever pain they may be inflicting on their friends. Pam concluded, "Human nature, unattended to spiritually, is bereft of a soul or conscience when it comes to hurting someone's feelings or, for that matter, even sharing."

Pam had to smile when she watched the parents come to pick up their children; she'd always hear them say to their young ones (as she also did many times during the day), "Say, 'Please.' Say, 'Thank you.' Now, share." And then it hit her, as if God were standing right there in the room explaining sin nature to his child, Pam. "You can, as human beings, be taught manners, but you cannot be transformed without my Son, Jesus Christ. Don't you realize that reconciliation of any sort is impossible without the presence and power of the Holy Spirit. And yes, my little one, it is *my* school, and it is *my* idea, and *I* will bring it to pass in my time." How Pam loved it when God spoke to her close up and personal; and suddenly she was ignited with enthusiasm again, knowing from the bottom of her soul that the vision she shared with Ham, Eleanor, Tonya, and the handful of others who had committed to make the Hope School happen, was God's will! She said to herself, *Because he who is in me is stronger than he who is of the world!* And with God's words on her tongue, a radiant, explosive warmth came over her, and she knew she was experiencing the presence of God. She felt his arms around her, holding her, encouraging her, making her feel safe, empowered, important, and heard. She wasn't wrong to have such a mighty dream. And Pam knew, deep down, that God was surely pleased with her.

Chapter 13

-Casting Call-

I rene's car was parked down the street from the high school, smoke swirling out the driver's seat window. Irene and Lauren were crunched down in the station wagon at odd angles, peeking out of the windows like some *Saturday Night Live* spoof on women detectives gone awry. Lauren whispered as she choked on Irene's cigarette smoke, "You say I'm ridiculous! This is ridiculous! Why are we spying on Chelsea?"

Irene hissed, "I gave in about that boy driving her to school, but you said that I would be picking her up!"

"Rene, that would be so dorky. You don't want Chelsea to feel . . ."

Irene cut her off, "Where do you get these words? 'Dorky'? 'Nice'? What? I'm just trying to make sure my daughter's not getting a ride to school with the latest ax murderer."

"Gosh, Rene, you're a bit over the top, don't you think?"

"No, I don't!" Irene slapped her hand down on the dashboard.

"OK, OK, we'll follow them home, but I've got to pick up Tucker in a half hour, and I don't want to smell like a smoke stack. So they have to come out soon, or I've got to go." Just then, the bell rang out in the distance as masses of kids exited the high school. Thankfully, Irene spotted Chelsea amongst the first wave of teens; she was walking along next to Trace, laughing and flirting away. As they reached his VW, he pulled the top down on his car, and they both got in.

Irene shook her head in disgust, "Whatever happened to chivalry? Why don't boys these days open doors for girls?" Her eyes narrowed. "I don't like him. I don't like him already. He's too cute for his own good! Look how cocky he's acting."

Lauren watched her sister fiendishly puff away on her cigarette, "Irene, you can't be too cute as a boy. Plus, it probably gave Chelsea a big boost to show up with a hotshot at school. I'm sure he's very popular."

Irene flicked her cigarette out the car window, "That's my point! He's popular. *Popular* means 'trouble.'" Horrified that her sister had just flung a lit cigarette out the window, Lauren exited the car to snuff out the culprit.

Irene went wild. "Get down! Get down so they won't see you!"

Lauren chided her, "You can't throw a lit cigarette out the window!"

Irene reeled from inside the car, "We're not in a barn! There's no hay around!"

"I don't care!" Lauren snipped as she mashed the cigarette into the sidewalk. "It's disgusting. It's a disgusting habit!"

Little did the sisters realize that they had parked within earshot and eyesight of the real estate lady's favorite café she'd taken them to earlier for sweet tea; their antics were being observed by all the locals out for afternoon coffee and sugar breaks. Lauren and Irene were clearly not making good first impressions on the busybodies of this small town, notorious for putting newcomers under their proverbial microscope and into their local gossip columns. As Trace whizzed by Irene's BMW to escort Chelsea home, Lauren threw herself on the ground so as not to be seen while Irene disappeared under the dashboard. Once safely out of view, the "dynamic duo sister team" took off down the street under the wary eye of the local sheriff, Chet Monty, who'd been watching their odd behavior with great interest. By the grace of God, literally, Lauren spotted the black-and-white cop car parked behind a UPS truck. She screeched at Irene to slow down to the school-zone speed limit of fifteen miles per hour.

"No, I'll lose them!" Irene protested.

"OK, Irene, do you want to get busted by the local police? Then we can't follow them at all. And I'm not going to be late picking up Tucker, so slow down!"

Annoyed, Irene slammed on the brakes. "Don't get your panties in a wad. I'm simply not going to let Chelsea out of my sight with that boy!"

Stunned, Lauren adopted the calmest demeanor she could muster at that particular moment. "Please don't ever use that expression in front of Tucker."

"What expression?" Irene zoomed down the street. Finally out of the school zone, she managed to maneuver herself two cars behind Trace's VW.

Lauren's lips curled with emphasis. "The 'panties in a wad' expression!"

Irene just laughed her off. "There's nothing wrong with that term. It just means you're a wiggly worm who can't sit still and your undies bunch up.

Lauren made a repulsive face, "Please, Rene."

"Alright, so noted," Irene threw one of her sister's sayings back at her. "And speaking of censorship . . ." Irene turned to Lauren, unfortunately taking her eyes off the road.

"Wait, wait, wait!" Lauren slammed her fist on the dashboard. "They're turning right!" Instantly, Irene swerved her car, almost hitting a divider along her pursuit.

Lauren grabbed her seat belt for protection, "Oh, that was a smooth move Marian Andretti."

Irene tugged at Lauren's sweater by the elbow and twisted it into a painful knot. "Shush! We're back on track, aren't we?" Lauren shrank down like a chastised puppy. Satisfied, Irene released her stronghold. "So, what I was saying before I was so rudely interrupted was, do you have some sort of block on my TV? I can't get any of my favorite shows."

Lauren raised her hands as if she had just won the lottery, "Yes, of course. I don't want Tucker watching some of the junk that's on TV. Personally, I don't want to watch it anymore."

Offended, Irene countered, "I don't watch *junk.*"

"What?" Lauren wagged her finger at her sister. "You watch shows with bad language, bad themes, and a lot of sex."

"And you don't watch them because . . . *why?*" Irene pushed Lauren's finger out of her face.

"Because I find them offensive, that's why!"

"And, since when, Miss Goody Two-shoes, do you find them offensive?"

"Excuse me!"

Irene calmed herself. "You know, Lauren, I think you've gone a little bit overboard since you've gotten into this God thing."

Lauren could barely contain herself, "And what exactly is so attractive about swearing, having premarital sex, cheating on someone, or murdering masses of innocent people? It just doesn't appeal to me anymore, *OK?* And I don't want Tucker brought up with those images in his mind. Do you know how hard they are to erase? I've been trying to erase them for ten years!"

"Goody gumdrops for you," Irene taunted her.

Lauren lost it. "Stop that! Stop those stupid little sayings from our childhood!"

"No, I won't because all I have left are my fantasies, and I don't care to have them erased, thank you very much! You sound like you've been brainwashed by some cult."

Lauren punched Irene hard in her arm. "That's not funny!"

Irene dramatically rubbed her wound in defense. "I swear, if you bruised me, you're a dead woman! Don't hit me!" Irene pulled at her sleeve as if she could press the pain away. "And don't talk to me about my sense of humor. I amuse myself late at night with thoughts of revenge. Every time I think of Ford and my best friend, I want to send them a pretty poison package." Suddenly, Irene's face lit up as she observed Trace's car turn toward Lauren's house. "Oh, good! They're going directly home."

"No stop at Park Place or the local jail," Lauren poked some fun.

Both the cars turned onto Linden Drive. Lauren cautioned, "Slow down, slow down! They'll see you following. Just pull over for a second." Surprisingly, Irene complied, putting her car in park by the side of the road.

As the dust settled, Irene panicked. "Do I smell like a cigarette?"

Lauren released her seat belt, "You *look* like a cigarette. You're fuming with bitterness, anger, and revenge. It'll eat you up, Rene. Forgiveness is such a core issue. That's why God talks about it so much, because people who hold others, including themselves, in unforgiveness, are the ones that really suffer." While Lauren preached, Irene redid her lipstick in the rearview mirror. "They become bitter and angry, and their lives are robbed on a daily basis of joy and peace. Even if someone has eternal life in Christ, if they can't forgive, they're bound to their past and imprisoned by their anger."

Finally, Irene turned to her sister with a raised eyebrow. "Listen, Pope Joan III, I'll worry about my unforgiveness, and you worry about yours. It wasn't so long ago that you were a raving lunatic about how you hated Brian. How could he leave you?"

"OK, OK, you're right, but that's why I know what *not to do!* In my case, experience overrides theory because I've done everything wrong. Remember, hindsight is 60 minutes."

"20/20."

"Rene, I'm talking to you about this stuff because I've been where you are and I know that you've got to let it go. And you've got to let God in! Look, we're all just broken little girls, broken-hearted, wanting to have the leading role in an adventure that never seems to happen. We want to have a soul mate instead of people who stomp on our hopes. And what happens? We end up merely turning out like a harder version of ourselves every season of our lives that goes by without embracing any kind of happiness."

"Geez, Lauren, you sound like a greeting card," Irene tossed her sister a wink to take the sting off of her assessment.

But Lauren was not about to be foiled. "Why? Because I've finally figured out that nobody's responsible for my happiness but me."

That statement really got Irene's goat, "They may not be responsible for our happiness, but they sure are responsible for our unhappiness."

"No, no, no! You're missing my point, Rene. There's a place of peace, calm, security, and unconditional love that you can find only in God. Just because I'm a messy messenger, doesn't mean the message isn't *perfect!*"

Worn out, Irene let her head rest back as she responded in a half grunt, "Lauren, we've been through this a million times. I honestly believe that what you've found in your faith is lovely. It seems to be working for you, at least better than it used to. I also think if you hadn't found whatever it is you found, you'd be hanging like a bat upside down screaming into the night. So I am truly happy for you. But it's not for me."

Before Lauren could respond, Trace zoomed past them again in his VW on his way home from dropping Chelsea off. Irene fired up her car, and Lauren slammed her seat belt back on, "Rene, I just want to be able to talk to you about some of these things and not have it escalate into an argument. I'm probably approaching it all wrong, but I just want you to have what I have in my life now, something I never had before. My circumstances or feelings don't define who I am anymore. It's about something that doesn't go away when things turn out badly or wrong. It's hard to describe, but it's so amazing!"

As Irene pulled up into Lauren's driveway, she opened her window to air the car out yet again from the last vestiges of her cigarettes. Then she addressed her sister with as much patience as she could gather. "Well, that's good for you, sweetie. And you don't have to describe *it* because you have to pick up Tucker. So off you go, and I'll see you at home later. I'm cooking tonight. And I may be cooking for you for the rest of your life because those houses we saw today were flat out scary."

Despite the rejection, Lauren let out one of her heartfelt giggles. "Well, that was the sweetest shove-off I've heard in a while, but let me leave you with this one, big sister. You're welcome to stay with us forever. There's plenty of room, and I love you no matter what."

Irene responded weakly. "I don't know what I'm going to do, Lauren. I just know I don't want to feel like this anymore."

Lauren leaned over and gave her sister a giant hug and a blob of kisses; and when Irene looked up from Lauren's barrage of affection, she had tears in her eyes—deep, painful, sorrowful tears. "Lauren?"

"Yes, Rene?" Lauren answered softly.

"When did we switch places? When did you start taking care of me?"

Chapter 14

-Home Fires-

H am held Eleanor's hand tightly as they left the doctor's office that Monday afternoon. They didn't speak for almost the entire length of the block when he finally broke the silence, "Darling, are you alright with everything?"

She just looked at her husband for a moment, fighting back another onslaught of tears. "I just can't cry anymore. My skin will never fit on my face again. I'm goin' to end up with stretch marks under my eyes instead of bags."

He pulled her up to him, giving her a big hug, "Ah, that's my girl. A little levity is good for the soul. Please, try to stop worrying. Remember, a happy ending means there's some sadness in the middle. The doctor said we won't know much until you've had your surgery, so if you agree, I'd like you to go in as soon as possible."

"I agree. Waiting just prolongs the agony. I'm going to have to tell at least a few people what's goin' on with me—the principal, and, of course, the girls when I see them tomorrow."

He ran his hand affectionately along her face. "Laughter is the shortest distance between two people, so don't lose your smile. It is so delicious." Yes, this man could always bring happiness to Eleanor's eyes.

❧

Shooter was waiting outside when Tonya came by to pick up their son from Pam's. It didn't matter how many years Tonya had been looking at her man, her eyes always lit up when he was near. "How's my big guy?" She sauntered over to Shooter for a quick hug. "This is a sweet surprise."

"Yeah, well I got outta school, and I thought we could take Bobbie for a burger. You don't have classes tonight, right?"

"Nope." Tonya hopped up and down in approval. "That sounds festive. So how was school?"

"For starters, I don't like two of my teachers, and I know that I'm goin' to need Ms. Eleanor to help me with at least one class so I can keep playin' ball."

"I'll help you, baby." He was outwardly unhappy with her suggestion, which Tonya immediately picked up on. "It's just, I've already been through the classes. God just birthed me a year before you, that's all. No biggie."

"I don't like feelin' that I'm behind you, girl. Anyway, Ms. Eleanor makes it easy with the math stuff I don't get." Tonya regarded him, surprised at his sudden candor.

"What you're gonna get is all those college scouts looking for *you*." She rubbed his neck for a moment before Shooter shuffled up the steps. "Yeah, better be. Better be."

Bobbie squealed as soon as he saw his mom and dad walk through the door. In his excitement he knocked over a chair on his way to greet them. Although he was definitely one of the bigger kids in the group, he still had a sweet, protective spirit toward the younger children. Tonya always said that Bobbie got his kind heart from his dad, that he was a gentleman from the day he was born. "Her *gentle little man,*" she called her boy.

Pam was surprised but happy to see Shooter. "Hey, what's up? How's school?" They shared their infamous handshake to the delight of the kids in the class. "Alright."

Bobbie crawled up his dad's pant leg, then hung off his arm like a swing. Seeing father and son together always warmed Tonya's heart. Shooter gathered his boy up in his massive arms, giving Bobbie a tickle for good measure. "I'll meet ya'll outside. Bobbie and me are going for a quick run."

Tonya watched them go, turning to Pam. "I hope he hurries up and marries me before I rust. Truth is, I think I'd wait forever for that man." Then she laughed at herself, good-naturedly, "But if he don't make an honest woman out of me soon, I'll smack him up side the head till he does! I've got a lot invested in that dude."

❧

Dinner was a disaster. Never a fan of pasta, Margaret picked at her food, disappointment written all over her face. The only one talking at the table was Tucker—ten miles an hour over the speed limit, as usual—relaying every detail of his first day at school. If Lauren had had any concerns about her son, they had been appeased the moment she saw his beaming face when she picked him up after school. Tucker already had a best friend and a play date for that next Saturday.

Margaret sent Sam over to their apartment for what had to have been their fifth cocktail of the evening. Encouraged by the definite buzz he had going, Sam leveled a line of questioning at Chelsea, with whom he had shared nary a word since she'd arrived. "So what is the boy's name?"

"What boy?"

"The boy that took you to school," Sam frowned.

"Oh, him—Trace," she responded, barely audible.

"Trace who?"

"Don't know."

"How do you spell *Trace?*"

"I guess the way it sounds, like erase, T–R–A–C–E."

"Where is he from?"

"He's from here. He lives here."

"Did he live here all his life?"

"I think he moved here a couple of years ago."

"What does his father do?"

Chelsea had just about enough of this line of questioning, and hoped that her next answer would put an end to the interrogation. "He's dead. We have a lot in common."

Irene looked up on that comment. "Chelsea, your father's not dead. He's just not around."

"Well, he might as well be dead."

Then it was Margaret's turn to have a word. "Now that's quite enough, young lady. After all, he's still your father no matter if he's a good one or a bad one."

"Mother, please," Irene objected. "Her father is a dead beat, and you know it."

Now, Lauren couldn't help but get her two cents worth in. "Irene, I don't think that's the way you should be speaking about Chelsea's father. Even if he's not all he should be, it doesn't do any good to degrade him."

Tucker followed the conversation, his head turning back and forth as if he were watching a tennis match; the tension at the table escalated within moments. Irene downed her wine, then responded to Lauren, "Don't tell me what I'm supposed to talk about in front of my daughter. She's my daughter, not yours."

Sam interrupted, "She's no one's daughter. She acts like we all don't exist. She doesn't talk to anybody. She just sits there like a lump with that poor-little-me expression on her face." Sam pointed his fork at his granddaughter, "You need to straighten up and fly right, young lady. This is your home, and you need to acknowledge that there are other people in it."

"That's right," Margaret threw in for good measure. "Just remember the next time you want your Christmas money early or you want to go here or there. Your requests shall fall on deaf ears if you keep treating people the way you do." If looks could kill, Margaret and Sam would have been laser beamed by Chelsea who managed not to respond verbally.

"Mom and Dad, please. I'll handle Chelsea if . . ."

Margaret didn't let Irene finish. "Well, you haven't been doing a very good job of it. The girl doesn't even speak."

Then Lauren fell further into the fray, "Irene, you just said the other day that it would be good if somebody said something to Chelsea to make her realize that her behavior," she glanced at her niece, "is not becoming."

Tucker looked confused. "Becoming what, Mom?"

Before Lauren could answer, Chelsea slammed her fork and knife on the table. She pushed her chair back, almost decapitating the cat as it fell to the floor with a crash, then ran out of the room.

After a few moments of silence, Lauren finally offered up a bit of wisdom, which was heard but not received. "You know, guys, an eight-ounce glass of water, once boiled, can turn into an eight-foot wall of fog."

"You are *crazy*. What on earth is that supposed to mean?" Irene said with a good deal of sarcasm.

Lauren instantly became defensive. "Don't talk to me like that in front of Tucker."

"Oh, for goodness sake, Lauren! Will you wake up and come back from la-la land or wherever it is you've gone? You're simply not going to protect Tucker from the world. People get divorced, people get cheated on, people lie." As Irene went on, so did her emotions, tears welling up uncontrollably. "People get hurt, people get humiliated, people get lost. People get left behind!" Before she totally lost it, Irene now slammed her chair back and retreated from the room as well.

Lauren glared at her father. "Look at what you did, Dad."

Sam stared her down, not one to be chastised, "I didn't do anything. I just asked the mute girl some questions. And if that's not allowed, don't invite us to dinner. Margaret, let's go." Margaret shrugged her shoulders at her daughter, grabbed her drink as well as a slice of cake from the counter, and followed Sam into their apartment.

Tucker just stared at his mom with his fork midair. "How come everybody's so mad?"

Lauren took her napkin and wiped her son's mouth while she searched for some sort of right answer. "No one's mad at you, Tuck. You didn't do anything, buddy."

"Yeah, but Mom, why's everybody so mad?"

"I don't know," she relented, shaking her head. "We're just a goofy family, that's all. It'll get better though, Tuck."

She could tell her son had really been upset by all the ruckus; he stared down at his plate. "It reminds me of when you and Dad used to fight all the time."

Oh, if words were daggers, Lauren would be slain on the floor. She immediately wrapped her arms around her son, "I'm so sorry, Tuck. Sometimes adults are real idiots. You know that rhyme from one of your books, 'sticks and stones can break my bones, but words will never hurt me'?"

"Yeah," he nodded.

"Well, that's a lie. Words can really hurt us, so we have to be careful what we say to one another. We'll just do some extra prayers tonight and ask God to give us all more loving hearts. Except you, buddy. You've got the biggest loving heart I know."

"OK," he said simply.

"So why don't you finish your dinner, and then I'll read to you for a while."

He looked back at his mom for a moment, then finally picked up his fork again. "Ya know, I think I'll be OK on the bus in the morning."

Lauren tried to give him a smile of assurance even though her heart was breaking. She thought, *Oh no, he already doesn't need me.*

"That's great, Tuck. What a big boy you are! I'm so proud of you. But if you change your mind in the morning, just let me know."

He nodded, finishing his dinner, "OK, Mom. And if you're afraid to go to your new work, I can go with you the first time, too. Cause you'll see that it's really not so scary. You just have to do it."

"Ahh, out of the mouths of babes." Lauren mused, "Thanks, buddy."

⁓⁓⁓

Lauren caught the phone on the second ring even though her thoughts were miles away. "Hello? Yes? Yes, I'm Tucker's mother. Oh, hello! How are you? Yes, Tucker told me about Keith today;

they seemed to hit it off. Saturday, yes. . . . Oh, well that's not a problem; we can do it another time. Tomorrow? Sure, hold on. Let me just ask Tuck, OK?" Lauren cradled the phone to her chest as she addressed her son who had just returned from changing into his pajamas. "It's Keith's mom, and she forgot that they have to go out of town this weekend, but she wanted to know if you'd like to go with her after school. She'll pick you and Keith up to go play at his house, give you a little early dinner, and then bring you home. How's that sound? Would you like to do that?"

Tucker lit up like a Christmas tree. "Cool!"

"OK! Hello? Yes, that would be just wonderful. Let me jot down your number. We live in the last house on the left on Linden Drive. Oh, terrific, you're not far at all. If Tuck's home by seven, that would be perfect. Yes. This is so kind of you. Thanks so much! And I look forward to meeting you tomorrow. Bye-bye." Lauren thought: *Gosh, not only does he not need me to take him to school, but he has a date tomorrow afternoon! I should be happy. Why am I not happy? This is everything I prayed for. Hmm, maybe you are just a crazy person dressed up like a mom.*

❧

Lauren had read Tucker three and a half stories before his eyelids finally closed, heavy with the exhaustion of the day and anticipation for tomorrow. Lauren prayed over him while she looked at her son sleeping peacefully, "Thank you, God, for loaning me this wonderful child to be in my care. And I ask you every day, in every way, to prepare me and empower me and help me be a good example for this boy. I know he is yours, but for the time being he's mine, and I love him so much! And I love you for sharing him with me. In Jesus' mighty name."

Lauren could not let the night pass without checking on Chelsea; maybe she was a young adult, but she was also still a child in so many ways. She wasn't surprised to find the door to her niece's room locked, but Lauren knocked anyway to see if the girl was awake. No go. All Lauren got for her efforts was Chelsea's garbled voice saying she was asleep. So Lauren retreated, deciding that sleep was good medicine for pain. She knew, however, her sister would not be asleep.

Irene didn't answer the door at first, and suddenly Lauren felt like a little girl again, hoping her big sister would let her in so she could apologize for some faux pas she had committed or some nasty thing she had said. It finally hit home with Lauren as she banged again on the door that Irene didn't act like Irene anymore. She had always been so forgiving, loving, and protective; but now she seemed livid, lost, and lonely.

Lauren had prayed that she would have the right words to help mend her sister's broken heart, knowing full well that those words wouldn't be hers because she had no wisdom of her own. Instead, they would be the words she herself had come to rely on from the Bible. She so desired to be for Irene what her friend Suz had been for her—an anchor, a divining rod pointing her to the safety, covering, and grace of the cross. Oh, if she could only get out of her own way so she could be better for others.

Now Lauren tried the knob, but the door was locked. She banged again, "Irene, please, let me in, huh? I'm really sorry." After a beat the lock slowly turned; as Lauren entered, Irene retreated back to her bed.

The room was dark and shadowy, blanketed in an ambiance of sadness; Irene's mascara was smeared down her face from crying. She had a big pile of Kleenex on her comforter, but the most telltale image that Lauren saw right off was Irene's old journal, the one their father had ripped the pages from years ago. That leather-bound compilation of aspirations and yearnings reflected Irene's heart and soul yet had never been shared. Irene was a magnificent writer whose words now seemed trapped in a stranglehold of despair and messy details.

Lauren's heart ached for her sister, who just sat there on the bed, silenced by her pain. Her struggles had taken their toll; the light in Irene's eyes had effectively dimmed. And even with their sisterly share of joking and sparring, there was something desperate about Irene, unreachable. This was not to say that Lauren's hurts, pains, and travesties were all healed and wrapped up in a pretty bow. But at least they had finally been recognized, understood, grieved; and for the most part they were on their way to being healed. What's more, a lot of Lauren's negative tapes that she'd carried from her childhood had been silenced. Yes, those nasty recollections of unkind words or debilitating insecurities had been replaced by the promises of God and a growing personal relationship with Jesus. Her God, whom she cried out for in times of floundering, was her everything, her Lord of lords! She so wanted her sister to know that kind of security, to experience the joy and peace of unconditional love. But there they sat—together, alone.

When she finally spoke, Irene's voice was vacant, "Lauren, I really just can't take any more right now, so please, I don't need a pep talk, alright?"

Lauren cut in, "Absolutely, Rene. I'm so sorry. Hey, let's go out to lunch tomorrow, just like we used to, OK? We'll be wild and crazy. My treat, we'll just relax and have fun. Remember what you always told me Edison said, 'Don't call it failure; call it an education.'"

Irene sighed, "Lauren, you're 'pepping.' I'm not a lightbulb."

"OK, sorry. Listen, Tucker is all set for the day, and Chelsea obviously has her school rides organized." Irene blew her nose as her sister rattled on. "I checked on Chelsea before I came here."

Irene sounded like she was underwater, she was so stuffed up. "So did I, but she wouldn't let me in."

"I know. She's sleeping. Are you OK with her plans for tomorrow?"

Irene looked up and shook her head. "And if I weren't, what difference would it make?"

Lauren was desperate to encourage her sister, who was emotionally disappearing before her very eyes. "I have an idea! I think you need to go and meet Trace's mom. Maybe we'll do that after we have a magnificent, delicious, splendiferous, disgustingly fattening lunch. We'll go and meet her. Stephanie's her name. We should do that. Maybe that will give you a little peace. She seems like a super nice lady."

Irene just shook her head again, "Lauren, you are so naïve. *She's* not dating my daughter; her son is."

"Well, you know, the ole apple doesn't fall far from the flea." Despite herself, Irene couldn't help but laugh.

Relieved, Lauren chortled, "Gotcha! See! I made that one up. I actually made that one up to get you *to smile again!*"

Irene waved a Kleenex at her sister as she mercifully let go of a guttural laugh. All the while, tears streamed down her face. "Lauren, you are so ridiculous."

"I know, but I love you so much, Rene! Hey, you know that they say the Word of God is a living thing that gets inside of you, kind of like a cold. You sit next to someone with a cold, and they sneeze, and the next thing you know, you've got their cold living inside of you!"

Irene stared at Lauren in utter disbelief. "How attractive."

"Let me put that another way."

"No, please don't."

"OK, OK. I'm just so happy you feel better. Ha! I made you laugh." Lauren beamed.

Chapter 15

-Afternoon Delights-

Irene was literally up at the crack of dawn the next morning to ensure she wouldn't miss seeing her daughter before she was off to school. It was still dark outside, the sun just beginning to rise over the treetops, when Chelsea entered the kitchen. She was surprised to find her mom waiting for her, cradling a mug of coffee. Making her way to the refrigerator, she grabbed an apple as she crossed the kitchen to meet Trace outside.

"Do you want me to make you some toast?" Irene felt a little stupid as she hadn't made breakfast for her daughter since she was in elementary school.

"I don't want to be late."

"It's only quarter of seven. Why don't you sit down for a minute?" Chelsea fidgeted like a cornered animal, but her mom was right, she didn't have to be down the hill for a while. Reluctantly, she sat at the table and started to nibble at her apple. "Did you sleep alright last night?" Irene offered her daughter a sincere look of concern.

"Yeah, fine. Why?"

"Well, I know that you were upset when you left the dinner table, and you didn't want to talk last night." Now Chelsea looked vacantly out of the kitchen window. "I just want you to know that your grandfather doesn't really mean to be so gruff; it's just how he is."

Chelsea challenged her mother with a look, "He gets really mean when he drinks."

Embarrassed, Irene shook her head, knowing she carried the same kind of baggage, "Many people do. But you have to admit, you've been difficult to get along with, especially since we've gotten here. I don't want to get you all upset before you go off to school, but I really would like to spend some time with you and see if we can talk things out a bit."

"Whatever, Mom. I've gotta go." Chelsea headed for the door, tossing her half-eaten apple into the garbage. "Oh," she spun back to face Irene, "some of the kids are going to the mall after school. It's OK if I go with Trace, right? He's a really good driver."

Irene was about to object when she heard Lauren somewhere in the back of her mind saying, "Give her some space."

"What time will you be home?" Irene wanted to bite her tongue.

"I'll be home by eight for sure. And we don't have homework yet, so I'll probably just eat something at the mall."

"But it's dark by then. Alright, I want you home no later than *seven.*" Irene was getting red about her neck.

"OK, seven. Thanks."

And with the only thank-you her daughter had offered in years, Irene still couldn't leave well enough alone, "Do you have a coat?"

"It's not that cold."

Just as Chelsea was about to exit, Margaret and Sam made their way into the kitchen. There was an awkward moment of silence, then Sam directed his, "Good morning" directly to Chelsea.

The girl rigidly stared back at her grandfather, "Good morning."

Margaret elbowed her husband slightly in encouragement; his words came slowly as he was unaccustomed to apologizing. "Chelsea, I'm sorry if I upset you last night. We are just curious about what you're up to, and . . ."

Margaret finished his sentence for him, just in case he was about to embark on another diatribe, "We want to know how you're doing and how school is going."

For the first time Chelsea softened her stiletto veneer ever so slightly, aware that her family was making an effort on her behalf. She actually smiled slightly, "School's good. Everybody's pretty nice. I've got to go now." And with that she was out the door.

By the time the breeze from Chelsea's exit had left the room, Irene was up on her feet pouring her parents some coffee. "Dad, thanks. You, too, Mom. That was sweet. I really don't know why she's so distant, but let's try not to argue, and I'm sure she'll open up at some point."

On that note Lauren and Tucker waltzed into the kitchen escorted by Bingo and William. The animals took their respective places in the room as they waited impatiently for their breakfast. Meanwhile, Tucker made the rounds giving everyone a hug while chatting about how he was going over to a friend's house after school.

"Has Chelsea already left?" Lauren asked as she busily moved about the kitchen.

Irene nodded, "Yes, the vanishing gnome. She's been very motivated to get out of the house lately."

Ever the optimist, Lauren reasoned, "Well, that's a good thing, don't you think? She seems to be enjoying herself."

Irene poured herself another cup of coffee. "You would be proud of me, missy. I let Chelsea go to the mall this afternoon *with Trace!*" She grabbed her chest at the thought. "I'm about to have a heart attack."

"No, you've just had too much coffee. But speaking of heart attacks," Lauren turned to her son, "are you sure you want to take the bus this morning?"

"Of course he does," Sam cut in. "He's a big boy. Besides, that's why we came in." Sam shifted his weight, then rolled his head from side to side as if limbering up before a boxing match. "I'd like to walk Tucker down to the bus stop." This was, to say the least, an unusual request coming from Sam; Lauren was dumbfounded at first, which Sam interpreted as a no. Still, he insisted, "I could go with you, then. I know *you* want to take him, but I'd like to take my grandson down to the bus stop."

Lauren snapped out of her shock. Looking at Tuck, she ventured, "How about that, buddy! I'll just let Granddaddy take you down, OK?"

Ever the compliant one, Tucker graced his mom with a smile, "Cool."

The sun was now up over the hilltop, its rays glistening on the lawn and colorful tree leaves. Lauren watched through the window as her father escorted Tuck down to the bus stop at the end of her driveway. Her eyes filled with emotion as she thought: *What a picture! Thank you, Lord. I can't ever remember going for a walk alone with my dad. Maybe you can teach old dogs how to smile. Ha! I know you can.*

She watched Sam lean over and button the top of Tucker's jacket, and then, to her amazement, her father took her boy by the hand so they could continue the rest of the way down the driveway. Sam gazed at his grandson like he was seeing him for the first time and smiled, "You know why I want to hold your hand instead of letting you hold mine?"

Tucker pondered the question for a second, "Nope."

"Because if you trip, you might let go of my hand and fall, but if I have your hand in mine, I won't let go."

Tucker smiled, "Cool, Granddaddy."

Lauren and Irene were making their way through midday downtown Centennial traffic in Irene's BMW. Little sister was slapping on some makeup with abandon, "You should've let me take my truck. If we look at homes this afternoon and we're driving around in a BMW, everybody's going to expect that you have tons of money."

Irene wiggled in her seat, "My bum is still tender, and that truck is like a jackhammer. I don't know how you can stand it."

"It is not," Lauren quibbled. "It rides just like a car with big wheels. Hey, I've got one for you, 'How does the guy that drives the snowplow get to work?'" Puzzled for a moment, Irene eventually smiled.

"Aha!" Lauren poked her finger in Irene's cheek, "Another smile! OK, I'm going for a homerun here. Why do we sterilize needles for lethal injections?"

Irene waved Lauren off, "Stop, stop, stop. Alright, we're going to have fun."

"Of course we are!" Lauren squealed, "I was thinking this morning that raising a teenager is like nailing Jell-O to a tree."

"Stop . . . do we go right or left? Where are we going?" Having arrived at the center of town, Irene was now circling an enormous statue of a soldier waving a flag on a rearing horse.

"I think the restaurant is down Third Street. It's Italian. Oh, Rene! We're going to have so much fun. Just remember, we can't be complaining while we're praising."

"Don't start." Irene's voice hit a low growl, so Lauren decided not to press her luck.

"OK, OK. Did you know that a caterpillar has the same DNA as a butterfly? People see us as caterpillars, but God sees us as butterflies."

"Where do you get all this *stuff?*" Irene regarded her sister, taken by her enthusiasm.

"Stop! Pull over. There it is. Frank-Os. How original." Lauren looked like a kid about to go into a candy shop.

⁂

Sharing the back booth of the now-empty restaurant, Lauren and Irene were carrying on like teenagers; one could tell by the cluttered table and array of glasses and plates that these two had indulged in a fine afternoon. Practically lying in her seat, Lauren moaned, "I'm so unbelievably stuffed. Even *I* can't believe how much I ate."

"You?" Irene threw her napkin at Lauren, "I've probably put on twenty-five pounds, and it's all your fault."

"Yes, but it was fun, wasn't it, Rene? Just like the good ole days! And you have to admit that that meal would have cost about nine thousand dollars in Manhattan."

Irene swigged her last sip of wine. "At least."

Looking around, she cringed. "They're going to think we've taken up permanent residence. We're the last ones here." Lauren took a sip of her now-cold coffee. "Rene, they said not to worry. They're open all afternoon. And I quote, 'No hurry.'" With that, both ladies hunkered down a little farther in their seats, enjoying the moment.

"Wow, wasn't this morning groundbreaking—watching Dad take Tuck down to the bus stop. I almost lost it." Then Lauren shot up as if plugged into a wall socket, "Hey, they cloned Dolly the sheep last week. Maybe we can clone our new dad!"

"You're pie-eyed, sweetie." Irene grabbed her napkin and threw it at Lauren again. "Am not!" Lauren wailed, "I'm just happy. I'm fifty years old, and I feel new everyday. I don't know why I'm always so surprised, but what happened this morning is what I call 'divine intervention.'"

"It was pretty amazing," Irene concurred. "I can't believe Dad actually apologized to Chelsea. Maybe old age does mellow one."

"Does a chicken have lips?"

"Is that a question?"

"I'm just making sure you're paying attention. There will be a test later, you know."

"I swear, Lauren. I'm having trouble tracking your thoughts."

"I was talking about Dad. He melted me this morning. I think it's pretty unusual for him and Mom to have accepted living with me."

Irene rolled her eyes looking very much like Chelsea, "I think it's pretty brave of you to ask them. Besides, where else were they going to go? Mom and Dad aren't exactly rolling in retirement greenbacks."

"I'm serious, Rene. I'm honored to have them. I want so much for Tuck to know his family. And I love Mom and Dad—ever since I found my Father in heaven."

Irene rolled her eyes again. Lauren continued, "Stop that! And don't get mad. I'm just telling you how I feel, OK?" Irene finally nodded permission for her sister to continue.

That's when Lauren really flew into first gear, "Yes! So ever since I found my Father in heaven, Dad doesn't have to be anything but who he is because I know I'm adored by God. Rene, I know that both of us wanted more of Dad when we were kids, but he was always there for us in his own way. And Mom, too." Lauren retraced her childhood for a moment. "Still, I had this kind of ache, this hole in my heart, didn't you? When we were little?"

Irene considered her sister's comments, "What I *can* say is that you always seemed to be pretty sad, always disappointed. When somebody let you down, it really shattered you."

"OK, I admit, 'love is a many splintered thing.' But my point is, I kept needing Dad to be someone he wasn't, and it wasn't until I came to my faith that the emptiness was filled. And now he doesn't have to be anybody but who he is! That's what I'm trying to say. The same with Mom. Now my job is to figure out how not to pass my hand-me-down heartaches to Tucker. It's a generational thing, and it can stop with us, here and now. Isn't that exciting, Rene? Proverbs 4:23 says, 'Above all else, guard your heart for it is the well spring of life.'"

"Alright, now *that* I can relate to." Irene licked her fork clean of the rest of her tiramisu. "When I was younger, all I wanted to write about in my journal was romance, adventure, and beauty."

"Yes! And all I wanted to do was get Mom and Dad to come to just one of my horse shows. That was my adventure."

They both took a moment for reflection, "Lauren, do you think that Dad wanted at least one of us to be a son?"

Lauren laughed, "Definitely! I think that's why I was such a tomboy, always trying to be something I thought I was supposed to be. Always trying to please everyone. I was trying to win Mom and Dad's love, or earn their love, or be good enough that I'd feel loved; and that insanity continued through every relationship I ever had, from friends to men." Lauren released a sigh from within her very depths, "Gosh, do you remember in the seventies, Rene? The feminist movement? 'I am woman, hear me roar'? How pathetic was that? Who wants to be a man? I don't want to be a man. I don't want to be God. I just want to be a woman. Strong and soft while I survive myself."

"I don't know about the soft part," Irene was quick to point out. "No one could ever tease you, then or now."

"I know! Because I can't stand being laughed at. I always felt like somebody was going to leave me or laugh at me. I think I have a pretty good sense of humor—just not about myself . . . yet. Hey! Here's what I've concluded, that what we've all done to ourselves is far worse than what anyone else has ever done to us."

"Now, that I do not agree with. What Ford did to me was the lowest."

"OK, that's true. That man gives new meaning to the phrase 'filthy rich.'"

Irene almost shivered, "But it's not just men that hurt us. Now, when I think back on all our lousy friends we've cried over, I want to invent a new kind of torture. Karen was my best friend, and she stole my husband."

Lauren shook her head, "I know, Rene. It was awful. There are just not many people we can trust. That's why I want us all to be close and make sure our kids are OK. Women are really the warriors, don't you think? I remember Mom was always like a lioness with us. She was really protective of us. That's what I want to be with Tucker, and I know you want to be that for Chelsea too."

"If she'd let me. I'm having so much trouble understanding her."

"You should try having a son. I have to connect the dots as I go. Boys want to conquer and save the day. That's why Tuck loves his Batman getup so much. But as girls, we just want to dress up and feel lovely. Remember how we'd stay up all night and talk. . . . I don't know. As a little girl, I just wanted to feel irreplaceable; and as a big girl, I want to feel irresistible."

"Is that why you were always putting on some sort of show for everybody when you were a tot? You were always dancing or joking around."

"I guess. I wanted to be the center of attention because I felt so overlooked somehow. And, Rene, that's what I'm talking about that's so different now. Yes, I hurt just as much when Brian left me as I did when Steven left me. The only difference now is that I have different tools to deal with the hurt. Who I am is not who I'm married to or what kind of car I drive. It's who I am in Christ. In my first marriage I thought my only value was based on how Steven looked at me or treated me. That was who I was. And for my part, I was so incredibly, emotionally needy, which of course, is the fastest way to push everyone away. And I was a star at it."

"I think you're being too hard on yourself. You're a fabulous woman."

"No, Rene, you're the one that figured out how a woman was supposed to be—mysterious but not out of reach. I always envied that. Mom knows that, too. I just didn't seem to be able to get that part right with a man. Maybe I never will. Either way, I'm going to let God pick my next husband if I'm supposed to have one. I still want to be explored. I still want to be inspiring and intimate."

"Who doesn't, sweetie? We all want to be loved. But, obviously, we just can't seem to find the right man to fill the bill. Do you have any idea what it's like to admit to yourself that you were just like a piece of jewelry to your husband? I don't think Ford ever really loved me. I don't think anybody's ever really loved me. I think I've just always been some kind of an ornament."

Lauren grabbed her sister's hands, "Oh, Rene, that's so sad. You're beautiful and you're wonderful. Those jerks were crazy not to have taken care of you and truly loved you for who you are, not what they needed. That's why I keep talking to you about my faith. You're the apple of God's eye. Each of us is. We're supposed to feel altogether lovely to the core because God sees us that way. And when we know where our real esteem comes from, we'll make better choices, especially in men. For so long I just felt that God didn't have time for me, but now I always say, "If God had time enough to make me, he has time enough to keep me. And he loves me. It's my choice to accept that love. I can't count on any other person to make me whole. You know what they say, 'Girls have sex to get love.'" Lauren bounced up and down in her seat with a new burst of excitement. "It's such an amazing thing, Rene! The Bible is always talking about royally messed up people and how God still used them in a mighty way. God sees us as spotless and brainless so we can start again!"

Irene was getting restless, "Spotless and brainless? That doesn't sound very inviting, Lauren."

"Oh, no, no! I meant spotless and blameless. Sorry, sorry."

"I'm sorry, but I find this all so elusive. I don't understand when you say things about the Bible. It just doesn't make any sense to me."

Lauren was not going to be deterred, "Look, I know it's easy to believe in miracles if you see them. But the Bible says, 'Blessed are those who believe without seeing.' So if you want a modern-day miracle, don't think about the parting of the Red Sea, or raising people from the dead, or even creation. Just look at me. Look at my life. Don't you see a difference?"

"I've already told you that I see a difference! It just doesn't connect for me."

Lauren exhaled, "Fine, but I can promise you one thing that I'm absolutely and positively sure about, my big sister: I am not spending eternity without you, Mom and Dad, Chelsea, or *anyone* I love. So, I'm not going to stop praying!"

Irene had had enough, "Good, pray away. But let's change the subject for a while, please?"

"Fine." Yet Lauren refused to let go of her hope. "You just let me know when you're ready to give up the pain, the hurt, the loneliness, the anger, the bitterness, and the . . . "

"Stop!" Now Irene was mad, "Do you think I like feeling the way I'm feeling?"

Lauren leaned in for emphasis, "Of course not! You remind me of a person who's fallen into quicksand, and they're struggling and struggling to get themselves free. But for all their efforts, they're sinking lower and lower. And just before they are totally enveloped and die, they look up and see that there's a huge, strong tree branch above them. If they had just looked up and grabbed onto it, they would have been saved!"

"Oh, that's a good one, Lauren. Almost as cute as the one about the person with a cold sneezing all over you."

"Granted, that was a bad analogy, but the quicksand is relatable, no?" Irene simply shook her head. "Alright, how's this . . . God is better than New York cheesecake. When I finally got tired of being a chump for no change, Jesus came to the rescue. What a romance, and I'm God's leading lady! And yes, I now have someone who won't lie to me, leave me, or let me down. And if you don't want that, then you're the one living in la-la land!"

"Lauren," Irene warned.

"OK, OK, I'll stop, for now." She threw Irene's napkin back, falling into hysterics when it miraculously clung to Irene's face like one of her sister's favorite horror movies, "You look like the glob."

"Shush." Irene yanked the napkin to her lap as Lauren leaned back and scrutinized her sister.

"Have you ever wondered why you're so fascinated with horror stories? Why on earth would anyone want to be entertained by terror and fear?"

"Perhaps because I grew up with Grimm's Fairy Tales?"

"Oh, you're right!" Lauren squeeled. "How sick was that? No wonder we're all nuts."

Irene began to unglue herself from her seat to leave. "Case closed," she said.

Lauren followed suite, having to peel her pant legs from the leather booth seat. "In your dreams!"

Chapter 16

-Helping Hands-

Sam and Margaret settled in that Tuesday afternoon to watch the five o'clock local news; Margaret fiddled with her packs of TV control clickers, madly trying to tape one of her afternoon talk shows before the screen was commandeered by her husband.

"Margaret, the news is about to start."

"Oh, Sam, calm down. I'm just about ready. It won't kill you to miss two seconds of the local news."

Sam muttered to himself, "I suppose you're right. But we still should know what Southerners consider newsworthy, even if it's only who caught the biggest catfish and who has the biggest derriere. Some of those people at the grocery store need a forklift to get around."

Margaret surrounded herself with pillows, obviously a habit both her daughters had inherited from her. "I read somewhere that Tennessee ranks right up there with the most overweight in the nation." She laughed, although not maliciously. "I almost feel petite next to the general public around here. It's actually been pretty good for my morale. Poor things must be victims of all the fried food they eat."

"And the grits and biscuits and bacon and gravy and . . . Gee, I'm making myself hungry. Why don't we have an early dinner before Jennings's *World Report* comes on at 5:30?" Sam was practically licking his chops.

"Alright, I can heat up some leftovers." Satisfied that she was finally recording one of her shows, Margaret flashed to another channel. It took a couple of beats for Margaret and Sam to register what they were seeing on television; pictures of their daughter, Irene, and Ford Williams flashed across the screen looking much like a personal segment with Mary Hart on *Entertainment Tonight*. Caught by paparazzi cameras, the couple was previewed at a political fund-raiser, a high-brow wedding, then dining and dancing at New York's hottest club.

But it was the text of what Sam and Margaret were watching that was the real stunner; the newsflash reported Ford Williams's death, having been overcome by a heart attack that very afternoon in Manhattan. The local female reporter's voice heralded her surprise at Ford's untimely passing.

Shocking news just in moments ago. The death of
shipping magnate, Ford Williams, from an apparent heart

attack has been confirmed by our affiliates. Ford, age sixty,
was rushed by ambulance to Columbia Medical Hospital
in response to a frantic 911 call from an unidentified
female caller. That's all the information we have as of this
moment. What you're viewing on the screen are photos
of Ford and his recently estranged wife, Irene Williams,
noted by W Magazine as one of the "mover and shaker
celebrities" in the style circles and society columns of New
York elite. As a recognized couple internationally, there
had been rumors of discontent for several years in regard
to their marriage, but it was only confirmed a few weeks
ago that Irene Williams had left their palatial penthouse
apartment on Fifth Avenue with her seventeen-year-old
daughter, Chelsea, to move to our own Nashville area.
Although no sightings of the mother or daughter have been
reported locally as yet . . . Oh, wait a moment. Flashing on
the screen a moment ago was a recent photo of Chelsea. At
this juncture no comments from any family or friends have
been gathered, including from Mrs. Williams, as to her
whereabouts, or more details concerning the sudden death
of her husband. We'll keep you posted as more information
is reported. Once again, Ford Williams, shipping tycoon,
dead of an apparent heart attack at age sixty.

Margaret and Sam were literally on the edge of their seats as
they stared at the TV, trying to assimilate the information that had
just crossed their screen. "Oh my," Margaret barely uttered while
Sam shook his head, "I just can't believe it. Where's Irene?"

Eleanor, Stephanie, Pam, and Tonya sat in their usual back booth at Norros taking advantage of the quiet time between meal shifts and crowds. This was their "circle of friends" haunt, a place they would gather at least once a week to catch up on what was going on in one another's lives. All four were determined not to let their friendships diminish due to lack of time or too much busyness in their packed schedules.

Eleanor, being the eldest and mentor of the group, would remind her dear friends that it takes time and focus to nurture relationships, and theirs was a unique group who watched over one another like hawks. They encouraged one another and, when necessary, held one another accountable by pointing out potential wrongs, directions, or decisions that one or the other might be tempted to pursue. And each had found out, through their individual experiences as well as the inevitable crossroads they had faced in the past, how valuable their network of friends had become. Yes, over the years, each had faced challenges of seemingly monumental size. And as Eleanor would also remind them, those challenges were not just random events of their past; they were an ongoing part of life. That's why God had enabled each of them to form a solid bond with the others as well as share the unshakable power of agreement in prayer. Never had those tools been more in demand than of late, and they all knew that not a one of them would be able to prevail without God's love, Word, truth, faithfulness, and covering.

Eleanor's face had almost recovered from her torrents of tears as she spoke to her sisters in Christ that day about what was for her the most daunting challenge she'd met in her years on this earth. If these ladies had been in the middle of Grand Central Station, nothing would have distracted their focus on Eleanor as she finished telling them about her ensuing surgery, fears about her cancer, and how much she needed their prayers and support. "Ham's hangin' in there as my shield, as usual, but I better be gettin' some of my concerns fleshed out with you girls too." She put her head down again, pushing back the tears she was so determined not to shed, "Because I feel so out of control, and I don't want to scare him." All four women had their hands gathered, one on top of the other in the middle of the table while Eleanor spoke. She stumbled over her emotions for awhile, then finally fell silent. Without hesitation Pam cleared her throat and began to pray, "Father God, I ask you to come right now and cover Eleanor with your mightiest angels. Bring her peace and a sense of well-being that can only come from you as she faces these difficult times. I ask you, Father God, to cover every person involved with her care from the surgeons, to the lab technicians, to the nurses, to the hospital bed. Let it be inviting as opposed to frightening. Let these times of doubt bring her even closer to you! And I confess, that my problems are suddenly dwarfed next to the situation Eleanor now faces."

All the women nodded and muttered, "Amen, Praise God," and "Thank you, Jesus," as Pam continued.

"I ask you, Father God, to cover Ham during this time. He has always been a source of strength for Eleanor. Let him not falter because he's such a mighty man of God and he loves his wife so much. Still, we know, Lord, that you are our pillar of strength; and we are like deer, panting for the living water that only you can provide."

Again the women moaned and called out their amens and praises.

"And so, Father God, I thank you in advance for Eleanor's healing and wholeness. She is your daughter, your child whom you handcrafted. You knit her together in her mother's womb, you know every hair on her head, you have amazing plans for her life, and your heart beats wildly for her. And we love her, too! God, only you know our hearts while we surround her in her circle of friends. We recognize that each of us will continue to have seasons in our lives that deposit us in what seems to be dark, lonely places. But Father, that is the only place that the seeds you have planted in us will grow! From the darkness comes the light, and we all stand in agreement that this fall season for Eleanor will survive the harshness of winter to spring forth with new growth and fresh fruit as well as the full bloom of a summer's day!"

Then it was Tonya's turn to pray. She assumed the voice of authority Eleanor, Pam, and Stephanie had come to expect from this young prayer warrior. "I rebuke you Satan in the name of Jesus! You can go back to the pit of hell from whence you came! Lord Almighty, you are in control. You already know the end before the beginning! You have defeated death, sin, and illness, and we claim, by Jesus' stripes on the cross, and from his blood that Ms. Eleanor is healed! Satan, you have nothing to do, say, or be about in this woman's life or the lives of those she loves!

I demand, in Jesus' name, that your demons of fear, anticipation, illness, loneliness, or any of the plagues of the heart that you would be wanting to threaten us with while we're here in your domain be bound and sent to a fiery grave. We are all covered in the blood of Jesus through the power of the Holy Spirit and in the name of Jesus we pray!"

"Father God Almighty, Father God Almighty" Stephanie's voice melded into Tonya's as one while Eleanor and Pam continued with confirmations of "Praise the Lord," "Amen," and "In Jesus' name!"

As was her wont, and in her enthusiasm, Stephanie squeezed her sisters' hands in emphasis as she called out, "God Almighty, we lay all of our concerns at the foot of the cross. We know that you are a loving and merciful God who gave his only begotten Son for our sins. And we know that, with our fallen nature, comes illness. But you say in your Word that we do not have to accept disease, so I'm relying on your words and claiming them in Jesus' name! I'm claiming victory and the sweet aroma of contentment, knowing that we are yours and that whatever *you will*, we ask it to be done in Jesus' mighty name! And all God's people said . . ." The foursome agreed out loud, "Amen and Amen."

What had been a place of sanctuary suddenly was invaded by the all-too-familiar breeze that heralded the opening of the diner's front door entrance. Be that as it may, if these women at the table had not finished their prayers, it wouldn't have mattered if a bulldozer had begun to tear down Norros. Still, for some reason, all four ladies instantly felt compelled to look up in anticipation, knowing in their spirit that someone, or two, had just been invited into their circle of friends by divine appointment.

Lauren made her way into the diner, Irene following timidly behind, but before the two could even take a seat at the empty front booth, Stephanie was on her feet, arms held wide open as she moved toward them. And while Stephanie gave Irene and Lauren a warm southern welcome, Pam, Tonya, and Eleanor pulled themselves together, held their hands high in victory, and exchanged abiding looks of love and confidence.

Stephanie gathered Lauren and Irene up like a mother hen, escorting them down the row of empty booths to greet the others; Irene couldn't help but be drawn to Trace's mom of whom Lauren had spoken so highly. Yes, she was a very nice woman. But then her thoughts turned on her like a pit bull, *Almost too nice.* Stephanie's genuine and outgoing welcome seemed, for Irene's city-slicker mentality, almost too good to be true. Still, she was curious—and she had to admit, something new and different was in the air. She could also tell Lauren was sincerely excited by it, so Irene decided to take a breath and give all this southern hospitality a good look-see before she gave it a run for its money.

All six women made themselves relatively comfortable in the back booth; Irene was feeling that her personal space had been invaded as she pondered, *Why on earth am I here talking to . . . who are these women?* But the more she listened to their kind offers of hospitality, interest in both Lauren's and Irene's respective children and extended hands to help them house hunt, the tension in Irene's shoulders began to relax. And then she saw a most unusual vision before her: her sister Lauren in fellowship, surrounded by women who obviously held the same faith as she. There was an instantaneous comfort and ease between these new acquaintances that Irene had never obtained with any of her friends of years. What had eluded Irene her entire life seemed to be like instant pudding to these women, whipped up and as delicious tasting as if someone had spent a lifetime preparing a one-of-a-kind recipe for happiness. Irene didn't like to admit it, but she was somehow drawn to their conversations that sped past superficial exchanges to deep sharing of what she had always considered "nobody else's business." Yes, before Irene knew it, she had been included in this elite group of trusted friends who were aware of one another's private matters such as Eleanor's impending surgery and fears, to concerns about their children, to Pam's sharing the vision for Hope School, to the surprise and shock of laughter from Tonya when she realized that it was Lauren's son, Tucker, who had played with her Bobbie at the circus. And it went on to Stephanie's loss of a husband, love of her son, and concerns of being a good single mom—concerns Tonya, Lauren, and Irene also shared. Irene's attention suddenly turned like a swap meet; daughter and Trace were off "at the mall."

Oh, it was all too bizarre! Simply too strange to believe, Irene thought, but then Lauren winked at her amidst the flurry of conversation. Yes, despite herself, Irene felt happier than she could remember being for quite some time. Lauren whispered in her sister's ear, "Don't you just love God's choreography?"

With most of the details of their lives out on the table, and phone numbers exchanged, Irene and Lauren finally excused themselves since the dinner crowd was beginning to stream in. Stephanie was called back to work while Pam escorted Eleanor home, linking arms and singing praises to the Lord as they went.

⚜

Sam, Margaret, and Lauren silently watched Irene pace the living room like a trapped cat. Her hair stuck out in stems of disorder while she incessantly rung her hands; all were unsure of how to help or what to say other than just to be there for her.

"I don't care if the news reports no confirmation, Dad! The fact of the matter is, I called my apartment building, and I've been informed that my dear 'best friend,' Karen, has already tried to bribe everyone from the elevator man to my ex-house staff to keep her name away from any inquiries or ties to Ford. How ignorant is that?" Irene had to take a breath before she could go on. "Then I find out from the private detective, who found out about Karen in the first place, that Ford actually 'died in Karen's proverbial arms' in her apartment, not ours. And if Karen thinks she's going to sidestep the world press, she's been wrapped too tight at Eden Day Spa!"

Irene's description of her husband's demise hit her parents' funny bones, and despite how hard they tried to maintain their serious demeanor, Sam and Margaret couldn't help but chortle out loud. "What?" Irene screamed, as she stormed over to her mother and father, stomping her feet like a belligerent cow.

"I'm sorry, Irene," Margaret tried to calm her daughter. "I know this is all so shocking, but I never thought I'd hear you say, 'He died in her proverbial arms.'"

Fuming, Irene whirled around and aggressively flipped her hands back into her thrashed hair. "Well, you heard it, and it's true. That's who he is." She had to take a breath before correcting herself. "That's who he *was*. And I can't say that I'm sorry that he went down sailing that ship." She suddenly burst into sobs; everything that had been tearing at her soul had resurfaced like an old wound, consuming her as she crumbled to the floor in dismay.

Lauren was quick to reach out; cradling her sister in her arms, she rocked her back and forth. "Rene, I know this is horrible news, but don't let it take you down even further. You said yourself he never loved you, and I know that you were expecting your final divorce papers this week. My point is, he was out of your life, so don't let him control you now from the grave. You were right, he was not a good man, and he shouldn't be allowed access to more of your heart now that he's gone than he had before he was dead!"

Irene went limp in her sister's arms; then after a beat an almost inaudible high-pitched laughter born of intrinsic despair rose up in her that slowly transformed into an expression of frenzied relief. Irene belted out in jingle form, "Santa Claus has arrived! Oh happy days! Oh happy days!" She pulled herself away from Lauren and stood up like a jack-in-the-box, inspired. "You don't understand, do you! None of you do." She practically slapped her parents in her excitement. "I was supposed to sign the papers by courier. I was never divorced, so it doesn't matter what slimy-little-pre-nup-cheapskate garbage he pulled on me. I won! He's dead, his girly-girl is going to be slammed in the papers, and I'm rich!"

Sam stood up straight like a soldier about to salute. "Irene, are you telling us that you're still in his will?"

Margaret tugged on her husband's arm, recognizing the delicacy of the moment. "Sam, that's not the point."

Irene cut her mother off, "Yes, it is! It is the point! Sweet revenge! See Lauren, revenge is sweet! Sweet, sweet, sweet! Suites in hotels. Sweet life of ease."

Lauren wasn't thrilled with her sister's reaction. "Rene, you're just overwrought right now and understandably shocked. I can't say that I'm not happy you have more security in your life financially, but I wouldn't revel in Ford's death."

"Shut up, Lauren. Let's celebrate! This is all good news! He had his comeuppance, and for the first time I really think that there might be a God watching over me." And with that she crumbled back into tears, completely out of emotional control. Lauren looked at her parents, "I'll get her meds."

⁘

Margaret and Sam had retired to their apartment. Tucker had been read to and put to bed after his marvelous afternoon and evening with his new best friend, and now Irene and Lauren sat at the kitchen table between William and Bingo who were stationed in their favorite spots like statues; no one moved. No one said a word. Everyone heard the clock ticking.

Chelsea was late; it was 7:40 p.m. when the kitchen door finally creaked open. The girl was expecting to be chastised for being tardy, but she didn't expect to see the forum gathered before her. "Sorry, Mom." She tried to make light of her disobedience, "Trace wanted to come in and apologize. He had a flat tire and . . ."

Irene just shook her head, "Don't, Chelsea. The next time you go anywhere with that boy, it will be after I meet him and review him à la your grandfather!"

Chelsea's face soured while Lauren nudged Irene to calm down. Mother and daughter glared at each other until Lauren intervened, "Chelsea, I assume you have not been listening to the news."

Chelsea dropped her backpack on the kitchen table and started to head toward her bedroom. "I don't like the news."

Standing, Lauren shouted, "Chelsea, I have to talk to you."

Chelsea reeled, "I just want to take a bath and go to bed, OK? Sorry I was late. It's not a big deal, and yeah, you can give Trace the third degree if you want to next time, but I don't understand why. Why, when I finally meet somebody awesome, are you all being witches about him?"

Lauren pounced like a cat and grabbed her niece's arm, encouraging her with a dose of force to come back to the kitchen table. "Please, Chelsea, just sit down for a minute, and don't say anything, alright?"

Realizing there was no other choice, Chelsea acquiesced, adopting her most bored look as she expected to be in for some sort of lengthy lecture about dating. What she wasn't expecting was to hear the details of her soon-to-be-ex-stepfather's demise. What Irene and Lauren weren't expecting was her response. It was simple and definitive: "I'm glad." Then she got up and left the room before anyone could resurrect a counterpoint to the aborted conversation.

Stunned, Lauren turned to Irene, "What the heck was that about?"

"I have no idea. They used to be so close, and then it was like going to the North Pole every time I'd walk into the room when they were together." Irene wrapped her arms around herself as if she could stave off her painful memories. "Chelsea started to act as if she were in competition with me. She'd strut about. Oh, that was before her angry part started. I remember one night she came into our bedroom, and she had a bathrobe on. She literally sprawled herself across our bed at the foot of Ford, unconcerned whether the bathrobe opened or not, and flirted with him before my very eyes! He, of course, told me that I was just imagining it all. That she was just being a young girl and that I was just being 'frantic, middle-aged, and menopausal.'"

Lauren considered what her sister was sharing with grave concern, "Maybe it wasn't your hormones, Rene. Maybe it was him. Maybe he was just trying to play you and Chelsea against each other."

Irene threw her head back, "No! It's the children who play their parents against each other! I don't understand her reaction now. I didn't understand it then, and I probably never will understand it. The only thing I do know is that now I'm going to be financially able to put her back into a private school. Away from that boy Trace. Away from any potential trouble." Frustrated, Irene flipped her head again in despair. "She's always been in private school, and maybe she'll be able to straighten out in the few months that I still have some say-so over what she does."

"Rene, it's not all about what school she goes to. Anyway, who knows how long all of the financial entanglements will take with Ford's will."

For the first time Lauren had ever observed, her sister gave her a sly smile, one born of a contemptuous heart. "He was still my husband when he died. I'm going to New York. I'm going to take my rightful place at his funeral as well as in his finances. And if you think that's cold, I don't really care. All I care about is not being humiliated anymore. Believe me, I am absolutely capable of wielding a big stick when it comes to my daughter's welfare, education, and future, as well as my own!"

With Irene's statement of cause and action, Lauren knew that all of them—friends, relatives, and acquaintances alike— were in for the ride of their lives.

Chapter 17

-Twists and Turns-

Sam got up at dawn to take Irene to the airport, complaining all the while that her suitcases were too large and too heavy. He grilled her about how long she was planning to stay away considering her overabundance of luggage.

Before he left, Sam made time to visit Tucker in his bedroom, giving the boy a scratchy beard kiss on the cheek, "I'll be back later, Tuck, so maybe we could throw a little ball between my news and dinner."

Tucker came to life out of a deep sleep, "OK." Sam's face cracked in a smile.

"And I can walk you to the school bus again in the morning, if Mom says so, huh?"

"Sure," Tucker offered, now barely audible as he buried himself in the covers; but then, as fast as the boy disappeared, he clambered out from under his mounds of quilts and marched to the bathroom. "I have to go to the potty, Granddaddy."

Despite Irene's incessant horn honking heard in the background, Sam stayed until Tucker crawled back into bed. How sweet to discover early one morning such a love for someone, especially for your own grandchild.

In times of importance, Margaret invariably came to the rescue. She stood at the front door holding Irene's flight information for Sam; then he, Lauren, and Margaret dashed out. Lauren was determined to offer her sister encouragement while she reviewed Irene's last-minute instructions as to how she was to deal with Chelsea. "Keep her in your crosshairs. You drive her to school. No boys! Everything's on hold until I get back here! Promise?" Lauren promised, wondering whether she'd be able to keep such a tight reign on Chelsea, but there was no time to negotiate. She simply needed to step up to the plate and be there for Irene.

What a difference a day makes, twenty-four little hours, rang through Lauren's head again as she digested the fact that the Patterson family had literally been in Centennial, Tennessee, for a short five days. Lauren felt she had been thrown into some crazy time warp, or at the very least, she'd been cast as the lead in one of her mother's sad-sap soap operas. Still, she did feel a little better after having had a B12 shot of love and support from Susan's phone call late last night and now she was ready and willing to take on the headship of the family. Still, she prayed that it would be for only a short period of time.

Tucker had to get his own cereal when he finally trundled down into the empty kitchen; it seemed everyone in his family was running around that morning like a flea on a wild dog. And it also seemed that he was the only one in the crazy Patterson household who remembered that Bingo and William had not been fed. *I know how to feed them,* the boy told himself, and so he did, with only a little accidental food spillage as he tried to tackle the unwieldy electric can opener.

Tucker only heard fleeting phrases of the intense conversations that had flown around the house last night, exchanges even rougher than the night when everybody threw their chairs down and walked out on dinner. He couldn't remember Ford Williams, his auntie's husband, except for the time at the giant Christmas tree in Rockefeller Center. He did, however, grasp that the man had died and considered that was probably why everyone had gone nuts since he'd gotten home from his friend's house yesterday.

Once Sam and Irene were on their way to the airport, accompanied by Margaret (who never wanted Sam to venture off without her), the kitchen began to settle down. Not immediately, mind you; Lauren unwittingly fed Bingo and William a double portion of breakfast, which they guiltlessly scarfed down when Tucker reentered the kitchen and joined Chelsea at the table, where she robotically chomped on her cereal.

Lauren had promised herself that she was going to be Ms. Cheery this morning, no matter what else happened. "Tuck, if it's OK, I'm going to take Chelsea to school first, then I'll drop you off right after because your school starts a tad later than hers." The kids just continued to eat their cereal, playfully shoving the sugar bowl back and forth like a shuffleboard. Seeing Chelsea engage in anything but a pout surprised Lauren. "And no one's listening to me but me," Lauren said to herself, "so that's what we'll do. OK?"

Lauren decided to let her dog and cat out for a quick stroll when it struck her—Chelsea hadn't said a word, hadn't even objected to not being able to go to school with Trace. Now that behavior really rang a warning bell for Lauren.

"Hey, Chelsea? Did you tell Trace not to pick you up this morning?" As usual Chelsea just gazed out the window; Lauren flat out wanted to smack some sense into her, but she calmed herself. "Well, I'm going to call his mom and let her know he's not to come by, just until your mother gets home. And we can talk about everything this afternoon, OK?" No response. "Look Chelsea, you're not being whipped and beaten with twigs, we just need to be respectful to your mother's wishes and . . ."

Cutting in, "It sucks!" Chelsea took another bite of her cereal.

"That's enough!" Lauren heard herself scream, much to Tucker's dismay. "I will not stand for that kind of language. I'm in charge here, and you're just going to have to listen to me because your mother, no matter how you feel about her, is going through an intense time, and she does not need to be aggravated! She entrusted you to me, and I'm going to do a good job whether you like it or not!" By the time Lauren finished, she realized she was screeching at the top of her voice. Stunned by her outburst, she quickly hugged Tucker. "Sorry, sorry, sorry." Lauren looked at the

kids who at that point were at full attention. "OK, we can do this. We really can, and we can do it and end up loving one another! How does that sound?" Lauren whirled around the kitchen letting the pets in, shutting off the coffee machine, throwing the mugs and empty cereal bowls into the sink, checking that the stove was off, and closing the microwave, all in one fell swoop. By the time her housekeeping efforts were accomplished, Tucker and Chelsea surprisingly were all set to go out the back door.

"Thanks guys so much for not making this hard," Lauren cooed. "I promise I'll make it up to you, OK? Let's just get in the truck, and hey, Chelsea, do you want to drive?" Just as the teenager was about to nod, Lauren thought better of her offer, "Oh, no. No, wait. OK, let me drive Tucker to school and then . . . Oh no, you go first. Dang. Alright, you can drive. Now, here's what's going to happen. I'm going to drive Tucker first because I know that the teacher gets there early. Then you can drive because you're so amazing and sporty, and we'll go on to your high school, and we can have a little chat time, OK? OK. Let's go!" No one had agreed to any of Lauren's plans; nonetheless, the three exited. Just before Lauren vanished through the door, she did a mental check, "Wait! OK, Chelsea, you go down and start the truck. Put Tucker in the backseat, and make sure his seat belt's on. Don't forget to keep the truck in park, and don't forget the brake! I'll be right down, and it'll be your turn to drive right after that. I just have to make a quick call."

Lauren zoomed back into the kitchen; grabbing the phone, she dialed Stephanie's number. It rang once, then twice; she was fidgeting like a child having to hit the bathroom when Stephanie finally answered, "Hey! It's me, Lauren. I hope you're up. Of course you're up. I just wanted to call and tell you that we've had some pretty shattering events happen in the family since we saw you yesterday. And my sister, Irene, had to fly immediately to New York. I'll fill you in later, but her parting words were that I was to—at least till she gets home in just a few days, take Chelsea to school. . . . No, no! It's nothing. I'm sure it's just that she feels like everything's a runaway train. Her husband just died. . . . Oh, I know. I'll explain, but she just wants me to keep a close eye on Chelsea, OK? Just tell Trace so he doesn't come by and wait for her. . . . Oh, tonight! Of course, Wednesday service, right. Well, I have Chelsea and . . . Oh, well sure. That might be just super. Tonya's bringing Bobbie? OK. . . . Well, I don't know if Chelsea would want to come. That would be the open question here. You know I'd love to. I just need her to come along. I can't leave her alone, just at this juncture. Without her mom. Will Trace be there? . . . Ah, ha! OK, maybe that's how I get Chelsea to attend. Alright! I'll be there with bells on. . . . Right, five sharp. OK, Stephanie, and thanks again for yesterday. It was amazing. God bless."

Lauren dashed out of the house; like a jackrabbit she jumped up into the driver's seat giving a reassuring grin to both kids. "OK, zoom, zoom, zoom, we're out of here! Tuck, you be the navigator. Tell me if you can remember which way we go. Right or left? Can't do this without you, buddy." And with that, they were off in a cloud of smoke.

Chelsea straddled the stick shift as she moved into the driver's seat while Lauren let Tucker out of the truck, giving him a hand as he maneuvered the steep step of the raised 4x4. Lauren nodded to a group of moms gathered around the school. Taking in the their style of dress, she noted that hers was quite different, deciding that she looked more like a farmhand than one of them. Shaking it off, she decided that she didn't have time this morning to worry about fitting into the crowd. She gave Tuck a big hug, went over and shook hands with Tucker's teacher whom she'd met on his first day, and as soon as she confirmed that her son looked secure and safe, she was off like a shot back to the truck.

Frankly, it had crossed her mind that Chelsea might have driven off and left her behind, but thankfully, the teenager was there at the wheel, her attention now focused on the stick shift and clutch combo that was to be her next challenge in life. And as they were about to drive off, Chelsea looked absolutely petrified that she might take off in a "goofy stutter start." Lauren thought it was cute that she cared about not making a fool of herself in front of Tucker, or at least Lauren hoped those were her concerns. And she just loved that the girl was starting to show some interest in Tucker at breakfast. "Ah, a chink in the teenager's armor." Lauren smiled.

As the truck lurched into the traffic, Lauren tried to remain calm, controlling her flailing hand that had responded to an all too close altercation with a fire hydrant. "Whoa, hot shot!" she warned Chelsea. By then, both Lauren's hands were smashed against the dashboard as the truck barely missed sideswiping an oncoming car. It was then that Lauren recognized she'd simply lost her mind to have let Chelsea drive in traffic. "OK now," Lauren was literally sweating all the while patting her niece on the shoulder. "Just slow down. A stick shift is really hard to get a handle on, but you're doing just great!"

Chelsea's nose was practically pressed against the windshield, "Thanks." Her eyes widened as she set her attention on the road ahead. Then, Lauren patted Chelsea's knee ever so slightly, warning her in a soothing voice, "We're coming up to a stop light, so you need to slow down way before you get there. Then take an easy glance left. Then right. Then in front of you." Chelsea settled, listening to Lauren's every directive.

When the light turned green, Chelsea didn't lurch ahead. Impressed, Lauren continued to coach her. "Good, you've got to get a sense of what your arena is. Do you remember when you were a kid and I took you for some pony rides? I told you that if you looked down that's where you'll end up." Chelsea nodded, her knuckles white from her grip on the steering wheel. "This is bigger business than a pony ride, so pay attention, OK?"

By that time Chelsea had actually accomplished a pretty normal stop at another red light, and without looking too obvious, she took a deep breath of relief as Lauren continued to rattle on as they waited for the light to turn green. "So, I'm just going to be bold here and tell you that, no matter how I've let you down, I'd like to start fresh. OK? I want to be here for you. I want you to be able to talk to me, and I'm not the local reporter. Everything is not going to go zooming through the family, alright?"

For the first time Chelsea thought about what Lauren was saying. Finally, the girl responded, "I guess you didn't tell Mom about the fender or anything. And you seem to understand more about Trace—how I feel about him anyway—more than Mom does. It's just . . ." Then she suddenly stopped.

After a beat of silence, Lauren encouraged, "Ok, well let's just start at the beginning." But as the light changed, Chelsea gunned forward; her emotions escalated, as did her conversation along with the speed of the truck. "I don't want to start anywhere. I don't want to go anywhere. I am where I am, and I want you to leave me alone!"

Lauren allowed several blocks to pass in silence. As the tension diminished, so did the speed of their vehicle. Chelsea couldn't help but notice the space her aunt was giving her. But still, she wasn't about to open up.

The high school was just ahead; and when Chelsea looked out the window, and instead of being embarrassed about being escorted to school by her aunt, she adopted an attitude of triumph as Trace passed slowly by them on the inside lane. That's when he came close enough for her to see his look of respect for her driving her aunt's big ole Ford truck. And as Chelsea pulled over to the curb, she managed to conclude her driving excursion with a modicum of grace as she jumped out of the truck, grabbed her backpack, and waved to Trace. There was, however, an ensuing problem; the truck kept moving down the street with no driver onboard. Lauren panicked for a minute, realizing that Chelsea had left the vehicle in neutral, and although the girl had turned the ignition off, the truck was a runaway about to crash into a line of cars. Lauren barely managed to get her leg across the gearshift and depress the brake pedal with her left big toe, just in time to avert a calamity that surely would have humiliated Chelsea's entire senior year.

⚜

Lauren had procrastinated long enough; she drove into the relatively small parking lot of Dr. Burke's veterinary clinic, thinking, *Yes, Tucker, you're right, I'm nervous. No, Tucker, you're wrong; I don't need you to go with me. Yes, Tucker, you're right, I wish you were with me. No, Tucker, you're wrong; I'm not going to fold. Oh my, how crazy are you, Lauren?* She parked the truck, then bowed her head in prayer asking God to give her strength, vision, wisdom, discernment, and boldness as she walked into what she perceived to be the next chapter of her life.

As was the case with her new house, she had taken on employment at this veterinary clinic by way of the Internet and photos. She was sorry to admit that it wasn't actually a "partnership," just an additional veterinarian's position to appear during off hours until she proved herself and could move into a higher position in the establishment.

Lauren hated to be tested, but she loved a challenge. She loved competition. She loved getting *A*s in school; she excelled because she was a good study. But at the age of fifty, that game was getting old. She reminded herself that she had figured out, since she'd come to her faith, that her esteem wasn't connected to her report card, or her paycheck, or her husband (or lack thereof).

Lauren sat a long while in her truck, taking in the ambience of the veterinary clinic that was to be her next place of employment, and yes, she thought a few things through.

It was only 7:45 in the morning, and Lauren felt like she had already finished a full day's work. She remembered Irene, still airborne on her way to New York; and she wondered how her sister would fare in facing the intense scrutiny of what was sure to be the ultimate media feeding frenzy, the funeral of her husband.

Lauren felt that Irene hadn't even been graced with two seconds to repair her openly wounded heart from past events before this next onslaught of emotions emerged. And yet she was secure in the fact that Irene had a gift of tenacity and never-say-die resourcefulness surrounded by an elegant, sensitive, and artfully imaginative heart and soul. This had been true of Irene ever since she was a child—an elusive butterfly trapped more than twice, the fairy dust shaken off her wings to the point that it seemed she might never fly again. Yet there she was, flying back to Sodom and Gomorrah, as it were, to claim her rightful inheritance of "pay for time"; sadly, that's the only way Lauren could look at it.

She shook her head, knowing that she and her sister had always taken two different roads. Lauren wasn't proud of the fact that, in her case, she'd chosen men who could tickle her fancy but had work ethics as slim as their wallets. And it was then that Lauren had to concede and agree with herself that she chose the men she chose because she needed somehow to be in control. That way, when they left, she might be husbandless, but she still had her ability to make a living.

Lauren felt herself squirm for a moment, repositioning her shoulder pads under her nipped-at-the-waist khaki shirt with tails that fell softly over her jeans, which fit neatly over her paddock boots. There were things about this horse lady that Lauren simply refused to give up. Her gait, even at fifty, carried her with the stride of a teenager; yes, she was an athlete. But despite all that, she realized, as she looked at the red front door of the gray brick veterinarian hospital building that loomed before her, she actually had to get out of the truck and go in, introduce herself, check the entire office out, and let them check her out. She reminded herself that there absolutely needed to be a meeting of minds, hearts, medicine, application, caring, and passion that had to jell to be connected to this practitioner. *OK, Lauren, get going!* she told herself as she sat frozen in her seat. *What the heck's up with you?* She internally chastised herself. *Why do you feel like a kid going in to get your first job slinging burgers? You're an adult, and you're the best darn vet you've ever known. Oh God, please! If it's right or wrong, tell me which way to turn.* And suddenly, she seemed energized, noting that this first step into her new career in Tennessee was the least of her mountains to climb. She also knew she'd better get over herself quickly because all of the tough, life stuff was not about her. There definitely was a bigger purpose for her life; she just wished it would reveal itself *soon!*

As she stepped into Dr. Burke's waiting room, her gut told her it was a factory, not a house of healing. Prices were slammed on the wall, "Payment required before seeing any animal." Her suspicions became frighteningly clear when Lauren noticed a four-year-old girl in the corner cradling a limp kitten in her hands. Her mother, nursing a newborn, begged the attendant at the desk to care for her daughter's cat; they couldn't wait anymore. The receptionist, about eighteen, was more concerned with chewing her bubble gum than the needs of the little girl's kitten.

Lauren scanned the waiting room, which was packed full with an array of animals: big dogs, little dogs, cats, kittens, caged birds, tangled leashes, and people on edge. But Lauren quickly focused back on the little girl in the corner with the kitten, literally dying in her hands.

No, it wasn't prudent; it wasn't right, but Lauren rushed to the child, picking up the kitten, literally blowing into the little feline's mouth to resuscitate the animal. Instantly, there was a flurry at the front desk, "Excuse me, ma'am, can I help you?" the teenager thundered, gum stuck to her teeth. Holding the kitten up in her hands, Lauren quietly stroked her little teeny rib cage to try to bring life back while she roared back, "Where is the doctor!" The girl reeled in her chair taken by Lauren's rude authority; her gum fell out of her mouth.

"I'm Lauren Patterson, the new veterinarian here, and I need to get into a room immediately! This kitten is dying, and we're not waiting any longer!" Everyone in the place took pause; even the animals who were straining at their leashes stepped back. Lauren blasted through the clinic's swinging doors, searching desperately for some aid for this kitten, which she had immediately assessed was suffering from a severe upper respiratory infection and was within moments of death. "Feline bordetella?" She pondered. The little girl and her mother, with baby now asleep in her arms, stood respectfully in the doorway as Lauren took over, scanning the room for amoxicillin and a ventilator. Then she started screaming, "I need help in here!" Finally Dr. Burke came storming into the room; this large man with red hair and a red face squared off with Lauren. "Who do you think you are?"

"Dr. Burke, I'm Dr. Lauren Patterson, I've come . . . I'm one of your colleagues, and this kitten is in critical shape. I apologize for stepping in, but there is no waiting time for this little one. So please, let's care for this animal, and then we'll say our hellos." And with that, she once again attempted to care for the kitten while sending a reassuring smile to the little girl who was now in hysterics. "Doctor, where's your amoxicillin?"

Instead of answering, Burke pushed Lauren back, grabbed the lifeless kitten from her hands, and passed it on to a now-present assistant without a glance. "Back room, number six." He barked his order of dismissal and was free to address Lauren. "Don't you *dare* ever get into the middle of my practice or scheduling. This is not a triage clinic!" He slammed the door to the examining room on the mother and daughter before continuing. "This clinic is about taking care of clients and making money!"

"Please Dr. Burke, the kitten needs an IV and oxygen. It obviously has a URI, possibly bordetella! We're going to lose her if we don't do something right now!"

But it was Dr. Burke who lost it. "Have you gotten paperwork on this cat?"

Lauren's eyes narrowed. "You mean the little kitten that the little girl was holding? What do you mean, *paperwork?* She needs assistance now!" Dr. Burke adamantly pointed toward the door. "Leave my office immediately or I'll call the police!"

Lauren could hear the little girl crying through the door, begging Lauren to bring back her kitten. Lauren knew her hands were tied as she glared at the doctor, her voice low and venomous. "You are despicable. And you can be sure, I'll be back to shut you down!"

Lauren stormed through the waiting room, and it was upon her exit that she spied the lethal drop chute—the animal drop off for unwanted lives that she had read about and had discussed with Eleanor. She stood there, frozen with outrage as she listened to the cries of animals not only from the kennels but also from the woeful howling, not uncommon when dogs are in treatment. But then there was a different sound, a different wailing. Lauren had only heard it in the most offensive pounds that she had ever visited, those places that shouldn't even be called humane shelters because they weren't even slightly humane. And this place, Dr. Burke's Veterinary Clinic, was a nightmare of the worst kind. Then like a tidal wave, it hit her; she had come all this way, leaving Francis and Oscar and all her wonderful pet/clients from her clinic in California for nothing! She reeled, "God, why am I here?" And then a second wave washed over her; as far as her work as a veterinarian went, she was out of a job.

Lauren slammed her truck door as she collapsed inside and started to sob uncontrollably. And then she saw herself, out of control just like Irene had been, and she rose up in righteous indignation. Maybe she couldn't do anything about that disgusting death trap of a place right now, but she was determined to stop Dr. Burke from practicing veterinarian medicine. Then and there she decided that this was one of the reasons she had come to this town. Her purpose had just expanded beyond her family—she was a woman on a double mission.

Lauren pulled a pad of paper and pen out of her glove compartment and started furiously writing a letter to the editor. She wasn't going to wait; she was going straight to the local newspaper, and, even if they didn't want her thoughts on the animal holocaust she'd just witnessed, she would make herself heard one way or another. As she wrote, she prayed to God to give her just exactly the right words to say as she scrawled her thoughts down, which now came flooding out of her as if she had agonized over every syllable for days:

CITY-SANCTIONED CHILD ABUSE IN CENTENNIAL?

What if you're a small child, and someone
grabs you up by the arm, throws you into the car,
drives across town, and takes you to a smelly building. Then they drop you down a dark chute into
a cage full of people of all ages and types. Some
are killers; some are foreigners that speak strange

languages; many are diseased and undernourished. There is fierce fighting throughout the dark night, and you are alone to fend for yourself.

Sound like some dark fantasy from the age of Communist Russia? Well, if you're an unwanted animal in Centennial, this could be your fate! It must be a dark secret in such a southern jewel of a town; the local animal dump at Dr. Burke's office, where unwanted critters of all kinds can be conveniently disposed of down a drop chute with no more effort than returning a late movie rental in the middle of the night to avoid extra charges.

The real irony in this story is that the address of Dr. Burke's nightmare is not on Elm Street but rather on Church Street! Stop by any day of the week, and watch your tax dollars at work.

One must wonder who is worse among the offenders in this all-too-real scenario. Is it the heartless citizens who, in a selfish attempt to rid themselves of unwanted animals, simply drop them off like their garbage and drive away? Or, is it an elected city government, so caught up in backroom deals and good-ole-boy politics that they have no time to consider the well-being of these defenseless creatures?

As a citizen of Centennial and a licensed veterinarian, I hold them both accountable for these atrocities. How about you?

⊰❧⊱

Lauren stood behind the metal desk of Brandon Chase, senior editor of the *Centennial News*. He looked to be somewhere in his fifties and attractive in a conservative "Brooks Brothers" way. Lauren couldn't help but notice that he wasn't wearing a wedding ring. *Oh, don't go there, Lauren,* she thought.

After having demanded to see the man in charge, she was admitted into his presence by a rather unpleasant, pointed-face, annoying secretary named Mary Ann. Lauren wondered, as Mr. Brandon Chase was reading her editorial, why everyone seemed so pleasant when she first came to this town; and now it seemed that every time she came across the locals, she found them to be cold and snooty. Thankfully, this gentleman before her certainly didn't have that tenor. (She was to find out later that Brandon was from the east coast and had just taken his position in the newspaper to liven up the local news.) When he finally looked up at Lauren after reading her written words, he clearly was engaged by her story as well as by Lauren herself.

"You write well," he commented.

Brandon's voice brought Lauren's attention back to the issue at hand, "That's not really the point, but if it qualifies me for your editorial space, then I'm glad."

He smiled, "Well, this is a bit of a sticky wicket. People around here, as I've come to learn, treat animals differently from, say, the way I would, coming from Connecticut."

Lauren countered, "I don't care where they're from or what they purport to be 'loving care,' this is an atrocity in anyone's language or locale. Perhaps if you're as aware of correct humane animal care as you say, then you'll be so kind as to include this editorial in your paper. But if you decide not to, please feel free to write one yourself. I don't care. I just can't believe in my wildest dreams that the general public is aware of these animal chutes!"

"If you don't mind," Mr. Chase suggested, "let me give you a little advice since I've lived here over a year now. Everybody moves at a slower pace, and it took me some time to settle down and be patient and . . ."

Lauren cut in, "I appreciate that, and I'm sorry for my intense meter right now, but I'm not going to slow down for an instant when animals are being tortured. So, if you can't help with this, then I'll go to the Nashville news. Plus, I will get on the local TV news if it kills me. I just need to figure out the lay of the land and who's who in the zoo around here politically, and then I'll be coming out swinging."

No doubt, Brandon was impressed with this woman. "Ms. Patterson, I'm going to put your editorial in Sunday's paper. As I said, it was well written; and frankly, although I'm not allowed to take sides as chief editor, I couldn't agree with you more. So please, if you would let me know if I could be of any other assistance to you, I'd be happy to do so."

Lauren paused for a beat, "What can I say? Thank you? Thank you so much, and I'll probably take you up on that assistance thing soon. I'm sure this is just the beginning of what will probably be a lengthy fight."

He nodded, throwing his Eastern upbringing hand out for a shake. "That would be a pleasure, ma'am," he smiled. "I got the 'ma'am' part from the local jargon."

"It sounded nice, coming from you." She felt herself blush. "Sunday, you say? Sunday's editorial?"

"You can count on it," he replied.

She returned his smile. "I'll do that."

Chapter 18

-Lifted Up-

As Lauren made her way through the kitchen that Wednesday afternoon, she was affectionately mauled by William and Bingo. Pausing for a moment, she recognized how much joy these animals brought to her life. With that, her disgust for Dr. Burke welled up in her again, but she calmed herself, finding comfort in having at least written the editorial to put her two cents' worth on the record. Lauren wasn't exactly sure whether her comments would lead to her being ostracized from the community or if she would be embraced by those who really cared about their pets. Regardless, she was not going to back off her beliefs.

The message light on her answering machine was blinking; Lauren leaned on the counter and pressed "play." Irene's voice sounded excited, "Just touching base, sweetie. I arrived in the Big Apple, and I have to admit, it's exhilarating to be here, even under these circumstances. Thanks for covering Chelsea for me. I cannot tell you how much I love and appreciate you for being such a good sister. I already have calls into the lawyer. I've adopted my "Joan Crawford" plan of attack. She's always been my hero. Oh, the way she took on the Coca-Cola Company moguls. I'm stunned at how challenged I feel. Maybe I was born for high finance and boardroom drama. Remember how I used to help you when you were a headhunter? Well, sweetie, I've got to run. I'll check in with you later. Kisses to everyone and, well, pray for me. I can't believe I just said that! By the way, you won't be able to reach me on my cell for a time. I've burned the battery low, so I'll call you when I get to the hotel." Lauren immediately went to report to her parents.

Sam and Margaret were gathering for their daily five o'clock news when Lauren popped her head in. "Hey guys, I heard from Irene and she made it to New York just fine. In fact, she sounds pumped. So, I'm going to take off and get Tucker and Chelsea. I just wanted to know if, by any chance, you might want to join us? I'm going to take the kids out to an early dinner, and then we're going to go over to Stephanie's church for Wednesday evening worship and youth group for the kids."

Her parents looked at her like she was speaking Greek. "Chelsea's going with you to church?" Margaret asked.

Lauren giggled, "I have a method to my madness. Stephanie said that Trace was going to be there, so I'm sure she'll be thrilled. Besides, if I can get her in a better atmosphere, maybe some of the good Word will rub off on her."

"Here, here," Sam said, feigning enthusiasm. "Well, we're just about to watch the news, so we'll be here when you get back."

"Maybe some other time," Margaret lied.

⚜

The church was brick, as most buildings were in Tennessee, but it did have some lovely carvings and stained-glass windows that adorned this midsize house of worship on the edge of town just off Main. Lauren aced a parking space in front labeled "Visitors," while Trace, accompanied by his mom, drove around the side to park.

Lauren, Chelsea, and Tucker were first to gather at the front steps to wait for Stephanie and Trace. Tucker was jazzed once he saw a whole bunch of kids his age arriving, one of whom was his buddy Keith. "So Mom, I get to go into class with the kids, right?"

Lauren ruffled his hair slightly, "Sure, if that's what you'd like to do. We'll take you over there, and then I'll pick you up right after the service." Lauren glanced around while they waited, taking note of the people arriving; they were of all ages and back-grounds—black, white, Hispanic. This place felt good to her, but then again, she already knew it would, having experienced the spirits of Stephanie, Eleanor, Pam, and Tonya.

Tucker squealed in delight when he saw Bobbie, his friend from the circus, tagging along behind Tonya, while Stephanie and Trace arrived from the opposite direction. Everyone exchanged hugs and greetings; Trace and Chelsea said hi under their breath, feeling awkward in front of the group. Still it was clear they were happy to see each other. Tonya took the young boys to class, Trace and Chelsea went to Bible study with Pam, and Stephanie and Lauren went to the service where they were to meet Eleanor and Ham.

❦

Once inside the church the music was simply exhilarating. Lauren had the pleasure of hearing Eleanor sing the classic hymn "Great Is Thy Faithfulness" with such conviction that it sent goose bumps up and down Lauren's entire body. Eleanor's backup was the church choir, and the music flowed from a full band— drums, horns, guitars, you name it. All Lauren could think was, *This place rocks!* Everybody was handclapping and swaying with the music when Ham waved over Stephanie and Lauren to join him on the front row. Barely able to hear over the music, Ham was introduced to Lauren, giving her a big welcoming hug.

The church was nondenominational and the percentages of whites and blacks attending were about equal. Lauren wondered who the pastor of this wonderful place of worship might be, and she looked forward with great anticipation to hear the Word of

God in such an anointed place. After five praise and worship songs, Lauren was caught a bit off guard when the gentleman sitting to her right on the front row stood up and took the pulpit. She was surprised because he was blond and young, not at all who she expected to be pastoring. She was also extremely curious as to how he had come to lead such an amazing congregation at such a young age. But as soon as he started to speak, her questions were answered. *What a powerhouse!* But just before he began, Ham leaned over to Lauren and whispered, "The difference in the people that come here to worship is that, usually after a great sermon, people leave a church saying, 'Wow, that *pastor* was amazing or anointed or powerful.' But when we leave this church after our pastor is used by God, we say, 'Wow, *God* was so powerful and amazing.'"

Pastor Mark took the podium, clearing his voice while sending an electric smile to one and all. If nothing else happened beyond the music and the warmth that Lauren had already received by the congregation and Ham, it would've been enough. But she was about to receive a real treat when Pastor Mark started to preach the Word of God. And, as with most people who stand before the Lord eagerly awaiting his personal and intimate message for their lives, Lauren felt that what the pastor touched on in his sermon that day was meant just for her. She thought, *Oh what a God we serve!*

Pastor Mark began:

> We're here today to lift up our diversities and
> embrace our common denominators, to engage
> and encourage one another, to edify and not envy, to

abolish the lines of denominations that separate our purpose in Christ. We are here to establish friends and fellowship through the power of the Holy Spirit and prayer in Jesus' name. We are here to stand in agreement with one another, knowing that God wants us to take the high road when most people choose the middle road and others decide on the low road. But God's people are called to excellence in all things including how we treat one another in Christ.

We thank God for his grace, which he shows us every day with his unmerited favor. And so we have purpose. We know, as children of God, that if we face persecution for his sake, it is simply positioning us for God's will in our lives. And we know that we are not forsaken when we are persecuted. Quite the contrary, God prepares us for those difficult times so he can propel us forward; and the preparation time, as with the making of a good meal, can seem almost endless. But while we savor the fruits of our effort, it turns our toil into a glorious banquet. When our God says to us in Matthew 11:28: "Come to me, all of you who are weary and burdened and I will give you rest." But he also tells us in his Word that the Great Commission is not a request; it's a command.

So I say to you today, we can't give what we don't have. God speaks to us about resting in him, through his power, being healed of past recriminations through forgiveness, so we, in fact, become billboards for the truth.

By how we are, not by what we say, we compel others to want what we have—eternal life in Christ, based on a solid foundation spiritually, knowing that when a moral code is broken, so are our hearts. John 15:5 says, "I am the vine, you are the branches. If a man remains in me and I in him, he will bear much fruit. Apart from me, you can do nothing."

So this evening I'm going to talk about allowing God more of ourselves, knowing that we are his and he does love us unconditionally. In preparing this sermon I felt in my spirit that many of you are going through what is referred to as "valleys" or difficult times. And I'm here to encourage you—to let you know that God will never forsake you. He's telling us every day that we need the refilling of the Holy Spirit, that we need to abide in him, seek his favor, and his answers. We need to be calling things into being that cannot be seen but are based on faith, and that calling forth will bring our miracle. There is a new way of praying in the church today to call for the blessings, the needs, the requests through agreement, and at the same time, reject those strongholds of generational sin and repeated areas of disappointment in Jesus' name.

So I ask you first, do we have to learn to lie as human beings? No, that comes naturally to our sin nature. We have to learn to tell the truth—we have to learn to confess and we have to learn to rely on our Almighty God through the blood of Jesus.

Lauren was absolutely transfixed, and as the sermon went on, her entire demeanor relaxed; she glowed with an expression of peace, and her eyes were transformed into pools of love. Oh, she was so happy to be once again in fellowship and worship! Then her mind wandered for a moment toward the end of Pastor Mark's teaching to her personal praise and thanksgiving to God for his covering and his love. And as the sermon concluded some twenty minutes later, Lauren was renewed and refreshed by the Spirit, ready to take on whatever the world would put before her.

Ham's eyes were gleaming as he held Eleanor's hand, who glowed with God's assurances. And then Ham turned to everyone in the circle—Stephanie, Lauren, Eleanor—and addressed Lauren. "We're so glad you're here, and we welcome you from the bottom of our hearts." Lauren almost started to cry as Ham continued, "I asked Eleanor this morning why she thought that in Revelation 4:8 it says, 'All those in heaven who surrounded God keep repeating "Holy, Holy, Holy"' as they circle around him in praise and worship."

Eleanor laughed, "Yes, Ham loves to see if I'm paying attention when I'm readin' the Word." She looked adoringly at her husband. "All in heaven say 'Holy, Holy, Holy' as they circle God because, at every turn, there's more and more magnificence!" With that thought, they all joined hands in prayer, a profound and deep lament for the children in the youth group, the young ones in the classroom, those in the congregation, and those in the circle of friends. Ham followed with a special prayer for the kids starting the school season, and for Eleanor, his love, for the medical challenges she faced. And as he ended his prayer, he said, "Father God, you say in Philippians 4:11, 'I am not say-ing this because I am in need, for I have learned to be content whatever the circumstances.'" Then he looked up and smiled at everyone, "Don't you just love that the Bible is so simple because God knows that life is not?" He put his arm around Eleanor, pulling her close. "One thing we learned a long time ago is that the only sure way to be victorious over any fight is not to get in the ring."

Lauren was a little puzzled with his statement, which didn't surprise Ham. "God's already won every battle. He knows every-thing that has happened and will happen. So we don't have to fight. He puts on the gloves for us, and he will smite our ene-mies." Lauren found great security in his words of wisdom.

Chapter 19

-The Let Down-

Sam's hands were literally shaking as he read the morning newspaper in his favorite chair; the sun was just rising when he glanced out of the window. "Margaret!"

"I'll be right there. I'm just finishing the bed." Sam stood, his eyes riveted on the folded front page.

"Margaret, get out here, now!" He walked over to the kitchen table and slammed the paper down.

Margaret stepped into the room wearing a fuzzy bathrobe and slippers, annoyed at Sam's insistence and tone. "Why are you in such a hurry this morning? I'll have your eggs ready shortly."

He just pointed at the paper on the table, and when she saw what was before her, she could only gasp. The headlines read:

The Search for Ford William's Widow Ends Here in Centennial

Underneath the headline was a New York City school picture of Chelsea and next to it a photo of Irene in her BMW scrunched down in the driver's seat, obviously yelling at Lauren who was standing outside the car smashing something into the sidewalk.

Sam was seething, "They look like crazy people! What on earth are they doing?"

Margaret was dumbfounded, "I have no idea. Oh, this is awful! Oh my gosh, this is not good." The caption under the picture read, "Irene Williams and her sister, Lauren Patterson, across from Franklin Café on the first day of school."

⚜

Also garbed in her bathrobe, Lauren read the article out loud to her parents who were now standing in her bedroom, still in shock. Lauren's eyes widened with every sentence. Her face flushed in anger.

Irene Williams, 52 years old, and the widow of the recently deceased shipping magnate, Ford Williams, moved to Centennial last weekend. It is reported that she is looking to buy a home locally, but in the meanwhile, Mrs. Williams is living with her sister, Lauren Patterson, her son, Tucker, and their parents, Sam and Margaret Patterson. Tucker is attending first grade at the public elementary school in Centennial while Mrs. Williams's daughter, Chelsea, is part of the senior class at

> Greystone High School. Irene Patterson married
> Ford Williams in New York City in 1984, and they
> resided on 5th Ave. with their daughter Chelsea,
> born in 1979. Mrs. Williams and Chelsea now
> reside at 1815 Linden St. in Centennial.

Lauren screamed at the top of her lungs, then threw the paper down on the floor. Sam and Margaret stepped forward, trying to calm their daughter as she rattled on: "I don't believe it. I don't believe it! Did you hear that? They gave out our address! They talked about Tucker! They said that Chelsea was Ford and Irene's daughter! That's terrible; they might as well have just said she was the illegitimate daughter of . . . How could they get their facts wrong like that? How could they do this? How could they put us on the front page of the paper? Did you see that picture?"

Margaret and Sam just shook their heads, "Yes, Lauren, that's what we're wondering about. What on earth were you two doing?"

"OK, OK, I know I have to explain this. That looks so awful! Irene had a cigarette, and we were making sure Chelsea got in Trace's car OK, so we were going to follow her home the first day of school." Lauren was stuttering, "You . . . you . . . you . . . know how Irene is. She was just concerned, and then she flipped the cigarette out of the window. Who would have taken such a picture? How could anybody do that?"

Then came a light bang on Lauren's bedroom door; it was Tucker. "Somebody screamed." Then Chelsea arrived on Tucker's heels. "What's going on? Did somebody scream?" Then William crammed through the door, almost knocking Tucker down, wildly looking around the room as if he were going to protect somebody, when in fact, he was more frightened than any of the people. Behind the dog sashayed Kitty Bingo to check out the ruckus.

Lauren practically did a backflip over the room as she sprawled her body across the newspaper on the floor, trying to hide it from Tucker and Chelsea; she was too late. "What's that?" Chelsea moaned.

"It's nothing!" Lauren spread her robe out like a fan in an effort to cover the telltale evidence.

"Mom, why are you lying on the newspaper?" Tucker moved forward to try to peer underneath his mother's bathrobe where a piece of Chelsea's face appeared upside down from a corner of the tabloid. Tucker looked up innocently, "It's you, Chelsea."

"Let me see that." The girl grabbed for the paper, and instantly a tug-of-war ensued between Lauren and Chelsea, while Sam and Margaret shuffled Tucker out of the room. "Come on, son. Let's go get some breakfast and let the girls talk for a minute, OK?" Sam offered.

"But Granddaddy, Chelsea's picture is in the newspaper."

"I know, they were probably just welcoming her to town." Margaret piped in. "Tucker, let's go feed the animals." Sam whistled for William and Bingo who shot through the room in a race to be the first in line for morning nibbles.

Caught in a standoff, Chelsea held the now pathetically wrinkled newspaper tightly in her hands; as did Lauren, unwilling to give up the fight. But after a long beat, she regrouped, as she looked at Chelsea, "This is all beyond ridiculous." Lauren let go of the paper causing Chelsea to fall backwards over a bedroom chair.

Finally recovering, Chelsea looked down, her eyes scanning the headlines and pictures; the girl was horrified.

◆◆◆

Chelsea sat mute in the backseat of Lauren's truck. For the first time since he had gotten there, Tucker had nothing to say, occasionally glancing at his mom and then at Chelsea.

Lauren checked her niece out in the rearview mirror. "Are you sure you want to go to school? You don't have to, you know. I'm going to call your mom when I get back, and I'm sure she'll agree that you could stay out of school. I just want to gather my thoughts and . . ."

Before Lauren could finish, Chelsea said flatly, "I'm going. I want to see Trace. I want to explain to him that I have this crazy family and that it's not my fault and that I'm not illegitimate!" With that outburst under her belt, she now stared down at her lap. "How could this happen?"

"I wish I could tell you." Lauren ached for her. "Believe me, I'm going to investigate."

Chelsea mumbled, "What were you doing in the car?"

"Well, I'm not going to lie to you, Chelsea. We were just checking to make sure that you got home OK with Trace."

Chelsea rolled her eyes, "I don't believe this. I can't wait till I'm eighteen. I'm going to go so far away, you'll never know I existed."

"Now, come on, Chelsea. It's . . ."

"Yes, it is that bad."

"Well, I'm sorry, and I'm embarrassed, too. I'm going to address this matter as I'm sure your mother will."

"It doesn't matter. It's done."

"It does matter, sweetheart. We'll get this straightened out, promise."

⁂

Lauren circled the kitchen table, the newspaper spread out in the middle. She had already bitten her fingernails to the nub as she challenged herself about how she was going to present this to Irene. Somehow she felt it was all her fault; they were all in this stupid little town because she had suggested it, and now look. Then a bizarre thought crossed her mind: *Well, maybe Irene could use this to get a job as a soap opera author. Oh shut up, Lauren! Just call her and get it over with.*

She took a deep breath, carrying the paper with her to the phone, knowing her sister would want every detail. But before she could dial, the phone rang. "Hello? Yes, this is her aunt. Yes, Mr. Principal, sorry, sorry . . . Mr. Hassock. Of course I can come get her. Is she alright? We had the situation in the . . . Yes, I know. . . . It's understandable that she's upset. I really didn't want her to go to school, but she insisted. Please tell her I'll be right there. . . . Thank you very much."

Lauren took a deep breath and picked up the phone to dial Irene, tearing at her nonexistent nails until her sister finally replied. "Hey, Rene. Hi . . . um, I was, well . . . uh . . . No, I'm not hemming and hawing! I . . . everything's . . . Well, everything isn't OK. The kids are fine. We just had a little issue here with the newspaper. . . . Well, I've got to go get Chelsea at school. . . . No, she's fine, she just . . . Well, Rene, OK! It's got some pictures of us and . . . Alright! I'll read it to you, but you need to come home. Yes, right away!"

Lauren escorted Chelsea out of the high school to her truck, which was parked by the welcome sign. Today it read,

"Hard times are not to break you. . . . They're to make you."—Ham

Lauren digested the sign, again feeling like God was personally sending her a handwritten note.

Precariously balancing two steaming bowls of vegetable soup and two glasses of milk on a tray, Lauren knocked on Chelsea's bedroom door. Eventually, she heard a weak reply, "Come in," from inside. Lauren almost threw the entire lunch tray on the floor as she tried to open the door. "No, you have to come out and open the door, Chelsea. I don't have a free hand."

It was several moments before Chelsea complied, greeting Lauren with, "I'm not hungry."

"Look, Chelsea," Lauren made her way into the room and not so delicately placed the tray down on a trunk at the end of the girl's bed. "You need to eat something, but more importantly, we need to talk. You didn't say word one coming home except that the kids were mean to you, and I want to know what they did so I can . . ."

"So you can do what? So you can tell their mom on them?"

"No. But they can get punished."

"They can't get punished for staring, pointing and whispering about somebody. It's just stupid! This whole thing sucks!"

"Chelsea, please don't use that word. That's so ugly. Oh, never mind. You can talk to me however you want, but you just have to talk. And as far as the kids at school, I don't know if it's possible, but I know your mother is on a mission to get you into a private school, so we can change that whole scenario if you want."

Chelsea went ballistic, "I don't want to go to another school! I don't want my mom to do that! I don't want to go to some stinking private school like I have spent my whole life in. I hate them! And I don't want to be away from Trace! He's the only good thing that's ever happened to me!"

Lauren physically took Chelsea by the hands and sat her down across from her on the bed. "Sweetheart, something is going on with you, and you've got to tell someone. If you don't want it to be me, let's find someone. Maybe . . . Did you like Pam? Do you want to go to a counselor? I don't know. I just know in my spirit . . ."

Chelsea objected immediately, "What are you, psychic or something?"

"Good heavens, no! No, I'm not talking about being psychic. I'm talking about the fact that I know something's wrong! I know you."

Chelsea whipped her hands away from Lauren, "You don't know me! You don't know me at all! You just left me like everybody."

"Sweetheart, I explained to you why I went to California. But you're right; I let you down. I let the ball drop. I didn't come visit as often as I promised, and your mom and I just seemed to be growing apart over the years. But I shouldn't have allowed that to affect our relationship. The point is we're all together now. And yes, I didn't handle a hard time I was going through with Tucker's dad very well, and I hurt people, and I hurt you, and I hurt myself! It took me several years of coming to my faith to recognize how self-centered I was and . . ."

Chelsea just stared at her, "I don't want to be lectured, and yeah, you did let me down. But I don't care anymore. I just wanted to come home today; it didn't mean I wanted to become best friends."

"OK," Lauren thought for a minute. "Tell me at least why you don't want to go to another school if you're going to have trouble in the one you're in? Changing schools doesn't necessarily mean that you have to stop seeing Trace. I just think that your mother wants to get to know him and know that he's a good boy and a gentleman."

Again, Chelsea totally exploded, "What do you mean she needs to know if he's a gentleman? She couldn't tell a gentleman if he . . . Never mind. I just don't want to talk about Mom. All of a sudden, she wants to be mother of the year or something, but it's a little too late for that."

"What did she do to you, Chelsea? What's going on with you two? Why are you so angry with her? I know that she loves you very much, and she is so wanting to have a relationship with you, but you make it really hard."

"No! She makes it hard! She makes it impossible because she doesn't care. Because she doesn't see, and she doesn't know what's going on, and she doesn't know anything about me!" And with that, the girl burst into tears.

Lauren immediately prayed in her spirit, "God, please open the floodgates here. Please let Chelsea talk!" Lauren tried to take the girl in her arms as she said, "Everything's going to be alright, Chelsea."

But the girl pushed back with a vengeance, "No! It's not going to be alright. It'll never be alright. It's already too late. It's already too late for me. I'm glad he's dead! I don't want his lousy money! I don't want anything from him!"

"Are you talking about Ford? I thought you liked Ford?"

"I hate him! I hate him, and I'm glad he's dead." Chelsea's behavior was disturbing to Lauren.

She proceeded with caution, "OK, you hate your mom, and you hate Ford. And you're mad at me. Do you hate me, too? What's wrong Chelsea?"

Then she finally exploded. "He messed with me, OK! Is that what you want to hear? Yeah, he did, he messed with me! He messed with me and said he loved me and said he cared about me, but he didn't. He just messed with me!"

Chelsea's rage took Lauren's breath away. She definitely did not want to make a wrong move at such a crucial time, "Sweetheart, your mom told me about that—that you two were really close for years, and then all of a sudden he didn't spend any time with you. Is that what's hurt you? That he didn't spend any time with you? That no one spent any time with you? Your mom? Me?" Chelsea could barely get her words out in a low, sulteral tone. "No, he spent the wrong kind of time with me. I told you, he messed with me!"

Panicking, Lauren hoped she wasn't hearing what she was hearing. "What does *messed with you* mean?"

And in a burst of emotion, there it was, the very thing Lauren never wanted to hear from Chelsea, or anyone for that matter. "It means he had sex with me, alright? It means I'm not the sweet little girl everybody thinks I am! I'm . . . I'm . . ."

Lauren just sat back in her chair. *"He had sex with you?"* Now Chelsea was beyond control as she screeched, "He did things to me. He didn't ever totally do *that,* but he did things to me and gave me alcohol and drugs and took me places and bought me things and made me feel like he cared about me! Made me feel . . . I don't know . . . I don't know anymore! That part of me doesn't feel anymore, and then . . ." Chelsea panicked, "I don't want to talk about it anymore!" She jumped up and ran into her bathroom, slamming and locking the door behind her.

Lauren remained where she was as if a bolt of lightening had hit her. She just kept murmuring, "Oh my God, please no. Oh God, please! Please!" Way back in the distance, Lauren could hear the doorbell ringing, but it seemed she was caught in the twilight zone until her father banged on the door.

"Lauren?"

She jumped out of her skin, her father's stern voice always prompted that reaction in her. "Yeah, Dad, what?"

"Lauren, there are some people here to see you. I don't know whether to let them in or not. There's a black lady and three other women. Eleanor something or other."

"Oh! Yes, Dad, let them in! We went to church with them last night. Tell them I'll be right there."

"Alright, but I'm not going to be sitting there watching them. I'm just going to let them in your house, and I'm going to go watch my football game. So . . ."

"It's OK, Dad. I'll be right out. They're friends, alright?" She heard him stomp down the hall; her father simply did not tolerate any interruptions to his sport's time. Lauren took a deep breath and made her way to the bathroom door. She could hear Chelsea sobbing pathetically inside. She tried the knob, which was of course locked. "Chelsea, sweetheart. Look, I'm going to leave you alone for a little while alright? I'm here if you need me. I'm just in the living room with Eleanor. And Chelsea, there's soup. I know you don't want to eat. I know you don't want to talk right now, but I promise you as sure as I'm standing here that this is all going to be OK. I know it doesn't feel like it right now. I know it feels like the end of the world to you and that there's no way out, but there is and we're going to take care of you. I'm going to take care of you. We love you."

The girl finally screamed, "Go away!"

"OK, I'm right inside the house, and I'll be back in a little while. Please, just take it easy. I love you, sweetheart." Lauren finally backed away.

Making a rather pathetic gesture of pulling herself together, Lauren entered the living room to find Pam, Eleanor, Tonya, and Stephanie sitting in various chairs around her living room. William stood sentry in the center, and Bingo sat on the coffee table licking her paws. Lauren valiantly tried to put on a smile but was relieved that she didn't have to put on airs with these women. The four stood immediately and gathered around Lauren, holding her and encircling her with love.

Eyeing William, Eleanor whispered into Lauren's ear, "Just tell me that big black dog likes me."

Lauren stuttered, "William? He wouldn't hurt a flea."

Eleanor wasn't convinced since the dog kept staring at her. "I'm not a flea. I'm a big black woman that most dogs want to eat." She managed to get a smile out of Lauren, albeit fleeting, then Eleanor hugged Lauren closer to her. "We saw the paper. I can't imagine what you're thinkin'. This isn't a bad town. I don't know how they could have done such an awful thing. How's Irene?"

Now Lauren crumbled in their arms while they lead her to the couch. "I don't know, I don't know. It's worse . . ." She kept babbling.

The ladies surrounded her again, starting to pray over her. "What is it? Is it something else? Is it Chelsea? Is she alright?"

"No," Lauren sobbed, "she's not alright."

Tonya shook her head. "Those kids at school probably gave her a hard time, right?"

"Yes, they did," Lauren got out between gasps. Pam immediately got up and went to the kitchen and brought back a roll of paper towels; Lauren blew her nose. "She came home, but it's worse; there's more. I thought Chelsea might want to go to the private school that Irene could afford now. That's why she's in New York." They all nodded, already knowing where Irene was. "Is Chelsea OK?"

"No, she's not OK. I don't know if I should say this to you. I don't know, I don't know."

Eleanor just put her arm around her again. "Lauren, you don't have to tell us anything. God knows what's goin' on, so let's just pray. We're here to give you some coverin' and support for you and yours. We're not tryin' to be nosey."

Lauren said, "Oh, I know. I would have no secrets. I just haven't assimilated what's going on, and I haven't even told Irene. I can't say anything yet."

Pam comforted her, "You don't have to say anything."

They all bowed their heads. Pam put her hands on Lauren's shoulder, and Eleanor held Lauren's hands, and Tonya started to circle the group praying hard.

Eleanor whispered in Lauren's ear, "God is here, God is here, and prayer is our language of dependence. It just means that we know we can't do anything without him. Tomorrow is only about God's will and not our plans. We just need to be still, whatever it is. We don't need to know the details; God knows. The Bible says that God's grace is sufficient for us because his power is made perfect in our weakness, and he asks us to be patient because he is in control. So whatever's happening, we're going to pray over it now. We're going to lift you up, and we'll stand in agreement in Jesus' name." And then they began.

Chapter 20

-Enemy Camp-

auren's answering machine was blinking again, which she noticed when she went into the kitchen to get some water. Her head was spinning with questions, fears, and confusion. The message was from Irene, sounding highly agitated as she told Lauren that she was getting on a plane and that she'd be landing in Nashville from New York on American Airlines at 7:52 p.m. She said she'd meet Lauren outside baggage claim.

As Lauren erased the tape, she glanced at the clock figuring that she'd missed Irene's call earlier when she was talking to Chelsea. Adding up the time zone change, she realized Irene was well on her way and that she'd barely have enough time to get to the airport. One thing she did not want to do was leave Irene hanging out in the cold with nine thousand bags before she had to tell her even more bad news. She didn't even know how she was going to tell Irene the news. At first, Lauren wanted to go in and talk to her parents about everything but quickly thought better of that. Besides, she didn't even have time to think! "OK, just don't panic." She made her way down the hall to her niece's room. As she had assumed, Chelsea's door was locked. She muttered, "Maybe that's good. At least she's out of the bathroom."

She knocked on the door, but there was no reply. "Chelsea, I have to run to the airport right now to get your mom. She's flown in from New York. Your grandparents are here if you need anything. I'm going to tell them to keep an eye on Tuck; I know you probably just want to rest in there. So, I'll have my cell, you have the number if you need me, sweetheart. I love you . . . Chelsea?" Lauren exhaled, "Look, Chelsea, I can't leave till I hear that you're alright. So if you want to be alone, I'll respect that, but otherwise, I'm perfectly capable of knocking this door down and taking you with me. It's your call."

After a moment Lauren could hear the girl directly on the other side of the door. "Just leave me alone. And I don't want to see Mom when she gets back."

Lauren started to object, but due to lack of time, she decided she wouldn't be able to make any headway, so she simply said, "Chelsea, I respect that, and I'm sure your mom will, too. I'll encourage her to do that. It's a lot to assimilate, and I promise you that everything will be alright. But in the morning we'll have to sit down, or you have to sit down with your mom or somebody, and address this. It's not just going to go away. I know you're in pain, sweetheart, but we'll get you all the help you need. OK?

I love you." Again there was no answer; Lauren had no choice but to head out to get Irene.

❦

As fast as Lauren drove without getting pulled over and as much as she prayed, Irene was still standing outside the baggage claim surrounded by mounds of luggage looking like she was about to kill someone. Lauren jumped out of the BMW and rushed around to help Irene with the bags. "Sorry, sorry, sorry. I didn't get your message till late and, anyway, I brought your car because you like it better than my truck. You know how you don't like the way it drives. I wanted you to be comfortable on the way. Does your bottom still hurt?" Irene just looked at her, "Lauren, you're babbling. It's OK. Let's just get the bags in the car and go."

The drive home began in silence, Lauren and Irene gathering their thoughts before tackling the first issue on the top of their agenda. In fact, Irene didn't know they had an agenda. She thought they were only dealing with the insanity of the newspaper article. She began by asking Lauren for the paper.

She smacked herself on the forehead in frustration, "I forgot to bring it."

Irate, Irene pulled a cigarette out of her purse and lit it. "I asked you! You promised you were going to bring it! I've seen nothing in New York in the papers. I have to see what they've said! Why didn't you bring it? Do you have copies?"

"No, I don't have copies. I probably should have gotten copies, but it's all there at home. Don't worry; I gave you the gist of it anyway. It was just a picture of you and me outside the school looking like blithering idiots, and it talked about Tucker's school and where I lived and the address and the . . . Ah! . . . The worst of it was the picture of Chelsea on the front. It talked about you, reported Ford's death. I went over all of this with you. They said Chelsea was yours and Ford's daughter but then made it end up looking like she was illegitimate."

Irene was fuming. "I thought I was going to be able to calm down about this, but every time I think about it, the madder I get. What kind of insane place have you moved us to?"

Lauren took the blow knowing that she was going to take more than a lot of heat for everything. "OK, I know I had us move here, but you can't blame me for that stupid newspaper article. It's part of the 'Jannette/Nannette' whatever the heck newspaper chain you've had so much trouble with before. They seem to have it out for you, or in for you, or whatever."

Irene cut in, "I didn't see any other coverage in the New York press." Lauren countered, "Well, I wouldn't hold your breath, especially with smoke in your mouth, because I'm sure it'll be all over the country knowing that creepy news chain."

"I do remember a few years ago that Ford actually wanted to take that newspaper to court and sue them. They had put in some garbage about a Far Eastern oil deal that was flat out untrue; at least that's what Ford told me. But who knows? Maybe he was doing everything they said he was doing." Lauren looked at her sister, hating that she was going to have to add insult to injury with what she had to tell her about Chelsea. As the car filled up with smoke, Irene rolled down the window a crack so Lauren could breath.

Finally, Irene turned around, eyes blazing. "I hate what's happening to my daughter!"

Lauren just sighed, "Rene, I've got to talk to you about something that's difficult. It's more important than this reporter stuff."

Irene threw her head back, "What could be more important than being plastered all over the front of the newspaper where you've just moved into town? I think the best thing to do is just move someplace completely different."

Lauren shuttered, "No, Rene, don't run away. We need to be together right now, and we need to deal with this. Don't let some stupid newspaper run us off as a family! We're here. There are just more important issues to deal with right now, and another move is not going to help Chelsea."

Irene looked at her sister, "What's wrong with Chelsea? Where is she anyway? Why isn't she with you right now? I told you to keep your eye on her, completely!"

"She's in her room, and she didn't want to come out. She was very upset. I did keep my eye on her, I watched her like a hawk. When you left, we all went to church together."

Irene almost swallowed her cigarette, "You went to church together?"

"Yes. Everyone was there, and everyone was fine. I took her home in my car, and Stephanie and Trace left in his."

"Trace was there?" Now Irene lit up another cigarette.

"It was at church, Rene! Let me finish what I'm saying because I have something important to tell you!"

"What?"

"Well, she . . . That's when everything happened. When we got up the next morning with the newspaper thing, she wanted to go to school. I told you that on the telephone. And I took her. Then the principal called for me to come get her because she was upset."

Irene was really getting impatient: "You told me all of that! That's why I came home. I'm here! Didn't she want to come to pick me up? That's so rude!"

There was a long pause while Lauren just stared straight ahead. "She doesn't want to talk to you right now, Rene. But it's not your fault."

Irene just looked out of the window, crushed. "Oh, that's great. I didn't do anything to her. Why is she so mad at me? I just don't know what's the matter with her. I'm going to get her in a private school, and I'm going to get her straightened out, and I'm going to get her some security and . . ."

Lauren held her hand up like a crossing guard, "She's not going to a private school. She doesn't want to have anything to do with Ford's money or anything that comes from him because . . ." Then she paused.

"Because why? Why would she care where the money came from? It's my money. I'm his wife!"

"Because he molested her!"

"What?" Irene gagged. Scared, Lauren slowed the car. "Maybe I should pull over, and let's just talk a minute before we go home."

"He molested her? He *sexually* molested her? My daughter? She said that? She told you that?"

"Rene, she . . . Yes, she said that."

❧

Chelsea climbed out of her bedroom window, making her way through the woods down to the street where Trace was waiting in his car. She jumped in, and they took off like two thieves in the night; she was breathing hard, and he was looking very confused. "Are you alright? What's wrong? I mean you sounded so weird on the phone. I thought I wasn't supposed to see you alone?"

"You're not, but it doesn't matter. I don't care what they say. I just needed to see you, OK?" Trace nodded his head, a little uncomfortable; Chelsea seemed so intense. "Hey," she said, "let's just drive around for a while. My aunt went to the airport to pick my mom up, so I don't have a lot of time. I just needed to get out of the house and go for a drive, OK?"

Trace put his arm around her for comfort. "OK, take it easy. Do you want to go get a burger or something? We could just sit in the parking lot for a while."

"Yeah, that'd be great." Suddenly she realized that she had exposed her emotions to him. That meant there was no more game playing. He could see that she was upset, and she knew she had to gather her thoughts and get in control quickly. One thing she had learned from her mother was, the more she demanded from Ford, the less she got, and Chelsea did not want this boy to go out of her life.

Trace's hand moved off her shoulder and back down by the car's stick shift. Chelsea took his hand and held on as if it were some sort of lifeline for her. And although this boy didn't know what he was getting into, or really who he was sitting next to, he knew he wanted to protect Chelsea from the moment he had laid eyes on her. Frankly, he was struggling with how strongly he felt about her, feelings that he'd never experienced before and didn't know exactly how to handle. "How long do we have before they get back?"

Chelsea shook her head, "Don't know. I left right away. How far is the airport?"

"It's only about—I don't know how fast they drive—about a half hour."

"I've got to be home before they get there, that's for sure so. I guess we've got an hour."

He squeezed her hand. "OK, good. Well, I'll get you back in time. Just relax."

⚜

Irene was out of her car that was parked on the side of the highway. She was sitting on the ground, screaming and sobbing at the same time. Lauren stood behind her as the oncoming car lights flashed across their forms in a strobelike fashion; the whole situation seemed surreal.

"How could this be happening? One disaster after another. I'm going to kill him! I'll kill him with my bare hands!"

Lauren ventured a step closer, "Rene, he's already dead. We have to help Chelsea now and not get caught up in the anger thing with Ford." Suddenly, Irene turned around and grabbed her sister by the legs, tackling her; they both sprawled out on the ground. Lauren had never seen Irene like this, not in their entire lifetime. It was as if her heart had been amputated. As she pressed Lauren's hands above her like they were in some sort of wrestling championship, Irene screamed, "Don't tell me what to do! If I want to kill him, even if he's dead, that's what I'm going to do!"

Lauren nodded slowly, cautious, as if she'd just been attacked by an escaped lunatic. "OK, Rene. You call the shots. But I know we have to get home, and I know we have to calm down, and I know we have to . . ."

Irene released her steel grip on her sister. Sitting back up, she remained there, stoic, mesmerized by the car lights. Lauren carefully pulled herself up into a sitting position, waiting to see what her sister's next move might be. Although Irene was destroyed, distraught, disillusioned, and drained, she finally turned to Lauren, "I'm so sorry," she cleared her throat. "Oh, my poor Chelsea. I don't know where to begin except that we have to get her some help. I'm not going to be able to do it. She won't let me. If I could have helped her, none of it would have happened."

Lauren felt safe enough to move toward her sister. "Rene, it's not your fault. But you're right. For now, Chelsea doesn't want to talk to you. She doesn't want to talk to me. It's not like she could talk to me more than to you. She just did because . . ." The passing traffic lights suddenly changed into a red whirling floodlight as a police car pulled up to the side of the road. The big burly policeman who had his eye on the sisters in town exited his car with caution, ready to investigate the suspicious activities before him. Irene and Lauren froze.

༄༅

Trace had managed to find a secluded back lot parking area, way behind the movie theater complex beneath the sway of a heavily laden oak tree. His VW was all but invisible in the night. The remnants of their hamburgers and sodas were strewn across the dashboard, and although it was chilly, Trace had let the top down so that they could stare up, starry-eyed, at the sky filled with the galaxies of wonder.

Spellbound, Trace pulled himself away to check his watch, ever the responsible one as he had promised to be. "We gotta go."

Chelsea moaned and then looked at him. The lighting was perfect, like Hollywood movie perfect, the moment right out of a romance novel. But instead of the boy being the one who advanced on the girl with a sweet kiss, it was Chelsea who made the first move, a move that surprised and excited Trace. A move that escalated quickly into passion that was way out of bounds for their relationship, and when he tried to pull back, she again called upon all of her female wiles to lure him to her. She was hungry for him. Hungry to be held, hungry to be loved, hungry to be cared for. Needing his attention and believing in her heart that this was how she was able to attract men, she had learned early on to be seductive.

Her stepfather had awakened things in her that no young girl should or could be capable of digesting or handling. Chelsea's childhood and innocence had been taken away from her and was replaced with a deeply wounded heart and a twisted sense of true love. The attention of a man had fulfilled her need for the love of her father who had abandoned her so many years ago. There was no understanding on her part about the devastating difference between the two, and Chelsea became easy prey for the sick attentions of Ford—attentions that started out by simply spending time with her, talking, walking, buying her presents, making her feel special, especially when Aunt Lauren, who used to fill that place of making her feel especially loved and important, moved away. There was a chasm that needed to be met, and the manipulations of a pedophile were set on fire by this innocent yet emotionally needy child—a child that he would soon turn into his playmate, teaching her how to lie, how to make plans with him and not tell her mother. Yes, he taught her how they could chart their course together. Chelsea wasn't tied up in a closet; she was not threatened into silence, and what continued over the years escalated when Ford planted the seed in Chelsea's mind that he would be all hers once she came of age. Yes, Chelsea had believed that she would eventually replace her mother.

Trace pulled back from Chelsea's embrace; he needed to come up for air. Despite how excited he was by her attentions and her wherewithal, he was feeling outmatched and overwhelmed. He took a breath; then she sat up, immediately defensive. "Did I do something wrong?"

"No, no," he said straightening his shirt, "I've just got to get you back." She looked at him again, doe-eyed. She started to put her hand on his lap. "Chelsea, I don't want you to get in trouble. I need to get you back now."

She pulled away; he could tell that her feelings were hurt, and she looked scared again like she was when she got in the car. He didn't know what any of it was about, but he could feel her pain as sure as she was sitting next to him. And still, and even more, he wanted to take care of her.

He remembered when his mother had a miscarriage years ago. He had overheard that the baby was a little girl, and he didn't know what to say to his mom when he heard her cry. But his dad sat him down and tried to explain. "Your mommy is very sad. She's lost something that was a part of her—a baby we were both hoping for. But sometimes God has a different plan, and he took your sister home to him before we even got to meet her. And although she's in a perfect place, your mommy's very sad right now."

Trace remembered looking at his dad as a nine-year-old, really not sure what he was being told, but he sensed that it was important. Then his dad put his arm around him, "Your mom just needs to be left alone when she says she needs some time. But the best thing we can do is just love her, even if there is the slightest opening. Let's just get in there and hug her, and she'll be OK after a while. These are just things of life, son. Hard things that'll come up, but we'll always stay close and take care of one another."

Trace thought back on his memories, realizing that it was then that he thought God wasn't good. God scared him. Why would he take his little sister away and hurt his mom so much? It didn't make much sense then, and his fear of God was confirmed when his father was killed. Trace felt betrayed by life; life that he was always taught was given by a gracious God now seemed like a cruel trick. That's when his young boy's heart began to reshape, creating compartments that he would allow to feel and others that he put in a locker room someplace, awaiting another game, another day, another circumstance.

Trace stopped trusting, and strangely enough, that's what he felt instinctively about Chelsea. She didn't trust either. It didn't matter if their details were different; they shared deep pain. He could feel it. He could feel it even beyond what he was feeling as a young man set against her beauty.

"We gotta go." He looked at her. "But it was nice. Really nice. OK?" And those were the words that Chelsea needed to hear; she longed to be special to someone again. And that gave power, some meaning to her life. Chelsea felt better as they drove off into the night. And although she didn't want to leave when he said, he didn't want to get her in trouble; it felt good. And that was going to be enough to get her through, at least for a little while. At least until she saw him again.

It wasn't that Officer Chet Monty didn't believe the sisters' story of having pulled over to talk, and it wasn't that he recognized them from that morning's newspaper because they were both so incredibly disheveled; he simply deduced that they were drunk after having witnessed their previous antics outside the school. Unfortunately, his conclusion was confirmed by the smell of alcohol on Irene. She told the officer that she had ordered some cocktails on the plane. "I wasn't driving; I was trying to relax. The pilot was driving!" The more she talked, the more upset she became having started the conversation already on the verge of hysterics. She just wouldn't shut up. "I am an adult and I'm perfectly capable of having drinks. My drinks are none of your business! My sister was driving."

That's when the situation escalated, and he escorted her to the side of the road, "Get your hands off of me!" The policeman asked her to walk a straight line while shining the light in her eyes. Lauren was horrified as Irene became more and more belligerent due to her extreme emotional angst. She clearly didn't know what not to say and took this "southern pie," as she called him, excuse for a policeman on like a barracuda. The more Lauren objected, the more intense the fray became between Irene and the officer.

Lauren ran back to the car to get her license and registration, then politely told the policeman that she just wanted to take her sister home; but by that time this officer had an attitude bigger than his pot belly. His macho southern disdain for out-of-towners clicked in, and his control mode took over as he ordered Irene to take a Breathalyzer test, "So as to clear up any misunderstanding that you were driving intoxicated, ma'am," he said sarcastically.

Now Lauren lost her cool. "Officer, I was driving. I picked my sister up at the airport. We have to get home. Just release her to me, and we'll be on our way." She waved her license and registration in front of his face. "I'll 'breathalyze' anything you want! Here's my license; here's my registration. Why are you doing this?"

When Irene smacked the Breathalyzer out of the officer's hands, he escorted her to his police car and slammed her into the backseat. "You're goin' down!" he spat at her. Lauren just stood there horrified, looking at her sister behind an iron-mesh divider. Then, trying to block him, she begged the policeman to stop this insanity. But by then, he was into his full defiant mode and wasn't about to let Irene go. As he walked around to the driver's side, he ordered Lauren, "Ma'am, step back, or you'll be goin' with her. You can find her down at the precinct police station just off Main. I'm going to have to clarify a few details with your sister before she can be released in accordance to her behavior. She just struck an officer."

Lauren started to go ballistic.

"Ma'am, I'm warning you. Now, step out of my way!"

And with that all Lauren could see were the red lights and sirens screeching as Irene was carted off into the night.

Chelsea made it back through her bedroom window, feeling that she had just gotten home in time, when in fact, it would be hours before her mother showed up. She did, however, hear someone run into the house because William started barking, but the dog stopped quickly and then she heard the door close again. She hoped it wasn't some intruder, but she dared not go down the hall

to check on anyone, just grateful that her evening's escapade had
not been discovered.

⁂

Lauren made her way through the streets of Centennial, careful
not to speed yet close to losing her mind as she searched for the
police station. She had called for directions on her cell phone
and was impolitely told by some voice on the other end that, yes,
there was some female suspect down there, just picked up on the
highway; and she was in detention, waiting for arraignment by
the judge.

Lauren thought, *An arraignment by a judge! For what?* But
that was about all the information she was allowed. Lauren had
gone home to gather up some cash, having been told that after the
arraignment, depending on what the judge decided, the detained
woman may be placed on bail.

It was at 3:30 in the morning on Friday when Irene finally
emerged from the police station on Lauren's arm; she had no fire
left in her, no quips, no more comments worthy of publishing
in some novel. Irene had been thrown into the proverbial pokey;
she was taunted for seven hours, threatened to be charged with
drug possession, driving under the influence, and assaulting an
officier. Frankly, anything the officer could come up with in his
nasty little mind was fair game. And now that he recognized who
Irene was, he was having a ball with "Ms. New York Society"
as did the fat cop behind the desk who scoffed at her. The
black female police woman laughed out loud at Irene when she

298

wouldn't let "the prisoner" use the private ladies room. Instead, she made Irene go into an open-fronted urinal to humiliate her when Irene said she could no longer contain herself. And as Irene lay there on the metal bed between confrontations, she thought back on the TV series *In the Heat of the Night* or the movie *Cool Hand Luke* and realized that she now was experiencing firsthand what it's like for someone to be picked up in a small southern town by a redneck cop with cohorts who enjoyed making others squirm.

Chapter 21

-Set the Stage-

Now there were two newspaper cover stories spread out on Lauren's kitchen table, side by side. Everybody had read Thursday's edition except Irene, who now stood there numb as she reviewed the photos and story Lauren had told her about on the phone. But it was today's newspaper headline that absolutely floored the entire family. And it was something that was not going to be able to be kept from Tucker, Chelsea, or anyone for that matter. The headline read:

Irene Williams Arrested in Centennial

The article was short; the information, obviously leaked from the police station in the middle of the night was carefully constructed so that there would be no legal ramifications for false statements. It merely said:

> Mrs. Irene Williams, a recent resident of
> Centennial, was arrested by Officer Chet Monty and
> arraigned by Judge Baxter last night at 2:30 a.m.,
> allegedly charged with assault of an officer, resisting
> arrest, and public intoxication. Bail was set for fifteen
> hundred dollars, and Mrs. Williams was released into
> the custody of her sister Lauren Patterson. A pre-
> liminary hearing is set for one week from today
> where Mrs. Williams will have an opportunity to
> make her plea.

Lauren noted that the report in the paper was written by Brandon Chase.

The entire family stood around the table, staring at the vision before them; then the telephone ring broke the silence. Lauren grabbed it, "Who is it? Oh, Brian. Yes, I've seen it. We've seen . . . Yes . . . No, she wasn't. She was just overtired. As you've probably read in the newspaper . . . Sorry, I haven't even had a chance to tell you that Ford died. I wanted to give you a call because we've been splashed all over this newspaper here. Well, it's the local paper, not the Nashville paper. Yes, I know you get it. No, no . . . Oh, so you don't . . . Well, how do you know what happened? It was on the radio and TV news this morning? Brian, could you do me a favor and come and get Tuck for the day? Can you get out of work? I just need to . . . I don't think he should go to school. Maybe if you could just take him for the weekend. You were going to pick him up this afternoon anyway. Ah, thanks a lot. . . . Yeah, thanks a lot, Brian. I appreciate it. It will all work out; everything is ridiculous and not true. She wasn't driving; she didn't hit the officer. I was right there. . . . I mean she did, she knocked the Breathalyzer out of his hand, but I don't think that's assaulting a policeman. Yes, I guess that's a no-no. She did insult him though, but the rest of it's ridiculous. She wasn't driving. . . . Yes, she had a few cocktails on the plane, but she was just upset; that's what she was. . . . She was upset, not drunk. I was driving. . . . Look, Brian, I'll call you later. Thanks, can you come now? Alright, thanks." Lauren hung up; looking at her family, she realized that she'd just answered a bunch of their questions.

Chelsea just shook her head, "I'm going to school, so who's going to take me?"

"Brian will be here in twenty minutes. Irene, if that's OK, why don't we let him drop her off at school." Irene nodded as Lauren continued, "If that's what you want, Chelsea. You know it was horrible yesterday, and today could be even worse."

Chelsea just looked at her family and said flatly, "It can't get any worse. I just want to go to school and get away from here."

Irene tried to go to her, to put her arms around her daughter, but Chelsea pushed her away. "Alright," Irene gathered her thoughts, "I'm going to let you go to school if you give me your word that you won't leave there. I'm going to pick you up under the sign, right at the bell. Otherwise, you're not leaving this house."

Chelsea shook her head, "Yeah, I'll be there, but I don't want to talk, OK?"

Irene relented, "Fine. That's OK. You don't have to talk; you just have to be there. Everything's going to be alright, Chelsea. Just hang in there, sweetie. I'm so sorry for all this mess. I was just upset and . . ."

Chelsea cut in, "It doesn't matter, Mom. I'm going to get my books." She left the room.

Lauren gave Tucker a big hug, "Hey, buddy! Why don't you go and pack your things for the weekend. Daddy's going to come and pick you up in a few minutes, and you get to have the day off from school!" Tucker just looked at her for a moment and then said, "OK." But before he left, he went over and gave Irene a hug, holding her around her legs in a sweet gesture of support. Still, he was definitely looking forward to getting away for a few days with his dad.

Margaret sat down at the table with a woozy expression on her face while Sam started to pace. "Irene, I don't believe what is going on. You *hit* a policeman?"

Lauren broke in, "Dad, she didn't hit the policeman. She just smacked the Breathalyzer out of his hand! He was obnoxious, and he wouldn't listen to me. He didn't believe I was driving, and Irene was understandably hysterical!"

"What do you mean?" Sam blurted, "'Understandably hysterical'? How can you be *understandably* hysterical?"

"You can be, Dad, when you keep getting news like Rene's been getting every time she turns around."

Irene went to her purse on the counter and pulled out a cigarette; no one dared try to stop her. Even William and Bingo had
sense enough to lie in the corner of kitchen quietly, making no
demands for their breakfast. "Mom, Dad," Irene finally said in a
weak voice, "When the kids take off, we all have to talk. What
you see in this newspaper is not all there is. As a matter of fact,
it pales in comparison with what's going on with Chelsea. So just
please, go into your apartment; and as soon as they leave, Lauren
and I will be in. We want to get some advice from you." Her voice
was wavering. This woman was truly at the end of her tether.

Trace was waiting under the welcome sign at the high school
when he saw Shooter and a group of his friends appear across the
parking lot; they were clearly walking in his direction. Frustrated
from yesterday's events with Chelsea and not ready to entertain
any more comments about his girl, Trace prepared himself for a
showdown. *One word about Chelsea and it'll be on,* he decided
as he made a quick count of Shooter's group. They continued to
walk toward him, deliberate and steady. *After two years of bitter
competition, was it all going to come to a head right here, right now?*
Trace calculated how he might get the best of the clearly larger
nemesis. *No matter,* he thought. *I'll hit him first, before he expects
it. I've had enough of him and his downtown attitude and his three-
point jump shot.*

And then Shooter stood before him; the look he carried was
serious but Trace had no intention of backing down. "You picked

a bad day to get in my face, dude." Trace adopted a slightly side-ways posture, ready to attack the moment Shooter's nose came in arm's range.

"Not here to fight with you, bro," Shooter spoke calmly. His voice completely surprised Trace, but still he readied himself for whatever Shooter might do next. The muscled black arm slowly reached out toward Trace; the palm was open, not menacing. A handshake? Trace's mind calculated Shooter's real intentions, then chose to return the gesture. Their hands locked together; they studied each other for a moment, and then Shooter said in a low and thoughtful voice, "Listen, man. Your girl is having a hard time, and I just want you to know that we'll be watching out for her." Before Trace could respond, Shooter continued, "Now, I know, man, you can take care of your own. But I just want you to know that we all think it stinks that she's had a bum start here. We ain't into makin' people feel worse than they already do. I can remember back when Tonya got pregnant with my son. I was fourteen, and there was a lot of gossip. I didn't like it. I didn't like it for my girl."

As Shooter started to back away, Trace nodded at him, "I 'preciate it."

Shooter gave him a peace sign. "Yeah, well, I'll be seeing you on the court."

Trace smiled for the first time in twenty-four hours, "Yeah, I'm glad we're on the same team, man."

On the board for the morning statement, Ham had written:

FRIENDSHIP IS A WELL-WORN PATH BETWEEN TWO HOMES.—HAM

❦

Eleanor had been admitted to the hospital at six that Friday morning; she was awaiting her surgery, having been already prepped. Ham was ever by her side in the private room; there were flowers surrounding her on every open shelf available. "Oh, Ham," Eleanor looked around the room. "You know how much I love flowers. They remind me of God's creation. Each unique and so beautiful. An offerin' to us of his love. And when you bring 'em to me, my husband, they make me feel so wonderful."

He held her hands in his, looking down at his bride as he began to stroke her cheek ever so softly. "You are the love of my life. You know that. And you also know that what the enemy means for harm, God will turn to good. So, my love, no matter what happens, I know you're going to be better than ever. You are a flower to God. You are a bouquet to me, and I know our Lord will not let the enemy touch you." Eleanor's eyes filled with tears, tears she didn't push back this time because they were tears of joy; and she embraced that peace beyond understanding that she so longed for since this whole ordeal started.

Ham looked back at her, "You inspire the hero in me. Heroes want to rescue their damsel in distress. I would do anything to take this from you, to make it all better. It's hard for a man when he feels things are out of his control. The funny thing I've found out, my dear Eleanor, we're never in control; we just think we are. That's why we always make so many mistakes. But God is in control, and he must have a pretty big graduation day for you ahead because this is a tough one. I'm with you all the way, my love." Ham sat down by her side. "Are you sure you didn't mind my telling the girls not to come over this morning?"

Eleanor shook her head, "It doesn't matter where they're prayin' from, as long as they're prayin'. I just want to be with you."

"I promised I'd call them as soon as you're out of surgery. They told me they'd be at the diner holding vigil all day till they come here." And then there came a light knock on the door, and Eleanor knew it was time to go.

Some of the regulars banged on the diner door, confused as to why it was locked. Norro, the owner, approached the small gathering of clients from a side street. When they questioned why the diner was closed, he responded, "Stephanie's under the weather, and I have no other server. We'll be open tomorrow. Ya'll come back then." Everybody dispersed, a little frustrated, but anyone who knew Stephanie knew she would never call in sick. Norro glanced through the locked doors where he noted that Stephanie, Pam, and Tonya were sitting way in the back booth, gathered in prayer.

Just as he was about to leave, the secretary from the newspaper approached him. "Norro." He turned to her. "We're going to be needing more pictures of those sisters."

"Yeah," he said with a grin, "appears so, considerin' the headlines this mornin'. They've been in the diner already a couple of times, so it'll be easy for me to grab some shots without bein' noticed."

"Good," she nodded. "Just get 'em to me, and we'll do the same deal." He nodded back as she crossed the street toward the newspaper office.

⚜

Lauren and Irene spent the day visiting various counselors who might be able to help Chelsea. They both felt, after speaking with Sam and Margaret, that picking just the right one would be the crucial element in Chelsea's recovery.

Later that morning Pam had broken from the prayer circle to answer Lauren's call for some suggestions in helping Chelsea; Pam was right on target about who might be the right ones to help, as well as offering her services. Then Lauren prayed with Pam on the phone that she'd stand in agreement with the others in prayer for the swift and full recovery of Eleanor and mentioned that she'd be over to see Eleanor once she and Irene got Chelsea from school.

After speaking with all the potential psychiatrists and counseling centers, Irene finally agreed with Lauren that Pam might be the right person to help Chelsea. Lauren had told her that Chelsea had spoken highly of Pam when she met her at church. She seemed to like her and trust her. But more important, although Pam didn't have the credentials the doctors they'd interviewed had, what she did have was a real feel for kids who are hurting. Lauren explained to Irene how important Christ is in the equation of real healing. Irene argued for a time, reminding Lauren that her daughter was not a believer and that she was not a believer, but Lauren begged her sister, "I love Chelsea. She's a part of me. I've watched you struggle with your issues, and yes, I still struggle with mine, but I know that nothing was ever recognized, understood, grieved, or healed in my life until the grace of God became a part of the equation. And maybe Chelsea doesn't know Christ now, and maybe you don't, but please trust me here. The influence Pam can have on Chelsea will be immeasurable because of the love of God in Pam and the discernment that she has spiritually. I just don't want Chelsea to be put on a bunch of medicine and turned into a zombie."

Puffing on another cigarette, Irene bristled as they sat on the porch at Lauren's house. "I know that you have Chelsea's best interests at heart, Lauren, but sometimes medication helps."

Lauren looked at her sister, tears welling in her eyes. "Please, trust me. Let's try it without first, alright?"

Exhausted, Irene finally agreed, "OK, but if it doesn't work, I'm taking her immediately to a psychiatrist who can prescribe medication if he thinks that is the best for her."

"OK," Lauren said, relieved. She glanced at the wall clock. "We've got to go get her. We don't want to be late."

"Right," Irene stood up and straightened her blouse. "I just feel like I've been so late for everything with her." Lauren gave her sister a hug. "It's not too late. Promise, Rene."

Irene met Chelsea under the school sign where she was introduced to Trace. They shook hands, "I've been looking forward to meeting you." Irene said.

"Yes, ma'am." Trace put on his most polite front.

"Well, thank you for taking Chelsea to school. I met your mom over at the diner." Irene couldn't help but be taken by the apparent sincerity of this boy, and she certainly could understand why her daughter liked him. *He's handsome on fire,* she thought. And their looks of adoration for each other did not go unnoticed by her. *Wow,* she reminisced, *there's nothing like young love. Ah! Was she actually saying that?* She diverted her thoughts back to the conversation.

"Ma'am," Trace offered, "Would it be alright if I took Chelsea out to the movies tonight?"

Irene thought for a moment, "Chelsea and I have some catching up to do, but why don't you give her a call tomorrow afternoon. I'm sure Saturday night will be fine."

"Thank you, ma'am." Trace nodded. Chelsea exploded with a smile; Irene was thrilled to see a moment of happiness on her daughter's face. She put her arm around her daughter as they headed back down the street where Lauren was waiting in the car. She had watched the meeting from a distance and was touched by the image of her sister and her niece coming toward the car, Irene's arm around Chelsea. But it wasn't long before Chelsea pulled away, not wanting to appear like a little kid in front of everyone. Irene understood, stepping a bit farther from her daughter. "Thanks, Mom. I really like him."

"I can tell. Today I just wanted to stay home with you and . . . we need to talk, sweetie."

Chelsea just put her head down for a moment. "So Aunt Lauren told you?"

Irene quietly answered her daughter. "Yes, and we need to talk about it—we need to get you some help with this. I just want you to know that I love you so much, and I had absolutely no idea anything was going on. I don't understand how it could, or when it did, but let's just take one step at a time." Chelsea was chewing her lip nervously; nonetheless, there was some sense of relief in her countenance—the kind of release that comes from letting go of a deep, dark secret.

The sun was just beginning to descend behind the tallest of the treetops; light was streaming into Eleanor's hospital room where Pam, Lauren, Stephanie, and Tonya gathered around her bed. They all had their hands piled together on Eleanor's, whose arms were folded across her chest. The women had been in deep prayer as they raised their heads in thanksgiving, claiming victory and healing for Eleanor. There was not a dry eye, but there was also not even a glimmer of fear in any of the women's expressions. Eleanor concluded by saying, "Thank you, Lord, for all your blessings." Then they all said together, "Amen, in Jesus' mighty name." Eleanor brushed her tears away and regarded her dear friends. "Ham's gone to get me a triple Dairy Queen with chocolate on top!"

All the women laughed, "You go, girl!"

"He didn't much like hearin' from the doctor that we had to wait for the results. He wanted to know everythin' right away . . . what my prognosis is. But I kinda enjoyed it because Ham's always tellin' me to wait on the Lord, be patient, God's never late. Well, now we just have to wait on some test results."

"They're going to be just fine. I know it." Tonya said, "Ms. Eleanor, you're gonna be smiling through the rest of your life, and that's a request by the way, 'cause you look pretty darn scary when you cry."

Everybody laughed with relief while Eleanor basked in the joy of having her friends so dear to her, so near to her. "Thanks for comin' over, ya'll."

"Where else do you think we'd be?" Stephanie added, "Norro's seething because he had to close the diner all day, but I don't care. I wouldn't be anywhere but here." Then Lauren offered in a small voice, "I am so honored to be here, to be part of this circle of friends. I wanted to tell you, Eleanor, that Irene sends her love. We've got quite an issue with Chelsea that Pam's going to help us with. Irene didn't want to leave her daughter right now; otherwise she'd be here." Eleanor comforted Lauren, "Don't you worry about your sister or Chelsea. Whatever it is, we'll just pray over it. The details will reveal themselves."

Lauren giggled, "You sound just like my friend, Suz. Oh, you should meet her. She's one of us, for sure. Actually, she's going to visit me soon, and she's going to be so happy for me that I've found all of you."

Eleanor patted Lauren's hand reassuringly, "Honey, we are happy you have joined us. And don't be gettin' any ideas 'bout letting those pig-headed people run ya'll off either."

"Never. You know what they say, if you can't stand the heat, get out of the South! We're here for the long haul."